PHARAOH'S FRIEND

Printed in the United States of America.

For information address:
Durban House Publishing Company, Inc.
7502 Greenville Avenue, Suite 500, Dallas, Texas 75231

Library of Congress Cataloging-in-Publication Data
Linkous, Nancy Yawitz, 1951 –

Pharaoh's Friend / Nancy Yawitz Linkous

Library of Congress Control Number: 2004107755

p. cm.

ISBN 1-930754-61-2

First Edition

10 9 8 7 6 5 4 3 2 1

Visit our Web site at
http://www.durbanhouse.com

I am deeply grateful to my many friends who encouraged me through this long process of novel writing. I am especially thankful to have had the love, support and editing skills of my brainy and talented sister, Laurie Kirkpatrick; my equally brilliant (and amusing) cousin, Mark Glass; my creative and clever friend, Bob Gale, who gave me the opening line; and my over-the-IQ-wall buddies, Jodi Babcock and Gail Guidry. My heartfelt appreciation to Karen and John Lewis for pulling this story out of the slush and into publication, and unending gratitude to Robert Middlemiss, Editor-in-Chief, whose singular confirmation of my writing is enough to have made the struggle worth it. To my teachers, Venkatesh Kulkarni, Gail Donohue Storey, and Chris Woods, thank you for sharing your wisdom. And to Rhon, my husband, I could not have written this book with an empty heart — you fill me with life and love and challenge and the unbelievable bliss of feeling lucky. I would also like to acknowledge all pets, especially my many cherished ones (past, present and future), for their innate ability to provide solace.

For my family

CHAPTER ONE

September 15, 1991 *Houston, Texas*

WHY CAN'T A CAT ATTEND A FUNERAL?

When the gray cat jumped on top of her daughter's coffin, it didn't seem strange to May Worth. Maybe it sensed Susan was inside the lacquered box, under the wreath of pink tea roses. The cat had played so often with her seven-year-old in St. Francis' shady courtyard it had grown to know her, even waiting on her after services. Now sprawled across the top of the casket, the cat duplicated the flowers' arrangement. Its graceful tail and long limbs were like the cascading sprigs, its pointy ears sharp as the green leaves. Harmony poised over such an unnatural event; how could such beauty be displayed at such an unbearable moment? It didn't make sense.

Father McFairly and a slew of others rushed forward, shooing the animal away.

May told them it was okay, something Susan would have liked. They insisted it would be distracting, not appropriate, not sanitary.

"That's ridiculous, tell them to leave it alone, Jason." But May's husband wasn't there. "Where's Jason?"

"Poor thing is sitting all alone in the courtyard," Grace Sutton, her best friend, told her.

May wanted nothing more than to be alone in the courtyard with him. Instead, strangers who were of no comfort at all surrounded her, pressed against her, smelling of coffee and mothballs, and said meaningless things. She wanted Jason with her as he'd been when they went to select Susan's casket, choose the flowers and decide which dress their baby would wear forever. "These won't be necessary," the man had said as he handed back the shoes and lace-trimmed socks: items dwarfed in his large hands — hands that were too smooth, too white, too sterile, as if he were wearing the same awful gloves the nurses had. Why had she listened to him? How could she bury her little girl barefoot?

She tried not to think of it, tried not to think of all the other funerals before this one, tried not to take that thorny path that always beckoned her, but there it was. It waited deep inside for miserable moments such as these to surface. The tiniest of openings and up it popped, painful as if it had just happened: her parents' funeral.

"Were Mom and Dad wearing shoes when I buried them?"

Grace grabbed May's hand and brought her face too close. Grace's black straw hat with dark taffeta bow poked her in the eye. "Susan's out of pain now, she's safe with God."

"Safe? She died!"

How could Grace say that? But it had always been like that with her friend. Even when they were young girls she'd been God's spokesperson. It had been easier back then to believe her, as if there really were a divine plan. She had even explained May's parents' spectacular death from a lightning bolt as a direct summons to Heaven. But now, almost thirty years old, and ever since her trip to a conference in New

Mexico last summer, Grace had increased her religious inventory to include channeling, past lives, cause and effect, karma, the Christ within, universal consciousness, energy chimes, psychics, crystal power. None of it made sense.

"How could God have let this happen?"

"I'll get Jason," Grace said.

May watched her friend's large black hat bob between people and head outdoors just as the children from Susan's first-grade class appeared. Dressed in their special-event best, they shuffled single-file past the closed white casket, their smallness exaggerated by the vast surroundings of the chapel. They followed the chalky-faced teacher, Mrs. Thompson, as if on some kind of field trip.

Each child shook May's hand as Mrs. Thompson supervised, a pencil-thin eyebrow arched all the way into her hairline. Their little faces were so familiar May couldn't help but anticipate Susan's. At the sight of the last child, who stood before her in a designer outfit that was far too sophisticated for her age, she felt empty and angry and frowned when her own daughter did not appear. The girl frowned too and stared at the pattern of ducks embroidered across May's dress.

"It's the only black dress I own," she said to the child.

Mrs. Thompson's arched eyebrow dropped.

Someone pulled May's arm; the service was about to begin. As they walked to their seats, she saw the plump cat again, crouched beneath the first pew. She picked it up and placed it on the coffin, where it circled three times before settling in the exact spot it had before.

Now it was Father McFairly who frowned as he asked everyone to sit.

At last, Jason appeared.

"I feel like there's more we're supposed to be doing," she said. "I try to imagine our sweetie lying right there in front of us, and I can't. I try to imagine her cradled in God's arms, and I can't. I don't know where she is."

Jason put his arm around her, shushed her.

The priest's words droned. None of them made sense. She bowed her head and stared at the embroidered ducks on her own dress. They were restless, moved their webbed feet up and down, poked their heads under their wings, preened and fluttered, prepared to take off. She imagined she had wings of her own, stretched to her sides. A light breeze lifted her away.

Chapter Two

June 26, 1992 *Gullcrest, Texas.*

Night approached the Gulf Coast horizon. Light from paper lanterns swayed in the air conditioning over May's head. It moved shadows around the room. Pictures of Oriental fishing harbors framed by black bamboo faded into the Full Moon Cafe's red walls. She didn't like the darkness anymore and wished someone would turn on the fluorescents so she could see the people who sat near her.

But she knew it didn't matter; she would take their unfamiliar faces and turn them into ones she knew. She did it all the time now, seeing long lost family members at the grocery; her parents sitting a few rows ahead of her in the dark theater; Fluffy, sunning in the yard; a glimpse of Susan running down the sidewalk.

She turned toward the older couple seated in a booth behind her and, as expected, saw her grandparents on her father's side. Just like those faded photos, all that was left of them by the time she was born, this couple, too, was worn at the edges.

At the table next to theirs were her mom and dad, whom everyone in Gullcrest had known, even before their news-making deaths on that Thanksgiving Day. The man's large ears were just like those that had framed her father's kind face with such ballast. Those ears had heard things she never would: a winter frost coming, giggles from the unborn calf in Big Bessy's womb, stories that the doves and squirrels and mice who lived in his family's rice fields had told him. If only her father had heard the clap of that lightning bolt before it blackened the soil in front of them on that day in 1976. If only the crow or the snail had called out a warning to her dad; if only all the people she loved were still alive.

A young man who didn't look like any of her lost family walked into the cafe. His black hair, shaved close to the sides of his head, was long and wavy at the top.

Once inside the restaurant, he kicked the door shut with the heel of his boot, and the stuffed blue-neck goose mounted on the front wall quivered. The cook rushed in from the kitchen, then turned back when she saw him. The boy shouted at her in Chinese and reached inside his leather jacket with his right hand.

May looked at Jason, but he just stared out the cafe's rippled glass window at the darkening beach. She glanced at her family look-alikes. Not one of them worried about the stranger standing too close to the cash register. But wasn't the goose above the front door calling out? Couldn't the man with those wonderful large ears hear its warning?

"Get out! Get out!" She rushed at the boy.

"May!" Jason yelled.

"This just my punk brother come for his dinner," the cook said.

She saw the take-home paper bag. There were more people in the restaurant than she'd realized. Some of them stood beside their tables now, staring at her.

"I'm sorry," May said to all of them. "I'm sorry," she said to the boy.

"Mr. Tough Guy!" The woman slapped the back of her brother's head. "Always acting like the bad ninja in a Bruce Lee movie." She put the warm paper bag in his hand and shoved him out the door.

Jason led May back to their table.

"Nothing's been right since Susan died," she said.

"What does that have to do with you yelling at that poor kid?"

"I thought he was going to rob the restaurant. I felt like I had to do something. I keep feeling like I'm supposed to be doing something, or forgot to do something."

"You don't think I could have done something?" Jason stroked his sandy-colored hair. "It's good that we're getting away for awhile, you keep getting everything all wrong."

"It's the last thing I feel like doing. You and Grace go, leave me here at the beach house. I'll be fine."

"Leave you alone." His handsome smile looked suddenly sinister.

He poured her a cup of steaming tea that smelled like cloves. She sipped it.

"Why can't you wear your hair up like I've told you to? It gets all frizzy and wild looking when we come to the beach."

She smoothed it down, tried to tuck the long curls behind her ears. Everyone was still staring at her, while Jason talked about the things they had to get done that evening before leaving the following day.

"I'm so embarrassed."

"Let's just go," he said.

"But our fortunes."

"Let's go, I said." He threw some money on the table.

It was at times like this that she missed her daughter the most. She and Susan could hardly wait for the meal to end to read their fortunes. It was the reason to eat Chinese.

She picked up her cookie and followed Jason out of the restaurant.

▲▲▲

He drove too fast, as always.

"Please, slow down."

He drove faster. Past houses painted in vacation colors: blues, pinks and yellows, built high on spindly legs for protection from rising water, they crossed over the pass the town had cut right through the middle of Gullcrest in an attempt to reroute the ocean's current. Neighbors had built bulkheads of every imaginable material in attempts to save their property, but it was inevitable that the ocean and bay were bound to meet. The eroded strip of land was a smaller version of itself each year.

A stick near the bridge marked the height the water rose to during the hurricane of 1975.

"I wish I had a marker," she said. It would let the whole world know she'd reached her limit at twenty-nine years. After Susan's dying, she didn't think things could get worse, but now, nine unbearable months later, there were so many other problems. Jason, for one. He drank too much and was angry all the time. The simplest things could set him off: a friendly wave from a neighbor, a waitress messing up an order, TV advertisements, a traffic signal.

He pushed one button after another on the radio, then hit his fist against the dash. "Any damn station will do," he said.

She cracked open the cookie and held the white strip of paper near the window as they passed under streetlights.

YOU LONG
TO SEE
THE PYRAMIDS
OF EGYPT.

What a joke. She didn't want to go anywhere, especially with the ocean creeping closer every day to their weekend beach house, the house she had inherited from her parents. But Jason had insisted on a trip. The time away would do her good — different sights, sounds, scenery, as if a change of landscape would help her get over their baby's death. And Grace, of course, was convinced the universe had provided the free tickets, rather than the three students who had cancelled the archeological summer class with her cousin, Richard Sutton.

Jason laughed when he heard her fortune. "Was I right? What did I tell you! What's mine say?"

"I didn't bring yours, you said you didn't care about it."

"Well, thanks for thinking of me."

She stared out the car window. Gullcrest disappeared as she watched. Everything seemed temporary. Why even bother to cover the windows with plywood or shut off the water or turn off the gas or do any of those chores that they nonetheless did that evening in preparation for their leaving? Who's to say that the beach house would even still be there by the time they returned? Gullcrest might not even be there.

That same evening, after Jason was asleep, she put shells she and Susan had collected for years back in the very straw basket they'd used to carry them home from the beach. She moved like the tide, gathering them from bowls and drawers, off shelves and hooks in the wall.

It was three in the morning when she stepped out on the porch. A lizard pulsed its throat. Large and then small. Light and then dark. She scooped it up and placed it on her bare shoulder.

"Keep me company," she said. It scampered up her long dark hair to the top of her head, where it stayed perched like a fancy hair ornament.

Down an oyster-shell path to the shore, she wore her old nightgown that had a rusted safety pin at the neck where a satin ribbon had once been attached. The warm ocean breeze made it billow like a sail as she put all the shells back in their places.

A sound in the brush spun her, but there was only the moon, its face full, yellow and large. Then other faces, sad faces with weepy eyes and pained smiles, appeared, and a stained glass window and the wreath of pink tea roses. She felt for the lizard in her hair and stroked its tail.

"Good-bye. I'm off to Egypt, of all places."

Chapter Three

Fifteen miles northeast of Zagazig, Egypt.

Professor Richard Sutton was too busy playing solitaire to notice the massive shape inching ever closer. He placed the ace of hearts onto an unfolded map of Cairo.

"A few more days and May Worth will be here," he said.

"The girl you crushed in your youth," Azzis Musawi said.

There was enough light from the kerosene lamp for him to see his Egyptian assistant, who wore the orange and blue Houston Astros baseball cap he'd won from him in a poker game the week before. Azzis tipped the hat, as he'd done all week, and laughed.

"Not crushed, had a crush on. But you knew that."

"Professor!"

He turned the face of his Timex toward the lamp. Three am, an easy time to remember for the journal. He tossed the cards, hopped over Azzis, and ran to the roped-off section of desert where his students stood in a patch of yellow light provided by a generator. They were gathered around a piece of earthenware that was wedged in the ground.

When he pried the fragment loose, the delta wind whistled a song of unknown treasure, and the rustle of ancient footsteps gathered near. He blew at the dust that covered the piece like soft down, and the desert breeze blew it right back at him.

The tired students laughed as he wiped dirt from his eyes. He laughed with them. This was Egypt at its best, full of surprises. An ancient land of ancient people with a history measured in millennia. Everything about Egypt made him
feel so significantly small. The tiniest of cogs has a place on the wheel, the smallest life, significance.

He examined the jagged piece of pottery — inlaid mother-of-pearl set in a black paste formed part of an eye and the bridge of a nose. A procession of unearthed treasures, photos on glossy book pages, flipped through his mind before he found one that matched: the canopic vessel, a jar used to hold internal organs of the deceased.

"We might have ourselves a canopic vessel, which would mean this hint of a portrait is one of Horus' four sons." He held the shard up so they could take a closer look. "If it's Mesti, this would be a drawing of a . . ." He looked at his students.

"A human face," one of them said.

"And if it's Hapi?"

"The ape," another said.

"Qebhsneuf?"

"The hawk," several said.

"How about Duamutef?"

But instead of an answer there was a scream. Then another one. He looked up from the shard and screamed himself.

A lion-sized cat stood less than ten feet from him. It stretched its gray head inside their circle of light and sniffed at the air between them. Its fur was shiny in the artificial brightness and its eyes candescent yellow. It smelled like wet, warm sand and the bitter roots of alfa grass.

He clutched their find, and for lack of anything else hurled his watch at the animal. "Get out! Get out!"

It moved off through the veil of black desert.

The rest of the night, both weary and wary, the students took turns digging, one person always on watch for the cat. At the first sign of sunlight, Richard had Azzis drive him seventy-five miles in the open-top Jeep to Cairo to purchase a handgun. On their return, they stopped in Ajibba, a small farming village near the dig.

Azzis tipped the bill of his Astros cap as he greeted a couple of the poor fellahin who lived there. After each of the men had tried on the cap, he told them about the frightening visit by the giant cat and asked whether they would help kill it. They told him "no" in Arabic, while beseeching Richard with their gaze to let it be.

"Tell them how big it is," Richard directed.

"Maybe four, five hundred pounds," Azzis said.

The more slender of the dark-skinned villagers was dressed in the traditional caftan-like robe of Egypt but wore turquoise jewelry on his wrists and around his neck. How, in his impoverished state, did he afford it?

"They've seen the cat also," Azzis translated. "They think it's just a Reed cat, though they've never seen one of this size and with markings like a tiger."

The man's companion had a broad, flat nose and wore turquoise rings on each of his fingers and even his thumbs.

"The cat is common to Israel and the Jordan," the villager said. "It runs very fast, but only feeds on rodents and hares and snakes. No threat to our work animals or to us. Besides, the *meau* brings good fortune."

"No threat, the cat brings good luck," Azzis interpreted.

A tethered goat behind them suddenly bleated and scratched at the crusty ground.

Richard had heard many stories about the fellahin's allegiance to the animals that helped them work their cotton and sugar cane fields in lieu of costly farming machinery. Time and again he'd seen a single power-driven tractor alongside donkey-drawn plows. These impecunious villagers took such great care of their stock that they let the animals sleep in the clay-brick hovels that were their own homes.

"It's true, I was able to scare the beast off," he said.

A fat man with a napkin tied around his neck and a fork still in hand rushed toward him from one of the dirt-floor shanties. Still chewing on a piece of his dinner, the villager stood on his toes in order to reach his arm across Richard's shoulders.

"Forgive my pagan friends! Such superstitions in their foreheads."

His English came out in heavy short breaths that smelled of raw onion. He let the man's gentle yet authoritative push guide him back to the Jeep that still hissed and pinged from the long drive to Cairo and back. The manner was familiar, that of an omda, the government-appointed fellah who was head of his own village.

"Something funny you can say to your American *sahibs* about the poor, ignorant *fellahin*, yes? But the cat, he is no problem."

Azzis followed them to the car.

"Where are you from?" the fat omda yelled as the open-top vehicle pulled away.

"Texas."

"A cowboy! So long, cowboy." The man stood at the edge of his small, dusty village and waved good-bye with his fork in the air.

As they drove away, Richard noticed the glint of a large satellite dish behind one of the brown-dirt dwellings. "What superstitions? What was he talking about?"

"Who knows," Azzis said. "I grew up in the city. But the *fellahin* drink from the River Nile because they believe it is magic, and they wear turquoise jewelry to scare off the evil spirits."

"I saw the turquoise. But the fat man wore a gold Rolex!"

Azzis pulled on the bill of his cap.

Richard reached for the prized possession, but his assistant was faster, slapping his hand away and reeling off something in Arabic. He laughed, though he had no idea what Azzis said. As they drove, Ajibba's jeweled residents, the baffling omda who'd rushed them out of his village, the huge satellite dish, the talk of superstition and the possible danger of the giant cat began to overwhelm him.

"What do you think, Azzis?"

"Eeee, I think what a fine dinner that tethered goat in Ajibba would make."

Chapter Four

Within thirteen hours of the American professor's visit to Ajibba, the black Mercedes skidded to a stop in front of the omda's home. Teliah Motrinsh had been expecting the visit. Still, the roar of the car's engine made him grip the rough edges of his dining table. He sat in front of uneaten sweet cakes of grain and honey while his two children slipped under the table and clung to him. But his wife stood when the door to their house flew open.

"Have your morning meal with us, Jabby," she said.

Jaber flinched when he was called by his boyhood name. "Come with me, fat man," he said, barely audible and in English, as always.

Teliah searched the young brute's face as they walked away from the house toward the desert. Though only twenty-one, his pockmarked skin looked as worn as the pyramids, and his eyes, set as deep as the catacombs, had no life. There wasn't a trace of kindness in his countenance.

"Get those American pot hunters the hell out of my desert," Jaber yelled.

"But they are here with government approval. How can a mere *omda* change that?"

"Did I not tell you that idiotic legend you made up would bring nothing but trouble?" Jaber ran his fingers through his gelled American-styled hair and lit one of his filthy brown cigarettes. "Rumors of your fucking legendary cat and its 'good fortune' have already reached Cairo."

"Not in ten centuries would I have ever imagined that a giant cat, of all Allah's creatures, would appear near our Ajibba!"

"Kill it."

Teliah glared at the youth's stony face until his own fright made him look away. He turned toward the empty horizon, still able to see an image of the restless cat. "But think of this incredible coincidence." His throat tightened as he spoke the words. "What if, by my making something up, it came true?"

"You ignorant farmer!" Jaber grabbed his wrist and pulled him close.

The clutching hand was still cool to the touch from the car's air conditioning. When he brought his mouth close to Teliah's ear, he was afraid he might bite it off.

"You fix your mess or I'll take back this gold watch and your arm with it." Jaber squeezed the intricate band of the Rolex until it cut into Teliah's flesh, then spat on the village leader's sandaled feet and left.

When Teliah returned to his house, his children were busy painting turquoise handprints on the front door to keep evil spirits away. He smiled briefly at their innocent faces, the smile leaving at the thought of the evil Jaber al-Sabath, his business partner. Despite his young age, this man had already established a reputation ghastly enough to have spread far beyond their small farming village.

Rumor was that Jaber had done some terrible thing involving his twin sister, lovely Katia. Those who had known Jaber before that day were convinced that torment over this wrong eventually rotted him from the inside out.

He knew what Jaber had done and thought of it often, that day the twins left Ajibba for Cairo. But the brother returned alone, wearing a gold necklace worth six times the amount of money they'd left with.

Teliah had rushed to Cairo in his horse-drawn wagon that night with images of poor Katia trying to swim the Nile in the long cotton skirt the boy told them she'd modestly refused to take off. Over and over he imagined how the muddy current had pulled at her, how the skirt had billowed and how like a river perch in a seine it must have dragged her under. But when he arrived at the city the next day there was no talk of a drowning. Teliah went to the authorities. He spoke to the shop owners, and stood on the muddy bank of the river and asked everyone — tourists and beggars, if they knew of Katia's bad fortune. He wandered through the winding maze of Cairo's dusty streets, and even viewed three decomposed female bodies in the basement of the old hospital on the Corniche el-Nil.

He could find no trace.

After two days of searching, he returned to Ajibba, to the mother.

"Where is my child?" She cried like a wounded jackal.

Teliah held the woman's fragile hand as neighbors squeezed in around her front door. They pressed against the sheer yellowed cloth in the window and spoke to each other in whispers that sounded like scurrying scorpions.

"Everyone talked of the tragedy," he told the grieving woman. "The river police dredged the water with their motor boats and the *Hukumdar's* grimy dogs searched the phragmite reeds, but our beautiful Katia has vanished. The River Nile has claimed her," he lied.

The scorpions grew quiet, and in the darkest corner of the room he saw Jaber close his fierce eye in deference to Teliah's shrewd business sense.

Six years later, he still regretted that moment when he and the insolent brute youth became partners. Not a day went by that he didn't wonder if Katia would have been returned to them if he had not lied about her disappearance. And now that he had children of his own, he could not help but see the sweet girl's face every time he looked at his own daughter. Every day brought the possibility that his greedy deception would come back to harm him or his family. He accepted Jaber's cruelty as his punishment. He took responsibility for the tyrant's mother. He governed his small village altruistically and, without their knowing, shared his unscrupulous wealth with them. Every day was nothing more than another chance to make up for this sin.

He rubbed the dried blood away from his wrist where the gold watchband had cut him, then hugged each of his children before going into his home. Kneeling on his rug, he prayed that the American professor would lose interest in the mysterious cat. He prayed that the three hundred and fifty-two people in his village would not speak of the legend he himself had made up. He prayed that the cat would go away. And, as always, he prayed that Allah would forgive him for his greed.

Two days later, the black Mercedes was again parked in front of his home. Teliah ran his chubby hand across the hood of the car, still warm to the touch, but not hot. The young heathen was most likely visiting with his mother, the only person in Egypt who didn't know her son for the scourge he was.

Teliah crossed the dirt road and rushed down three narrow alleys, afraid of every shadow. Inside his office, he locked the door with a metal slide bolt and shoved a heavy wooden table in front of it. He leaned on the table as he caught his breath and prayed that this moment of cowardly retreat would not be his last. With the shades pulled, he rolled back a Turkish rug until the small steel door in his office floor was exposed. A series of numbers, his first child's birth date, entered into the LED recessed in the door's frame, set it in motion. It hummed, a resonance, much like the black Mercedes sounded from a distance. A second door, reinforced with a twelve-inch plate of pure copper and operated with the numbers of his second child's birth date, released seven large bolts and allowed him passage to the cool, dark vault beneath.

Lights in the space below automatically came on when he placed his sandy balgha on the first metal step. He checked the thermostat — fifty-five degrees — then put on the red knit sweater that hung on the wall near the bottom of the stairs. He checked the generator, then each fourteen-inch reinforced concrete wall for damage. He checked the concrete floor for condensation. He inspected thirty of the two hundred glass cases, and the treasures inside them. Only then, in the intoxicating scent of his ancestor's creations, was he able to relax.

Time alone with the antiquities always passed too quickly. He went to the case that housed his favorite artifact: a cat statuette made of turquoise.

"At least Jaber and his thieves are professionals," he said to the small statuette he cradled in his hand. "Not like those looters who bulldoze and even dynamite to get at treasures such as yourself."

If the insurance company would not pay the ransom on this favorite piece, he could possess it that much longer. Or at least until Jaber found a private buyer. Maybe he could even purchase it, though the black-hearted thief would ridicule him.

He placed the stone carving back on its bed of silica gel packets and forced himself to go back up the stairs to the world above, a world for which he had only himself to blame. But after setting the alarmed steel doors and rolling the dusty rug back in its place, he felt too tired to move the table that still blocked the entrance. Instead, he sat at his desk and pulled his latest copy of *Sotheby's Current Auction Prices* from the drawer. Underneath it was a two-year-old publication from Interpol, the organization headquartered in Saint Cloud, France, that monitored art thefts. Twenty items on this list had been in his tenure under the floor of his office at the time of the magazine's printing. Any other day he might have enjoyed figuring out how many pieces he could currently account for, but not this day. The mysterious appearance of the giant cat had put everything in a different perspective. How was it possible for something he'd made up to come to be? Surely, Allah was punishing him.

The weight of centuries pushed down on him, pinned him to his chair. But seconds later he was on his feet, face to face with Jaber, the snake's hand coiled around his neck, smelling of his vile cigarettes, forcing him toward the front door that was suddenly wide open.

Jaber did not let go until they came to a stop at the satellite dish behind Ajibba's community building. As the youth paced around it, the painted matte image of the mysterious cat on the dish's metallic surface grew larger. The fringe of blue beaded necklaces strung from the dish's edge clattered louder in the relentless wind. The villagers' offerings of barley, sugar cane, onion, maize and field mice at the base of the dish suddenly smelled rancid.

"How could you allow this?"

Teliah dabbed at the sweat on his face with the sleeve of his striped gellabeya and felt as though he were about to swallow his own tongue. "Our people have embraced the magic of television. They think they can communicate with our legendary cat by using the same transmissions."

"Our legendary cat? Your legendary cat, you shit-eating hayseed." Jaber spoke in Arabic now, which for some reason made him sound more threatening. The thief turned toward the dish and kicked the elaborate display of candles around it with his Italian-made shoes.

"I am about to achieve a deal of a lifetime, our American mule is on his way as we speak, and you and your ignorant farmers have drawn attention to this stupid village! My half-wit cousin says there's even an item in one of those in-flight airline magazines about it — your damned mystery cat is being used to advertise Egypt."

Jaber grabbed him by the back of his neck again and brought his mouth close, close as in a kiss, and his black eyes sucked him under like bottomless pools of smoldering crude oil.

"It's simple, fat man. Either the cat dies or you do."

Chapter Five

The loud drone of jet engines reverberated through the skin of the Egypt Air 747 and then through May. Jason and Grace had headed toward the first class section over an hour before. They'd left her surrounded by people who snored, some with their mouths open so wide she could see their silver fillings. The man across the aisle started a conversation, his mustache of several colors riding his upper lip like a nervous caterpillar. He passed her his business card, leaned across the space between them and clutched her arm. She pulled away.

"I don't need life insurance. With my bad luck I'll live forever." She moved to the window seat, took a roll of Lifesavers from her pocket, and popped a red, orange and yellow one into her mouth all at the same time.

Two gray-haired women seated in front of May whispered to one another. They turned and glared at her as if she were trying to eavesdrop. What did they expect? There was no place for her to go. She certainly couldn't join Jason and Grace after they'd left without even asking her along. Everyone was crammed in on top of one another, and yet these two scowled at her. She tried to make herself smaller, but it wasn't easy in the space. She didn't know how larger people like Jason and Grace traveled. Perhaps they had headed to the first class section simply for more room? She tried not to think about them, or the two ladies' incessant whispering from the row in front, though certain words kept seeping between the blue cushioned seats: money, artifacts, banker. She worked a crossword, read the airplane magazine, then rested her head against the hazy double-pane windows and fell asleep.

She dreamed she was drowning. Her lungs ached and she struggled for breath, just as an enormous black cat dove beneath her. Clinging to the short hairs of its neck while straddling its back, they surfaced into a sea of waves.

She woke up, remembering the cat from the funeral, how it had sat on top of the coffin, never making a sound or move through the whole ceremony, as if it were protecting her daughter.

Back in their seats, Grace and Jason stared at her.

"You were making noises," Jason said.

She straightened up, trying to smooth her curly dark hair into place.

"I sold a half-pager!" Grace said. "One of the good ol' boys in first class owns a pest control company. Thank goodness Houston roaches don't know bad from good economy!" She laughed and flung her silky blonde hair over her shoulder. That hair, always the reminder to May of what opposite images she and her friend were. Blonde. Tall. Fair-skinned. Bossy. Loud. And Grace could talk forever about anything — at that moment, the ad. She didn't stop until their dinners arrived. Once the servings of roast beef with string beans or chicken breast and noodles were wedged on the trays in front of them, the entire plane grew quiet. Too quiet, the silence suddenly uncomfortable for May.

"How's your dinner, Jason?"

"It's airplane food. Same as always."

"Same as always?" But nothing was the same as always. Everything had changed since Susan died. The length of the day. The weight of thoughts. The sound of footsteps. Jason.

He took another bite.

We might as well be on different planes, she thought.

Grace pecked at the food on her plate with her fork like some baby bird, a habit since they were children.

After the meal, only a few tiny beams of light stayed on — reading lamps above those passengers who chose to stay awake, or had never mastered the art of in-flight slumber. The space grew so black May was afraid she'd drifted outside of the plane. In the darkness, she looked for the large cat from her dream. But there was nothing. She held on to Jason's hand while he slept so she wouldn't float away.

The twenty-three hours of different flights had been grueling. The sun no longer set and rose by the clock, meals were served at unexpected times, sleep took over without warning, then left too abruptly. The plane became its own little continent, its citizens tolerating each other less with each hour, seeking the illusion of privacy in a novel, or in music, or in the movies that played continuously on the large screen. By the time they reached Egypt, Texas felt like a memory.

With land in sight, newspapers rustled, children cried, the smell of coffee permeated the air. Grace left her seat to talk to the group of Rice University students who were meeting her cousin Richard Sutton for the second semester of his class.

May raised the window shade for her first glimpse of Egypt. Spread beneath her was a country of brown and ocher hues that stretched from the blue edge of the Mediterranean Sea to the horizon. She'd flown through a dark sky of emptiness only to set down on a land of the same.

Chapter Six

Two days after the cat's appearance, Richard Sutton still had not tired of watching his students endlessly re-enact the encounter for those who had not been on shift at the time. But no one did it as well as he, especially acting out the very moment that, when confronted by the cat, he had thrown the only thing available — his watch.

"As a professor of archeology, wasn't it appropriate to use a piece of time as my defense?" Everyone would laugh. The humor helped their uneasiness over not only the gun from Cairo that he kept strapped to his belt at all times, but also the cat's steadfast presence.

Daily, he watched the gray cat like some afternoon shadow creep close to their camp. At times the animal, looking like a mixture of tiger, lion, jaguar, and friendly house tabby, didn't seem real. Its existence cast a fantastic light on all their activity, making everything appear just like the adventures he'd imagined as a boy so long ago, in the gravel yards his father and uncle owned in Houston. Even then he pretended to be a great archeologist. It was easy to turn a hot Texas day into a parched Egyptian dream. He saw golden pyramids and tombs of treasures, an oasis and single-hump camels. When his cousin, Grace Sutton, was there, she became his trusty assistant. And if her best friend May was along, she, unknowingly, became a beautiful dancer in flowing, tissue-thin garments without any underwear. But he never imagined a lion-sized cat.

Then again, he never imagined that a student program could turn up real treasures. As each day's dig brought forth another, he knew conclusively they'd uncovered a mastaba. Of course, they hadn't yet unearthed coffins, mummified bodies or even any body parts, but his students never gave up hope.

What they had found were pieces of obsidian, lapis lazuli bowls, a small gold vase, the body of a harp, and silver earrings in the shape of a crescent moon. Each item was tagged, numbered, weighed, photographed, sketched and described, just as he'd taught in the beginning classes.

There was no time to worry about the lurking cat; the days were too short, too thrilling. He put Azzis in charge of the mundane: the meals, the tents, the generator. It wasn't until the assistant shoved a calendar in front of him and pointed to a notation in Richard's own handwriting that he realized he'd lost track of time.

"Our next semester students arrive tomorrow! And with them, my cousin Grace and her beautiful friend May."

"And May's husband," Azzis said.

"It's more than fifteen years since I've seen the Little Orphan."

"Your cousin?" Azzis said.

"No, May. Little Orphan was what our family called her. Not to her face, of course. We always fussed and paid special attention to her, drove Grace crazy."

"Americans are pathetic people," Azzis said.

"No, just my dear cousin at times."

He remembered the Little Orphan's deliberate movements, precise hand gestures, cautious ballerina footsteps. She was lovely, in spite of the heavy burden of losing both parents at such a young age. "She's the same age as my cousin, close to thirty now. I'm just four years older than her, but back then…."

"I know, rubbing the cradle," Azzis said.

"Robbing the cradle. But you knew that."

Chapter Seven

May was last. Behind Jason and Grace and the archeology students, she was last to retrieve her bags, last to check through Alexandria Airport Customs, and last to emerge from an endless hallway into the passenger pick-up area.

An Egyptian wearing an Astros baseball cap held a large white sign with Professor Sutton's name scrawled across it. They followed him to a dusty white bus idling loudly in the airport's parking lot.

"Hello!" An American climbed down from the driver's seat and tried to hug all the students at once. His beard covered a tanned and smiling face, and his sandaled feet were as dusty as the wheels of the old bus.

One of the students pointed to it. "Is this the first of our Egyptian relics, Professor?"

Everyone laughed, including the man in the baseball cap who affectionately slapped the side of the bus as if it were the ass of a donkey.

The professor kissed Grace on the cheek.

Grace introduced him to Jason. "And you remember May," she said.

"Of course, I remember May! We played together in your back yard, Grace. I was the famous archaeologist and you both were my assistants."

"I wouldn't have recognized you," May said.

"It's the beard." Richard stroked his chin and then hugged her. "Wasn't quite this heavy when I was a boy."

"I remember the hidden treasure always ended up in the pool," May said.

"The Red Sea," he said.

"I remember one of us always ended up in the pool after it," Grace said. "And it was usually me."

Richard punched her lightly on her arm then turned toward Jason. "I'm glad you were able to use the extra tickets."

Jason shook his hand. "We had a hard time convincing my wife."

Richard looked at May.

"It's not that I'm not appreciative, I'm just not much of a traveler," she said.

He took hold of her hand. "But you don't travel through Egypt, Egypt travels through you."

While the man with the large sign took charge of the students, Richard told the three of them about his class, and how the students already with him for the first semester had unexpectedly unearthed something. Holding May's hand the entire time, his grip was comforting, not controlling. "We weren't supposed to discover anything, it was just an exercise. But now our dig has ended up in a completely different place than we'd scheduled. I had to drive my first semester students over a hundred miles to this airport so they could go home, and now I have to drive these kids and this old bus full of supplies back. My plan was to stay longer and visit with you, but I'm afraid I only have time for dinner tonight, as we'll be leaving tomorrow, and I was hoping ..."

He let go of her hand and walked away from them in the middle of his own sentence. Grace followed him while he loaded suitcases, cardboard boxes tied with rope, green duffel bags and bulging backpacks into the hollow of the bus.

"It's a land of miracles!" Richard called out through the open window when they pulled away. A few of the students waved good-bye.

A gust of desert wind swirled at May's ankles. It soothed her, like a warm blast from an open oven. A land of miracles?

Jason pointed at the long line of tourists in front of them. "We'll need a miracle to get a cab out of here."

Grace tipped a porter to flag down a ride rather than wait their turn in the hot sun. The man whistled a dusty, turquoise Chevy to the curb. An Asian man with a dull aluminum case on his lap was in the back seat.

"You share," the white-capped porter said as he maneuvered suitcases, bags, purses and people so they would fit.

Jason sat in the front of the taxi with the driver and three of their suitcases; May sat in the back with Grace, shoulder to shoulder with the stranger who sat between them. He smelled like lime. As they pulled away, May spotted the two gray-haired ladies from their flight. She smirked at them, happy she no longer had to put up with their snooty glares, but they stared at the man who sat next to her instead. May thought she saw him nod to them, but he was probably being polite — good manners, something she no longer had a grasp of.

"Hello," Grace said in that tone of voice that May knew really meant: I have space to sell in a Houston magazine.

He nodded again.

"You here on business?"

"Yes. And you?"

"Tourists." Grace introduced Jason and May. "What business are you in?"

"Trade. And you?"

"Jason works at the Houston Zoo. May and I work at *Houston Harbinger Magazine.* May's the art director, I'm in sales."

May couldn't bear to hear the sales pitch she knew was coming. "Can you believe a summer class of greenhorns actually discovered something? Did Richard tell you anything more?"

Grace twisted her mouth as though she'd just eaten something sour and gestured toward the citrus-smelling stranger. "My cousin said not to discuss it."

Jason laughed and shifted around on the front seat; he was always making fun of Grace's dramatics.

"A lot of the photographers who work for the magazine use that same case you have to protect cameras and lenses. A Zero Halliburton?" Grace said.

He nodded and tapped his fingers against the case. His heavy jade ring clanked three times as it struck the aluminum.

"Then you've been to Egypt before?" Grace said.

"Many times."

"And have you found it be a land of miracles?" May said.

"For Christ's sake, May!" Jason threw his left arm over the car seat and pushed on her leg. "My wife doesn't even know tourist bullshit when she hears it."

Grace reached across the aluminum briefcase and punched Jason in his arm. He turned back around. May popped Lifesavers into her mouth. The taxi driver began to whistle, but his passengers rode without speaking. The traffic inched down narrow streets lined with colorful shops.

Vendors yelled to them, sometimes pushing their wares through the open windows of the car: costume jewelry, loofahs, copper plates, leather goods.

"Americans first," the driver said.

The doorman at the Alexandria Hotel Cecil rushed to retrieve their luggage while the taxi shook in its own warm air. As it was about to pull away from the curb, the Asian in the back leaned out the window and touched May's arm.

"Miracles are overrated," he said.

She watched the cab until it disappeared behind a corner building. When she turned back around, Jason was at the front desk and Grace was with the porters. They hadn't heard this parting comment.

The Hotel Cecil's lobby was furnished in French formal rather than the Egyptian decor she'd expected. There were enormous couches in black and white striped satin, ornate shaded floor lamps and antique marble-top tables; everything was elegant but worn with age. Even the large crystal bowls of scented potpourri couldn't keep the air from smelling old. Heavy brocade draped the small windows, dusty chandeliers suspended from crushed velvet sheaths swayed precariously overhead, and the floral-patterned carpet was missing entire bouquet designs in the most frequently traveled areas. She found it endearing. Like Grace's Great-Aunt Ruthie, a distinguished matron who wore fancy white gloves at all times to cover the brown spots of age.

Three boys in white gellabeyas with red silk sashes and leather sandals that flopped away from their heels, carried the luggage to the elevator.

Jason towered over the dark-skinned youths as he gave them a tip. The smallest porter, who wore a black Casio watch too big for his wrist, handed him a business card: a torn piece of paper with a single name, "Bezhad," handwritten in crayon. When the boy wasn't looking, Jason crumpled the card and threw it on the carpet.

"You might want to hang onto your money, big shot. This is only the first day of our trip." Grace gestured toward the boys, who were admiring the American dollars.

When he turned back around he almost fell over May, who'd

bent over to pick up the discarded card. "Watch yourself," he said.

The British concierge, Mr. Kerrington, gave them brochures about the hotel and flyers on things to do in Alexandria. When Grace shook his hand good-bye, he pulled her close and glanced at the straps of her yellow sundress. "I must tell you that bare shoulders are inappropriate for this predominantly Moslem country. Since Sadat's death, there's been a shift back to more prohibitive styles."

"Thanks for letting me know," she said. But when she turned away from him she made her just-tasted-something-sour face again.

The Worths' room was three doors down the hall from Grace's. Jason disappeared as May unpacked their bags under twelve-foot-high ceilings and two slow-moving ceiling fans. She stirred the potpourri that was in a bowl by the door, the same scent used in the lobby. There was one telephone and a two-shelf refrigerator stocked with Coca-colas and bottled water. No television. In one of the bureaus, she found candles, matches and flashlights. Jason reappeared right before it was time for dinner.

"Where have you been?"

"Out," he said.

▲▲▲

Grace showed up for dinner in a strapless dress so sheer spiders might have spun it.

"What if the concierge sees you?" May said.

She tossed her sunny-blonde hair over one shoulder and headed for the hotel's dining area, her long stork-like legs exaggerated by the shortness of the dress.

Richard joined them just as they arrived at their table. It was on a balcony overgrown with bougainvillea overlooking Alexandria's Eastern Harbor. He put his arm around May, helped seat her and then sat beside her. She and Grace asked him about the dig; Jason was quiet.

"It was supposed to have been in El Maghra. But while we were visiting a small museum in Zagazig, one of my students noticed something strange on a papyrus map of the ancient city, a map that was drawn more than three thousand years before. Its execution was perfect — the line, the measurement, even the intricate border of small gold and blue triangles that framed it, but a large triangle drawn around the outskirts of the city was askew. There was a plaque describing the triangle as a symbol for the pyramids being erected along the western bank of the Nile at that time, but my student questioned it, and I agreed."

Jason gave one of his impatient looks May knew all too well, took a large gulp of wine and set his glass down on the edge of the table. She moved it back toward the center, pleased that the look didn't hurry Richard. If anything, he slowed the pace of his story.

In great detail he explained how odd it seemed for an Egyptian craftsman to use a symbolic image on, of all things, a document intended for accurate measurement of distance and location. When his student asked if he thought the three points of the triangle might designate important areas, he wanted to reward her thinking. It took some work, red tape and all, but he was able to relocate the dig to one of these very three points.

"No one expected to find anything. It was just summer curriculum," Richard said.

"But they did, land of miracles, blah, blah, blah," Jason made a circular motion with his hand like some big-shot director on a movie set hurrying his actor's lines.

"Well, mostly just bricks, but bricks, we believe, from a tomb. Also pieces of jewelry and pots and *canopic* jars." The look on their faces must have prompted his explanation. "They're clay vessels used to hold the internal organs of the dead."

May thought immediately of Susan's white glossy casket with the wreath of tea roses on it, the embroidered violets on the pillow inside. Fresh. Clean. Sweet smelling. But the image of a clay vessel forced its way in, ancient and chipped, stuffed with kidneys and intestines coiled in the jar's bottom like an old sleeping snake.

The waiters came with ahwa turki, thick black coffee served in china cups with handles too small for Jason's fingers.

Grace toyed with the crystal pendant at her throat and looked across the Eastern Harbor where hundreds of sailboats were moored. "Look, from here their empty masts look like tiny toothpick crucifixes."

"Only you would see something like that," Jason said. He set down the delicate cup and pushed at it with his index finger until it teetered on the edge of the table.

May placed it back in the center. Richard took her arm and walked her to the balcony's rail.

"I'm so sorry to hear about your daughter, I don't know what to say."

"Jason and Grace think this trip will help me, as if a sunny day makes a sad person feel better."

He squeezed her arm. They watched a boat maneuver into one of the slips.

"I wish you could come back to the dig with me."

"I wouldn't enjoy it, I don't enjoy anything anymore."

"Not even the mysterious cat that's been hanging around our camp?"

"A cat? A large cat?"

"Large? No, probably just five hundred pounds." He laughed.

Her breath stuck in her throat. "But how did you know?"

"I remembered you loved cats; I remember everything about you."

She felt light. Unanchored, she held on to the railing. "Is it black?"

He gasped, imitating her. "But how did you know?" He stopped smiling when she didn't laugh with him. "I'm kidding, it's gray and black, gray mostly. What's the matter?"

"I dreamed of a large cat on the plane. It saved me."

"From what?"

Grace walked to the balcony's railing. "So what do we want to see tomorrow? The promenade? The beach? I know, Pompey's Pillar. I think Jason would enjoy the Pillar. I read that it stands in the rubble of a temple that was dedicated to a god who manifested himself in the form of a bull!"

"More tourist bull." Jason laughed.

May walked back to her seat at the table.

"Richard, some of the girls in your class were flirting with you," Grace said, and then stroked his face. "Of course, you do have the Sutton family's handsome square jaw." She used that husky tone of hers that May detested.

Jason suddenly stroked his own square jaw.

"Now that I think of it, May, didn't you use to have a crush on my cousin?"

May felt Jason's foot press twice on hers under the table. She knew the drill. She pushed her chair back and yawned.

"Better get this party pooper to bed," he said.

"I'm gone in the morning," Richard said. "It was great to see you again, May."

She hugged him good-bye; Jason didn't even shake his hand.

On the way back to their hotel room, they walked on a pattern of disappearing bouquets on the hallway carpet. Jason draped a heavy arm over her shoulder, making her change the stride of her own step.

The hotel maid had turned down the covers, dropped the mosquito netting around their bed and sprayed the room with an insect repellent that still hung in the air even though all the screened windows were open. While Jason was in the bathroom, she lay on the bed. Turned diagonally at first, she then rolled into the center, stretching her arms and legs in each direction to get a feel for the bed's size. Sleeping had become a problem. In Houston their quilt seemed too small. No matter what position she started out in, during the night Jason's knees would knock hers and her hair would get trapped under his shoulder and his breath would come at her from all angles — warm and smelling of scotch. He'd complained about their three pet cats that slept with them. She suggested they buy a larger bed.

"Boo! I'm an Egyptian mummy!" He stood nude in front her, the mosquito netting wrapped around him. The white mesh flattened his upper lip so it covered one of his nostrils, and his right eye became a brown furry slit. His left eye stretched open so wide, the fleshy red of his lid showed. He lunged at her.

"You're too heavy, Jason." He was on top of her making mummy moans. She couldn't breathe.

He pressed against her, started to take off her blouse.

"Let me up."

He held her down. His breath on her face, this time smelling from the red wine he'd shared with Grace. "You don't want to hold my hand like you held the professor's?"

"Get off!" She pushed against one of his shoulders, drew her legs up and rolled out from under him. She ran into the bathroom, locked the door, turned the bath faucet on and cried into a towel. She pressed her face into it, then pressed harder. And harder. She hoped she would just stop breathing. But she let the towel drop, knowing her body would betray her. Even if she passed out, it would take in air. Even if she tried to stop crying, it would keep on. There was no controlling it any longer; it ate when she wasn't hungry, slept when she wasn't tired, spoke up when she should have been quiet and pushed Jason away when he wanted to make love. Here she was again, this time locked in a bathroom halfway across the world.

The doorknob turned.

"Jesus Christ, May. Open up!" He pounded on the door.

"I'm showering!" She always locked the door while she bathed — it was protection against the pranks he thought were funny. She couldn't count the number of times he'd dumped a pitcher of ice water on her while she stood in the shower, or the times he'd slipped cold noodles into the tub so they'd wrap around her feet like nesting water moccasins, or the times he'd replaced her shampoo with ketchup so that all she saw when she opened her eyes was the bloody bath scene from the movie *Psycho*. Once after she'd just turned her face toward the showerhead, knives pierced right through her back and buttocks. She screamed even before she felt the pain. When she looked behind her, her cat, Blue Bell, clung for dear life, dug into her backside, terrified of the water around and below him. Even after she had backed out of the shower and turned the water off, the traumatized animal wouldn't let go. Jason had to pry him loose.

Undressed, she turned her back toward the mirror to see the thin white scars that Blue Bell had etched into her all those years ago. She didn't mind them. It only seemed fair that her poor kitty had not suffered Jason's prank alone. She sat down on the cool edge of the tub, turned the bath water off and waited for Jason's snoring.

That first night in Alexandria, she again dreamed she was drowning. The water rushed into her mouth and down her throat. It tasted of sulfur, burned her tongue, bubbled up through her nose. She sank until the giant black cat caught her. When they surfaced, a dark figure paced on a nearby shore.

She coughed, took in a deep breath of air as she woke. It was only three in the morning, but Jason was already showered and dressed. His sandy-brown hair neatly combed, he wore his favorite outfit: a tan starched shirt with faded blue jeans, his black lizard belt and alligator cowboy boots.

"I keep having this dream about a huge black cat," she said.
He just stared at her.
"You okay, Jason?"
"Can't sleep. Guess it's just the time difference."
Time difference. Probably another hangover.

Chapter Eight

When Richard and Azzis returned to the dig with the new semester's students, a representative from the Cairo Museum and a government aide were waiting for them with Azzis's five relatives. The family members had been left behind to guard the discoveries. They rushed to Azzis, anxious to tell him about the days he had missed and how they had befriended the large cat.

"Something wrong?" Richard asked.

"They say the big cat sleeps and eats with them. He'll even do tricks for my Aunt Sada's *fetir meshaltet.*"

Richard looked around the site and immediately spotted the cat lazing in the shadow of the food tent. He laughed.

The new students were able to view all the treasures as he presented them for documentation to the museum representative, who asked many questions about the antiquities. But the government aide asked only about the large cat. Richard put him at ease, explaining the animal just as the neighboring fellahin had initially to him.

"He's an overgrown pussy cat!"

The aide wrote notes on a pre-printed form, checking boxes, no longer paying attention to Richard.

"He likes Aunt Sada's *fetir meshaltet*, for crying out loud! He's one of us."

In spite of what he said, the next day a military truck with four teen-aged soldiers in tan uniforms and M-14 rifles showed up at the site. They paid no attention when he tried to stop them. The tallest one pushed him to the ground. Azzis intervened.

The cat made no attempt to run. It didn't make a sound when the soldiers prodded it with the barrels of their rifles and forced it into the steel mesh cage on the back of their truck. They slapped each other's hands, as if they had truly conquered a feral beast, and then jumped into the cab of the truck. When they sped away, a cloud of desert dust concealed the cat from Richard's view. He missed the animal immediately.

The following days, he checked the white dunes around the dig. Nothing. He threw Coke cans at creeping afternoon shadows.

Three nights after the cat had been taken, he spotted hundreds of moving lights in the neighboring village of Ajibba, the same village where he and Azzis had stopped. He had the assistant drive to the village the next day to find out if there'd been a celebration.

"The *fellahin* had a candlelight vigil for the missing cat. They've made a shrine of the big television dish," Azzis told him when he returned. "They have painted the gray cat on its metal surface and have offerings of rodents and such at the base."

"Our gray cat? But why?"

Azzis pulled on the paisley-patterned scarf threaded through the belt loops of the American Levis he'd won from Richard in a poker game. "I am from the city," he said with pride, "they will not tell to me."

Richard drove to Ajibba the next day. Two young children at the large metallic dish dipped their hands into a pan of blue paint, side-stepped through lighted candles, dried-out breads and cookies, spoiling melons and apples, and decaying rodents at the base of the dish in order to make tiny blue hand prints on the flat surface above them.

He smiled at the young boy and girl, knowing their imprints were to guard the cat from evil spirits. He, too, approached the dish, stepping over small folded pieces of paper with inscriptions written on them, a pair of sandals, a terra cotta dish with water in it, and some yellow and blue plastic building blocks. He admired the painted image of the lion-sized cat on the dish's surface, then placed his own Timex at its base. When he turned back around, the omda stood in front of him, arms crossed.

"Hello again," Richard said.

The omda dropped his arms to his side and sighed. The sleeves of his gray and white gellabeya covered all but the very tips of his fingers as he gestured for Richard to follow him. They walked down a dusty alley into a small office, where they sat on creaking wooden chairs on opposite sides of a writing desk.

"I made up a little story." Teliah spread his hands palms down and strummed his fingers on the worn surface of the table. "You see, I have a small business on the side — something one might call a 'conflict of interest' for a paid government official. I wanted to share the profits with my fellow villagers, but they are proud people. I could not just give them money with no explanation, and to explain was out of the question.

"It was a story as harmless as your Santa Claus, or Easter Bunny. Not that they really believed it, but I think somehow they knew not to ask for the truth. I told them I dreamed of a giant cat that showed me where treasures were buried around our village. I bought *Pharoni* — imitation knickknacks made for the tourists in Cairo — then buried them myself. Days, sometimes weeks, later I would go out to the desert to discover something. I let the children go with me; it was great fun for them, and me, just a festive event that became a tradition. They didn't know I would dump these finds in Cairo. They thought the money or gifts I returned with were from sales. We were better for the story. My people all walked a little taller. We could afford the doctors in Cairo for our children. Better food. Better clothes. The big screen TV." Teliah stood and stretched his arms to either side of him. "We got to see who killed J.R., reruns, for goodness' sake!"

Richard turned away from the omda's unctuous smile and caught sight of a *Sotheby's Current Auction Prices* on the corner of the desk. He reached to pick it up, but Teliah snatched it first, his smile gone.

"I don't like your type," the omda said.

"Then why share a secret with me?"

"Because you foreigners dig and dig until you have answers that don't belong to you. Just like you dig for treasures that don't belong to you, either. You reap fame and fortune off my ancestors' sweat — riches that should go to me and my people." The government official paced back and forth, grew short of breath.

"So why tell me?"

The omda slammed the *Sotheby's* price list down on the table and plopped in his chair. He leaned back and looked at him as if he were staring through the bottom part of bifocals.

"Because the only thing you spoiled Americans understand is your happy Hollywood ending. Don't ruin this for my people. How could I have ever imagined a real cat would show up? But now that the government has taken it away, let it be. Let my neighbors have their happily ever after. Don't dig up this story for your *People Magazine* and your *National Enquirer*. I don't need the publicity."

Richard felt his face grow warm. He was an intruder. If anyone had claim on the mysterious feline it was certainly the omda, who without even realizing it had foretold the cat's appearance.

He stood and held out his hand. "You're right. Sorry for the intrusion."

He kept his hand outstretched, but Teliah didn't move. In the silence, waiting, there was a whirring noise — like a generator starting up. The omda stood suddenly, laughed loudly, came around the small table and noisily embraced him. Once again he was escorted to the Jeep as if he were an old friend, the official's hand on his shoulder.

"It's a remarkable coincidence, don't you agree?" Richard said. "That you should make up a story about a cat and then have one appear."

He started the car, put it in gear and then felt a touch upon his shoulder one more time.

"I see you are suddenly without a watch." Teliah laughed and removed the gold Rolex from his own wrist. "Take mine."

"I couldn't!"

"Then what?"

He looked across the hot waves of air drifting up from the desert sand. "A business tip. Your conflict of interest? Perhaps a venture I should look into?"

Teliah looked away, his brown face turned ruddy. The car sputtered a few times before he turned back again, this time with a broad smile and a gold-capped side tooth shining.

"Recycling," the omda said.

▲▲▲

The omda stood at the edge of his village, content to watch the open-top Jeep until even the wake of dust it created was gone. He became the barren landscape and the perfect blue sky and for one brief moment felt his world come to a halt, even the desert wind. The stillness was soothing, his mind as quiet as the tranquil green pools of

Nile water that occasionally slipped away from the churning current. Then he broke out in a great cool sweat. Soaked beneath his gellabeya, his body wept from every pore. He cried. He cried with relief, gleeful in a sudden clarity that Allah had not sent the magnificent cat to punish him, but to help free him at last from his past sins and the oppressive sentence he had endured under the tyrannical eye of Jaber al-Sabath.

Chapter Nine

That first day in Alexandria, May felt as if she were sleepwalking. She followed Jason and Grace, drifting in her own fog through the downtown streets, and then the Corniche, a fifteen-mile stretch of seafront promenade lined with restaurants, curios and small stores. She didn't even think of buying anything. Mr. Kerrington, the concierge from the Hotel Cecil, had made her too nervous with warnings about the rules of bargaining: visitors from a prosperous country were not to ask for much, especially along the promenade, where vendors paid a high price for location. But Grace adapted to the haggling as if it were some sort of sport, even drawing spectators with her loud negotiations. May was relieved when Jason suddenly got so hungry he made her stop so they could eat.

They waited with a throng of tourists in a chic restaurant on the Corniche while men dressed in striped gellabeyas flurried about, and squeezed additional tables into spaces that didn't exist. It took thirty minutes to be seated. The person who brought their water was different from those who took their drink order, brought pita bread, butter, silverware, napkins and meals. There were as many as seven waiters for every customer.

"*Baksheesh*," Grace read from her *Frommer's Guide*. "To share the wealth. Look at this, every one of them is supposed to get a tip. There's even a chart showing acceptable amounts for each service. First they tell us what to wear, then how to bargain, where to bargain and now how much to tip."

"What?" May had been watching a red-haired woman zigzag through the wash-and-wear outfits and the fancy-colored drinks in the room. As she passed their table, her camera hit the top of Grace's head and the automatic flash went off.

Everyone laughed but Grace.

"Why must you always say 'What, What,'" Grace mimicked her in a nasal childlike tone.

"What?" May said.

"See! You never pay attention."

"I was. You were complaining about all the rules."

"I don't complain. I was making a point."

"About rules? We have as many in our country."

"Of course you would say that. No one in the entire universe follows rules like you do," Grace said.

"What?"

"There you go again!" Grace tugged at her crystal pendant necklace.

"What are you talking about?"

"All those rules you follow!"

"Like?"

"Like," Grace hesitated, "never going even the eensiest bit faster than the speed limit. Never changing lanes without using your stupid blinker. Never sneezing without saying 'Excuse me.' Never burping. As long as I've known you, I've never heard you let out a good old belch."

May shifted in her chair.

"Or how about returning a library book late? Or, Heavens, not putting a return address on an envelope?"

"Or having too much to drink?" Jason said.

Grace laughed.

May's stomach started to hurt.

"Don't be so sensitive," Grace finally said. "We're teasing!" Grace looked at Jason, but he was silent, as he had been for most of the day.

"You need to meet my new friend, Beth Fields. She'd teach you how to loosen up." Grace pulled a gold compact from her purse and put on lipstick the color of a red chili pepper.

May stabbed a piece of lettuce with her fork. "I need to loosen up?"

"Well, just look at you," Grace said.

And then, for what seemed an unbearable amount of time, Grace and Jason did just that — looked at her.

She tried to relax, but the wooden back of her chair had become her spine. She sat too straight, her arms crossed too tightly. The embroidered butterflies on her blouse flapped their wings, and the high-neck collar choked her. She tried to cross her legs nonchalantly, but they stayed locked nonetheless, her knees clamped together and her feet flat to the floor just as the nuns at St. Mary's Catholic Girls School of Houston had taught her and Grace, so many years ago. She moved Jason's glass of water from the corner of the table toward the middle.

A waiter with a nose full of curly hair took her plate and then pointed at her in a friendly manner. "Very rare!" he said in English.

"What?" she said.

The waiter balanced the dirty plates in the crook of his left arm while he pointed to one of the butterflies on her blouse. "Very rare in Egypt."

"She's very rare, indeed!" Jason laughed.

She kept her eye on the waiter's pointed finger that was also thick with curly hairs, as Jason pulled her near. His hangover suddenly gone, now he would be friendly for the rest of the day, which made her feel unfriendly.

"Can't we just have a good time?" he said.

Jason steered them out of the restaurant, even paid for the meal, turning down Grace's offer for her part, and flagged down a taxi. "To the temple of the bullshit," he said, suddenly the cheerful diplomat.

Pompey's Pillar, the famous red granite landmark, stood on top of a grassy hill with large blocks of stone and remnants of broken statuary scattered all around it. Tourists sat in the shade of thick-foliaged mimosa-like trees at the hill's base, fanning themselves with guide maps, travel brochures, straw hats and flattened paper cups. They drank a variety of fruit juices: orange, carrot and pomegranate, advertised on a stand just inside the monument's park entrance.

Just outside the entrance three camels chewed on leaves from a pile of branches before them. They raised their lazy heads and heavy eyelids at each tourist who approached.

"Mister! Take a ride with one of your lady on a ship of the desert!" The owner pointed enthusiastically to his camels. Dust had darkened every crease of his gellabeya, making a vein-like pattern in the material. His mouth was wide, his nose flat and his upper body thick from working his animals.

Jason waved his large hand at the man. No.

"Then I take your picture with one? Three dollar American."

A cloud of dust floated toward them when the man slapped the saddle on the closest camel. They walked past him. Grace pulled a camera from her purse and took a picture just as one of the animals released a stream of urine. She laughed, but May saw the urinating camel had one wide foot raised.

"Jason, stop. It's hurt." She pointed as it barely set the foot down to turn toward them.

"I can't fix it."

"But that's your job."

"Not here it isn't. Besides, the owner would probably jump on the opportunity to sue a rich American even if I healed it."

"But that's what you're trained for. Just take a look, make a suggestion. What harm could that do?"

He started to walk away. She grabbed his hand.

"Maybe it's something as simple as a thorn, or a piece of glass? Remember when you were the only one out of the entire zoo staff that figured out what was wrong with that bear?"

"Well, I just figured out you must have something wrong with your ears, 'cause I said I wasn't going to fix it."

He walked to the crest of the hill. May and Grace followed. On the other side of it was a cemetery. Rolling hills of gravestones, rows of small and large markers in perfect order. There was symmetry in the layout, every plot and plant and path deliberate. Three Egyptian children slept in the shade of one of the headstones.

"I didn't come all this way to look at a graveyard." May headed back to the park entrance.

"So who made you the boss?" Grace said to Jason.

"What?"

Grace spit out the words through her red pepper lips. "First you ordered our lunch at the airport in Houston, then you made us get off the plane in Boston even though there wasn't enough time to go anywhere but the terminal's bar. When we switched planes in Greece you wouldn't let us leave the gate, then in customs you picked the slowest line and made us stand in it. Last night you decided we would eat at the hotel, and you selected the wine without even asking if I wanted white or red. Shopping this morning you actually told May to wait till we got to the restaurant to pee, and just a few minutes ago you refused a camel ride without even knowing if we wanted to go or not."

"You wanna ride one of those pissy-smelling animals? Who's stopping you?"

By the time May reached the camels at the entrance to the park, she could no longer hear Jason and Grace. Many of the tourists were leaving; the juice stand had closed, the sun low to the ground. She followed a skinny man in plaid shorts through the wooden gates and just kept walking. More than ten minutes passed before she stopped. When she looked back toward the Pillar, she saw the three plodding ships of the desert had followed her. The camels approached, the nearest one limping; they had a stench like boiling tar and hacked profusely as they lowered their heavy bodies to the ground, their bristly flanks touching, their crusty hooves tucked under them.

The delta wind stirred and a golden butterfly fluttered over their heads, the rare butterfly the waiter from the tavern had mentioned. The endless desert churned into shimmering fields of sandy ribbons, and the setting sun made the animals' darkened forms look like three giant cats.

The vein-patterned camel owner walked along the shoulder of the road. He shrugged his shoulders so that his light-colored palms faced her. "It is late," he said, his mouth looking even wider now that he did not smile. He made a clucking sound with his tongue. His camels stood, then trudged behind him single-file toward some buildings about a mile away.

On the way back to the Hotel Cecil, she sat between Jason and Grace in the back of a dirty-brown taxi and told them how the camels had followed her.

"They're just stupid, vile animals," Jason said. "Believe me, I take care of seven of them."

There was a time when Jason would come home from his job as a handler at the Houston Zoo and tell her about every animal he'd cared for that day. He called them by name and had framed photos of them on the shelves in their living room next to pictures of Susan. Now he even complained about their three cats sleeping with them, shedding hair everywhere. The grief therapist had told them to be patient with new and unexplained behavior. But Jason not caring about animals was abnormal, and his walking away from a wounded animal was unbelievable.

"You used to like those camels," she said. "Besides, there was something special about these three."

"Like what?" Grace said.

She saw the image of the camels transformed into giant cats. "Like they expected something."

"For Christ's sake, May!" Jason said. "Animals don't expect things, especially stinking camels."

She'd heard the lecture from him just recently. Anthropomorphism: giving human characteristics to animals.

"Look, it's been nine months since we lost Susan. You can't let the sight of a cemetery make you crazy," he said.

She thought of the nine months it had taken for Susan to grow inside of her, how being two people had felt so much more right than she just being herself.

Grace touched her hand. "You and Jason will have more children."

"We won't have Susan!"

They rode in silence. Jason looked out one side of the car and Grace the other. May sucked on a cherry-flavored Lifesaver and stole sideways glances at them. Grace rubbed her crystal pendant obsessively; Jason pressed his face so hard against the car window she was afraid he would break it. They weren't even fazed by the taxi driver's terrifying racetrack maneuvers. Neither of them budged from their separate corners, while she, in the middle, slid back and forth across the slick, vinyl seat cover.

That evening, May became ill. Against her protests, Grace had Mr. Kerrington call the hotel's doctor. A man in a white linen suit carrying a chrome stethoscope showed up at their door, accompanied by two middle-aged men, three women with coal black hair, an older couple who were bent in the same direction, four teenaged girls and five children that never stopped moving. Dr. Bedair Mubarak and his family had been on their way back from dinner when he received the call on his pager, so he brought them all with him.

While she was examined, Jason and Grace stepped into the hallway, where she could hear them answering questions asked in perfect English by the older children about J.R. Ewing. The star of the old television show *Dallas* had just been introduced to the Egyptian public through the wonder of syndicated American reruns.

Dr. Mubarak told her she had gyppie tummy, the tourist's disease. Her system would need two days to adjust to Egyptian food and water. He prescribed Lomotil and told her to rest, drink apple juice, peach nectar and lots of bottled water. He sat at a small wooden table in front of an open window to write the prescription. Sounds from the city below drew his attention outside.

"It's a pretty one tonight," he said.

She could see the moon from her prone position on the bed.

"It's the same moon you already know," he said. "You see? You're not as far away from your home as you thought."

She thought back just four evenings, when they were still in Gullcrest, at the beach house to do those necessary chores before leaving. Jason had flopped on the bed fully clothed, not even bothering to take off his sandy boots. She'd run to the beach with a lizard on her head to return the seashells, to replace what she'd taken, to set the universe back in order.

She felt the top of her head where the small creature had perched.

Dr. Mubarak watched her. "Your head hurts, also?"

"No, just a memory."

"Yes," he said. "Memories can hurt."

▲▲▲

Later that evening, after her fourth bottle of peach nectar, she kicked off the covers and stomped over to the table where Jason and Grace ate late night snacks from room service: taamiya, small fried patties of mashed bean and vegetable paste, and homan, grilled pigeon wrapped in thin filo dough.

"Till this meal, both of you ate the same food I did. How come you're not sick?"

"Just lucky," Jason said.

Grace looked away.

"Don't even say it, Grace," she told her. She didn't have to. May already knew what Grace was thinking; she'd heard it a thousand times in the year since Grace came back from that conference in Taos.

There's no such thing in the universe as luck.

Chapter Ten

As Dr. Mubarak advised, Jason insisted May stay in the room at the Hotel Cecil to rest. He wanted to spend the day in the city alone, but she threatened she would join him if he didn't look after Grace.

"We're not responsible for Grace. We don't owe that loony bitch anything."

"We wouldn't even be here if it weren't for the free tickets she got us," she said.

He met Grace in the lobby at nine in the morning.

She trailed him like a large looming shadow, her presence a mockery of his own. Into an already hot but breezy day, they walked along the busy Corniche without speaking, drawing admiring stares from shorter, plumper tourists. He took large strides, then larger, but her long stork-like legs matched his pace comfortably, until he stopped in front of a restaurant with windows open to the sidewalk and vases of orange-colored hibiscus on each table. He looked at Grace. She shrugged her shoulders, more with consent than approval, and walked inside ahead of him.

He stirred his coffee nonstop, banging his spoon against the inside of his china cup. A woman at a nearby table glared over her sunglasses. He took a long noisy slurp, loud enough for her to hear.

Grace read her menu until the waiter took it away. They waited for their food without speaking.

"*Iz zey yak?*" How are you? a cheerful face from outside the restaurant asked. As on their first day in the Hotel Cecil's lobby, the child wore the black Casio watch that was too big for his wrist and the same white gellabeya, but without the red silk sash. He gave them another of his hand-printed business cards. "Remember Bezhad?"

Jason was so relieved to have someone other than Grace to talk with, he laughed and extended his hand to help the little porter climb through the open window.

The head waiter, suddenly at their table, spoke in Arabic to the boy and lunged at him, but Bezhad ducked under the tablecloth. When he peeked out from the linen, the waiter grabbed for him again. This time the boy dropped to the floor and scurried right between the man's legs. Jason and Grace laughed while they explained that Bezhad was welcome at their table. Gloating, the child drew out the process of sitting next to Grace, pointing to the black coffee in front of Jason and ordering one for himself.

Grace treated the youth to the American Breakfast Plate.

"Let me be your guide to beautiful Alexandria," Bezhad said. "Twenty dollar a day."

Jason looked at Grace. They were bound to be stuck with one another until May felt better; it would help to have the kid for diversion.

"Ten," he said.

"Fifteen, and only because I like you."

He glanced at Grace again to see if she had appreciated their young entrepreneur's savvy. She smiled.

Bezhad started the tour with the grounds of Kasr Ras el Tin, a palace used by visiting dignitaries as a guesthouse; and the Tomb of the Unknown Soldier, in time to watch the changing of the guard. Alongside the grounds at the Roman Amphitheater of Kom el Dikka, they observed a Polish archeology team at work. At the Mosque of Abul Abbas, they removed their shoes before entering. Bezhad pointed at Grace's bright red toenails. "Very pretty," he said.

Jason looked at her long, slender feet. They were large, like the rest of her body, but nonetheless elegant. Smooth. Manicured. Feet of the wealthy. He followed her shiny red toes through the mosque, head down, padding behind her on the cool stone floor. May could afford to have feet like Grace's, but she'd never spend the money. They could have afforded many luxuries, but she made them live like ordinary people, hoarding her parents' inheritance, always saving for some unlikely catastrophe. Well, the catastrophe had happened — to their little girl. What good was saving? What good was there in being practical or dependable or honest if tragic things could still happen?

He started through his ever-growing list of what he would buy if he were in charge of May's money: Jaguar, Sony Stereo with large screen TV, everything in Orvis. Things that might make him feel better. He bumped right into a person who was part of a tour group that blocked the exit. Their guide spoke English:

"The cat has been permitted in the mosques since the time of the pharaohs." The guide prepared to open his white umbrella for protection from the roasting sun outside. "The priests allowed the wild cats access because they kept the temples free of rats and mice and snakes and such. Eventually, through this association with the priesthood, the cat itself became revered, and soon thereafter, deified. You see, the company one keeps can pay off!" The group followed the open umbrella into the sunlight.

Two brown-and-black-striped cats rested in the shadow of the doorway. A fat orange tabby sat on an ornate wooden stand next to the door. A striped calico slept on the first pew. A tan kitten batted an upside-down bug in the corner, and a gray cat suddenly rubbed its face against Jason's bare ankle. He picked it up, held it close to his chest and thought of the gray cat that had spread out on Susan's casket during the entire service. Bezhad petted the top of its head.

"Where did all these cats come from?" Grace asked, pointing at the movement in every dark nook and cranny of the mosque.

"I don't know what to do about May," Jason said, still holding the cat that purred loudly. "She steps off curbs without looking. She's always knocking things over and she can't remember anything — to lock the front door, pick up the laundry, flush the toilet."

"She thinks God has abandoned her," Grace said.

"Can't we leave God out of it for just one day? One god-damned day, Grace." He set the cat down, stomped outside and tried to ignore a sudden headache.

Their next stop, the catacombs of Kom el Shogata, was a burial place known by so few tourists there wasn't even an admission fee. Jason followed Grace and the nimble boy down a circular stairway to a subterranean chamber that was cool and dank and smelled like the jars of earthworms he'd kept as a child on his bedroom windowsill. Voices from other tourists traveled through the dirt corridors like ghostly rustling, growing louder the farther they descended. Electric lights, strung on hooks against the wall, hummed and cast furry shadows in the scooped-out corners of the room. The farther into the catacomb they went, the cooler it grew, and the better he felt.

They approached an area designated as a picnic ground for the families who had visited their dead. Tapestries spread over the dirt floor were a welcome relief to tourists needing a few moments to rest after the long descent.

"Maybe we should stop for a while," Bezhad whispered to Jason.

He subtly pointed at Grace, who seemed a little out of breath.

"Well, you really are a good guide. A real pro," Jason said.

They sat amid the others' quiet conversations. After a few minutes Bezhad crawled closer to Jason.

"Perhaps a real pro should charge a little more than I do?"

"Oh, that's the last compliment you get out of me, kid!" Jason shouted and reached for the boy, who deftly rolled out of his grasp and stood. But he caught the guide's small ankle and wrestled him to the ground. They laughed. Grace laughed. The surprised sightseers laughed. Their gaiety curled through the catacombs all the way up to the surface.

He held the boy tight and inhaled his salty odor, a scent like the Harbor wind, and listened with delight to the strange rapid language that spewed forth.

There was so little about Bezhad to remind him of Susan.

By the time they returned to the hotel, afternoon shadows were long, shopping bags were full, and tired tourists were draped across the large formal sofas in the lobby, drinking from tall glasses. Jason and Grace found May in her room seated at the window near her unmade bed, still in her robe and not showered. Pages torn from her sketchbook were all over the floor.

"Feeling better?" he asked.

"There's something strange going on out there."

He walked to the window. Their room overlooked a small, neat garden of leafy Lebbakh trees and three wooden benches under different-colored umbrellas.

"You see the bench to the far right under the turquoise umbrella?" May asked. "Those two old ladies from the plane spent practically the entire afternoon there." She rifled through several pages near her and handed him one. It was a drawing of the courtyard, the turquoise umbrella and two women sitting on the bench beneath it.

He looked at Grace. "What ladies?"

Grace shrugged her shoulders.

"These ladies!" May pointed, and practically stuck her finger right through the sketch he held. "The weird ones in the row right in front of us on the plane. Beady gray eyes. Surgeon-tightened foreheads and chins. Wore these horrible-looking wigs."

He shook his head. "I don't remember them, but what of it? It's a nice enough garden."

"You don't think it's odd to come all the way to Alexandria and then sit most of a day in a garden that doesn't even have a view of the Harbor?" She looked at him and then at Grace.

"Well, we could say the same about you, May," Grace said. "I mean, if we didn't know you were sick, we might think you had come all the way to Alexandria to sit in your hotel room to stare out the window at two weird ladies with bad wigs in the garden." Grace laughed.

May turned back toward the window. "Around three o'clock this slick-looking Egyptian guy smoking these thin brown cigarettes sat down with them." She reached for a different sketch and handed it to Grace this time. "They all kept acting as if they were just looking out at the garden, but they were having a conversation. They talked out of the sides of their mouths for twenty minutes like this!" Then talking out of the side of her own mouth to show them, she added, "Then he stood up, handed them a piece of paper and left."

"They were talking about the garden or the nice weather," Grace said.

"He handed them a business card," Jason said. "Why get yourself upset about it?"

"Because I am upset!" May accidentally spit orange Lifesaver saliva. "I'm upset about everything!" She walked away from the window and kicked at a pile of drawings on the floor.

"This is just like when you thought that poor kid was going to rob the Full Moon Café. You're making stuff up, it's crazy," Jason said.

"Crazy would be a relief."

"You need to put your trust in God again," Grace said.

Both May and Jason glared at her.

▲▲▲

The next day, May stayed in the room again. Jason was glad to be free of her. All through the night he heard about the clandestine courtyard meeting, and then in the morning she talked of nothing but her giant cat dreams.

"For four nights in a row, I dreamed I won the Sweepstakes," he told her. "But it didn't mean anything. No money. No call from a hotshot celebrity.

"Look, first there was that cat at the funeral, the one you insisted could sit on top of Susan's coffin, and then Land of Miracles Richard tells you about this big cat at his dig and, of course, he makes it sound more mysterious than it is. It's just power of suggestion, it's gotten stuck in your brain. Let it go, for everyone's benefit."

He went to the hotel lobby early, preferring to wait in the peaceful quiet an hour and a half for Grace. Bezhad showed up ten minutes after Grace did with maps of the sights they would see that day and the restaurants they would visit. Strangely, the more time they spent with the boy the more fluent he became. At last he confessed his poor English was an act. Years of experience in the tourist trade had taught him fewer American words brought more American dollars and even American gifts. He pointed proudly to the large black watch on his wrist. Jason taught him a new American word: shrewd.

Bezhad told them silly jokes, sang for them, and called Jason "The Duke," because of his croc cowboy boots, Texas accent and pigeon-toed swagger. Grace bought the boy a belt with a brass buckle, and Jason let him win at arm wrestling. He carried the street-smart urchin on his shoulders. Both he and Grace let Bezhad keep any coins they got back from purchases. "This is real money," Bezhad said, fascinated by the various metals and sizes of his own currency. "Not like paper. I always keep coins right here in my pocket so I can hear them sing. Bezhad be a rich man one day."

"Don't get hung up on a dream, kid," Jason said.

They returned to the hotel shortly after dinner with bags full of purchases to share with May: Egyptian cotton blouses and shirts; silver picture frames; balghas — heelless slippers made of light-colored leather for each of them; blue bead necklaces to ward off evil spirits; and lots of goofy Pharoni — worthless souvenirs.

She was at the window again. Jason recognized the look on her face: the same distracted expression that took over when she worked crosswords or jigsaw puzzles.

"Now what?" he said.

"The Asian man from the taxi. He was in the garden today."

He dropped the bag on the bed. "So?"

"He's not even staying at this hotel."

"Maybe he is," Grace said.

"He didn't get out of the taxi when we did. Oh, forget that," May went on, "he met with the same two women who were in the garden yesterday with that Egyptian. On the same bench." She looked back and forth between him and Grace. "Under the turquoise umbrella. The two women who sat in front of us on the plane!"

"May," he pulled her away from the window, "you're a good distance from that bench. You wouldn't know if it was the same guy from the taxi."

"He had the Halliburton with him. The chrome briefcase."

"You haven't had enough to do these last two days," he said. "Tomorrow you're going with us, healthy or not."

▲▲▲

The next day Bezhad took the three of them ten miles east of Alexandria to Montaza Palace, a former residence of the royal family that was built in 1892. Painted in white, bright pink and grass green, it was a garish sight — as over-decorated on the inside as its fancy archways, ornate pillars and baroque molding adorning its exterior. The palace was situated on acres of beautifully landscaped gardens stretching to one of the cleanest public beaches on the coast.

When they got to the shore, May scanned the sunny sky one last time for the thundercloud that she knew would not come — it was another gorgeous day.

"I can't take these perfect days," she told the small guide. "Does it ever bother you? Don't you ever want the sky to just blow apart and make us all run for shelter?"

Bezhad laughed.

She took off after him, chasing him across the beach. "Run for shelter! Run for shelter!" He howled. They ran all the way to edge of the water, darting back and forth between the sunbathing tourists, circling back to where Jason and Grace had spread the towels Bezhad had told them to bring from the hotel.

"Aren't you a fickle little friend," Jason said to the boy.

Bezhad stood near May, who was bent at the waist and panting for air, his arm slung across her shoulders. "I don't understand," Bezhad said.

Jason had already stepped out of his clothes so that he was in his bathing suit. He walked toward the water without saying anything.

"It means you're a quick runner." May stood and put her arm across his shoulders.

They watched Jason for a few minutes, then Bezhad left to buy their drinks. Grace undid the small bows at her shoulders and stepped out of her cotton dress. "He's just grown fond of the kid the two days you stayed in the room. First time I've seen him happy in a long while," Grace said.

"Since when do you stick up for my husband?"

"Well, you weren't there," she said. "They sort of have an understanding." Her red bikini shimmered in the yellow light. May pictured her own body while admiring her slender friend's, recalled all the times she had consoled Grace about her bony hips and flat chest when they were girls. Who would have ever thought Grace's shapelessness would one day become so fashionable?

May sat on one of the hotel towels, well aware of her own weight as the sand gave way beneath her. The fifteen pounds she'd put on during the last half year felt like three hundred.

Bezhad brought lemonade, three twenty-ounce bottles of beer and a plate of desserts: baklava — a fillo pastry layered with nuts and syrup, and fetir meshaltet — a pie baked with butter and served with cheese, honey and molasses. She took a lemonade, covered the pastry plate with a hand towel and pushed it safely beyond her own reach.

"Want to go for a swim, kid?" Jason, dripping wet, had come back for his goggles.

"No." Bezhad sat down on the towel next to May. "I'm a little too fickle at the moment," he said and frowned at Jason.

"Suit yourself." Jason walked away.

"I'm game." Grace ran to catch up with him.

Bezhad pulled a worn deck of cards from his satchel. "Let's play Crazy Eights," he said, still frowning.

They played until an obese woman who introduced herself as D.D. Dodd ducked into the shade of their umbrella.

"Mind if I join you?"

Before May could reply D.D. had squatted and let gravity take hold, landing just inches from the covered pastries. Her flowered one-piece swimsuit was two sizes too small, and a gold necklace disappeared into the folds of her chin.

"All this walkin' got my hemorrhoids hurtin' me somethin' awful," she said.

When she learned that May was from Houston, she slapped her pudgy thigh. "Good night, girl! We're neighbors!"

Bezhad put his cards down and left.

From that moment on the woman never stopped talking. She answered her own questions, laughed at her own jokes and diagnosed her own ailments. May nodded, added an occasional remark and tried to be polite to her fellow Texan.

D.D. Dodd had come to Egypt with her church group. May listened as she droned on about all the places she'd seen, every meal she'd eaten and how, oddly, during the most disappointing day trip to the ancient city of Bubastis, she'd had the finest food.

"At that Temple of Bast, they got the most delicious gooey cakes in the sweetest little shop across the street, but don't waste no time goin' to that temple, sugar."

"No?" She had stopped listening. Her mind had drifted back to the meetings under the turquoise umbrella in the hotel's garden. The two women she'd seen there and on the plane were starting to seem familiar to her now — something about their snooty manner, the way they held themselves so erect, their grandly slow hand gestures. She thought of the many grownups' parties she and Grace had snuck into at Grace's home before being discovered and shushed out of the way. Two wealthy sisters were always in attendance at these elite gatherings. Bejeweled, with every hair teased and sprayed into perfection, surrounded by a small audience, they held court like royalty: a status, May imagined, that gave them lifelong expectation of the same no matter how many years later, or how remote a place, or how unknown they may be to their new audience. These two ladies had that same affect. The Egyptian and the Asian treated them like queens in the courtyard. But what was royalty doing in coach class, wearing department store wigs?

"Why, that goddess Bast is a beautiful statue, what with her dress and jewels and all, bur her temple is just a bunch of stones!" D.D. wiped the sweat under her chins and continued to gripe about the temple. Then she talked about how she was able to keep track of all the different myths and all the different relationships that the gods and goddesses had.

"Bast, for example, was Ra's lover."

"Oh."

"The sun god, Ra," she said. "I can remember most of them gods' names."

"How is that?" May asked, surprised to be listening again.

D.D. laughed and confessed that she had twenty years of practice from watching the soap operas back home. The Egyptian myths were just like her complicated daytime stories: everyone somehow related, a few of the goddesses mothers to the same children and a few of the gods in love with their own daughters. From one legend to the next, the same deities took on different names, powers and form. They cheated. They lied. In general, they weren't very trustworthy folks.

"I guess even deities have a hard time getting along," May said. She certainly couldn't get along with anyone lately. Strangers on a plane. Jason. Grace. Especially since Grace's return from the Taos conference, May felt the only remnant of their friendship was knowing they used to have one.

"You got kids?"

She couldn't see Jason or Grace among all the people in the water. She stood to get a better look, but D.D. tugged at her shorts.

"So you got children, hon?"

"What?" she said.

"Children?"

It was the first time since Susan's death that someone had asked. The people from the support group at Center Park's Hospital had warned Jason and her to be ready and had armed them with replies — none of which she could think of. She shook her head no, sat back down and reached for the plate of pastries.

"Girl, you ought to have a baby." D.D. helped herself to some melting fetir meshaltet. "It's the only thing made my miserable life worthwhile. Lord knows it weren't my mean husband, but my two angel-boys that brought my joy. Why, I'd had more if it weren't for the hysterectomy."

May ate the nuts off her baklava, then stuffed the entire pastry in her mouth. Then another and another. She stared at her own giraffe-patterned shorts and listened to the details of the female operation D.D. had undergone in the fall of 1977. When she paused just long enough to reach for another molasses treat, May grabbed her fat wrist.

"Please, I just can't listen to you anymore."

D.D.'s at-last-silent mouth fell open.

Jason and Grace ran up to the umbrella. Grace ducked under it and shook her wet hair all over May.

Jason looked down at the single piece of pie on the desert plate. "Gee, thanks for leaving us some!"

D.D. Dodd rolled onto her knees, stood and then left without a word. Grace dressed, Jason collected his things and Bezhad, who suddenly appeared again, ate the last pastry.

May watched the stout visitor waddle down the beach alone.

"Now what's the matter?" Jason said.

His lashes were dark and shiny with salt water, and the white towel flung over his shoulder made his tan look deep brown. A bird squawked, children laughed and she could hear the waves behind her making gentle lapping noises. It felt like an ordinary summer day, like any one of many they'd spent on the shore at their beach house in Gullcrest.

"I just can't seem to be nice anymore."

Jason cocked his head. "Who says you ever were?"

Grace walked up from behind him and punched him in the arm.

"Kidding!" he said. "Can't anybody take a joke around here anymore?" He pulled the white towel from his shoulders over the top of his head and walked toward the taxi stand.

"I can defend myself," she told Grace.

"Can you?" Grace said.

Bezhad took May's hand; they walked toward the taxi stand.

Grace followed.

Chapter Eleven

On the sixth day of their vacation, Alexandria's gusty sea air stirred the dust in the boulevard with playful short breaths. It circled May. She shut her eyes, held her skirt down and for one bright moment forgot who she was.

"May!"

Grace's finger poked her shoulder.

"Don't worry so much, we'll get to Cairo."

They'd planned to reach Cairo by train, only to find there were no tickets available.

"I'll get us there, I promise." Grace placed one hand over her heart, the other on her hip, and mocked a secret oath they'd made up in their childhood.

She smiled at the brief image of fourteen-year-old Grace in her navy blue skirt and blazer, the uniform of St. Mary's. But then the twenty-nine-year-old Grace turned abruptly, red skirt swirling at her knees. Her body long and lanky, like some fearless crane stalking a river, she crossed the crowded Shari el-Horreya Boulevard toward an outdoor market. Her wide-brimmed red hat bobbed between a variety of dusty vehicles: horse-drawn wagons filled with sugar cane, watermelons and pomegranates from the country; bicycles with mere traces of their original colors; and flatbed trucks spilling over with the day's garbage collection. Large commuter buses discharged heavy clouds of exhaust. Tiny automobiles, with passengers' legs and arms and heads stuck through the open windows, darted in and out of it all.

An enormous water truck rumbled past, wetting down the street in an attempt to control the dust. Its spray was quieting. Hush. Hush. As it doused the boulevard, barefoot children ran beside it and danced through rainbows. May sat on one of the eleven pieces of luggage the taxi driver had set on the sidewalk in front of the Sidi Gebir Train Station and flipped an orange Lifesaver back and forth with her tongue. Even so, her mouth remained dry from the dust. She worked the candy harder, twisting her mouth and pursing her lips. Then, as if the activity itself had caused it, she again saw the younger Grace in her starched school uniform: *Spit*, Grace said as they stood over a barren spot of ground. *I can't*, she told her. *Hurry*, Grace said, *before Sister Marguerite sees us.*

They'd taken two black olives from a serving tray at a dinner party that Grace's parents had given at their mini-mansion in River Roads, the wealthiest suburb in Houston, and planted the seeds the following day with great ceremony on the school grounds. This will be our tree. It will grow larger than both of us and everybody will wonder where it came from. But secrecy made the upkeep difficult. Since they couldn't be seen leaving the school with buckets of water, the only thing Grace could think to do was spit on it. Twice a day, they ran to the secret spot, gestured their secret oath (the very oath that Grace had mocked just moments before) and spit. *Spit! Spit!* Grace said. May could never work up the amount of saliva that her best friend did. *Why do I always have to do everything?* Grace said. *Now, spit!*

Then, grownup Grace was back. Glamorous and tall, she stood

in the shade of her own red hat in front of the Sidi Gebir Station. The crystal pendant on her necklace looked like a jagged piece of ice; and despite the heat, her skin was even-toned, no sign of perspiration; her make-up still as fresh as when they left the Hotel Cecil more than an hour before — not at all the image of the champion spitter May knew her to truly be.

Grace tossed her blonde hair over one shoulder and took a bite of something she held away from her body at an angle. "It's mutton!"

May watched her dab a napkin at the corner of her red lips. She wanted to taste it, but thought she'd better not test her stomach so soon after being sick.

Jason appeared, also with mutton. He held the greasy kebab in his large hands as delicately as Grace did.

"You both bought food and didn't think to bring me anything?" May asked.

Grace grabbed the smallest bag of her luggage and started across the boulevard again. "I'll meet you inside the station to the left of the big clock at the Cairo gate."

"But there are no tickets!" May said.

"The universe will take care of us, May! You're such a worrywart."

Four barefooted children, three boys and one girl, rushed to the luggage before Jason had a chance to flag down a porter. Inside the station, the signs were all in Arabic. "Cairo," Jason told the girl.

The bright smile that appeared on her small face reminded May of Susan's. Her child's smile was that moment before laughter, a wrapped chocolate, the fortune inside all those cookies they had shared at the Full Moon Cafe. Just the thought made her smile. Then a Halliburton case passed in front of her. She strained to see who was carrying it before the crowd blocked her view. The Asian? Here? She started to follow, but Jason caught her arm and pulled her in the opposite direction.

"Pay attention, May."

Grace arrived just as the train did. "Go!"

The crush of people getting on swept people getting off the train back in. Suitcases, umbrellas and open-mesh satchels full of lemons, onions and cauliflower were tossed through the windows ahead of their owners. May and Jason followed Grace.

"Richard told me to get in a closed window compartment," Grace said.

"But we don't have tickets," May said as a sheep was pushed onto the train, farther down in the third class section.

"My cousin said we could get seats by paying off the conductor."

"Bribing the conductor is not the same thing as the universe taking care of us," May said.

They were allowed to stay for an additional six pounds.

The section of the train they ended up in had once been a dining car. The upholstery on the booths was either missing or split wide, exposing tattered, yellowed Styrofoam padding. The wooden tables were spotted with black rings where objects too hot had once been placed. Graffiti was etched into them, like the tops of so many school desks, but the Arabic lettering looked more to May like the abstract art of some master than the scrawls of vandals. She ran her fingers over the uneven surface of the table. How many of the people whose names were carved before her were still alive?

Jason tossed their luggage into an overhead bin. Grace sat down opposite her, at last removing the large red hat.

It took some time for the train to get moving. Grace, as always, filled the lull with whatever folly was on her mind. She pulled her *Frommer's Guide* from her purse and pointed to a map of Egypt. "Even though we're traveling south, we're leaving Lower Egypt and heading toward Upper Egypt."

The reversed geography made sense to May. Her whole life also felt turned around. Perhaps she could find comfort in this land of miracles. Then she thought of her dreams, the mysterious meetings in the hotel gardens, the camels that turned into giant felines, her gyppie tummy, and all that time alone in the hotel room. She closed her eyes. Things had grown worse since leaving the States, not better. She sighed and leaned back against the seat, as the train finally pulled away from the station.

▲▲▲

Grace stared at May when she heard her long-winded sigh. That, and the way May answered "What?" to anything and everything had Grace grinding her teeth and biting her manicure. But worst of all were the endless supply of Lifesavers. May sucked on them at all times, her lips twisted in furious motions, making noises like those old people in the nursing home with her Great Aunt Ruthie. Sometimes she couldn't even understand what May said because of the candies.

"Must you always do that?" she said when May sighed again.

"What?"

"And that too. We've already talked about the whats!"

"What?" May said, louder.

"Nothing." But it was everything. Even the way May had acted in Houston's Intercontinental Airport before the flight, as if she were taking this trip just to please her. And the fuss she'd raised while deciding to go: the shots, their passports, the Egyptian food, the long flight, the worry about leaving that shack of a beach house for two weeks and, of course, those stinky pet cats. Even the weather had been an issue. So what's a little heat to us Houstonians, she had told her. You know Texas and Egypt are on the same latitude.

She frowned as May sank farther into the train's worn seat. The yellow Styrofoam, which had burst through the upholstery, looked like an exotic flower in May's hair, and a fly landing near its center, like a bee drawing nectar. Little clouds of cigarette smoke from a man in the booth next to theirs hung near May's face, softening the portrait with impressionistic style. Sunlight through the train's large pane window refracted off of Grace's crystal pendant, splashing May with the faintest rainbow of colors. This, more than the Lifesavers and the ever-present sighs and whats, bothered her most: May had a way of making everything around her seem beautiful, as if her artist's eye projected outward.

It wasn't that May herself was beautiful, the space around her was. May's features were ordinary: olive coloring, frizzy black hair, a boring mouth and dull brown eyes with lashes that could use some mascara. Her teeth were too small; her fashion ridiculous, always sporting some animal design on her clothes or jewelry. Still, May emanated elegance.

Grace swatted at a fly with her large hat and frowned at the hat's bright red color. A strand of her brassy-colored hair moved back and forth with the train's motion. Compared to May, she felt cheap. May was a seven-course meal; she was fast food.

"What's that?" Jason pointed to a brown paper bag on the seat.

"A little surprise I bought before boarding the train," Grace said. She pulled out three plastic cups and one bottle of Nefertiti, a light-colored Egyptian wine. She poured as they held the cups as steady as possible against the swaying of the train. They bumped their plastic rims together clumsily to toast.

"To the new Curator of Mammals of the Houston Zoo!" she cheered.

"I'm still in the trial phase," Jason said.

"You'll do fine," she said. "Congratulations."

"It's nice to hear a vote of confidence." He gave May a strange glance, which didn't surprise Grace. May had confided she wasn't sure Jason could handle the new position. He'd come through the ranks in an unusual manner — even his schooling hadn't met the requirement. His training began on his family's farm and through their friendship with the local veterinarian, who'd given him an after-school job and gotten him into the University of Iowa when his grades couldn't. He'd started with the Houston Zoo as janitor, keeping the facilities clean, eventually getting to know the crew, and assisting them with animal duties. His persistence and outgoing nature brought the promotions that put him in position to prove he could be an animal keeper. He'd worked with all of the mammals, and was good at the daily regimen of cleaning, feeding, observing, administering medication, planning diet and supplements. But the organizational, budgetary, managerial skills he would need as curator — May said he didn't have. Grace still remembered a time when he'd botched supervision of the six hundred-some volunteers during a special event.

"Yeah, congratulations," he repeated and drank to his own success. His lack of etiquette didn't surprise her either. He had, after all, grown up on a farm in some God-forsaken little town in Iowa. Bezhad had it right when he called Jason "Duke" the first day of their tour through Alexandria. His pigeon-toed, shoulder-heaving swagger was John Wayne's, his manners were no better than some cowpoke farting away at an open campfire, and his way with women was definitely from a black-and-white western.

"And now a toast to my promotion!" Grace paused to build suspense, but also because the wine, too sweet, had made the tip of her tongue curl. "To the new publisher of *Houston Harbinger*!"

Jason offered his congratulations immediately, but May didn't say a word. Grace told them a memo announcing her promotion would be sent to the employees the third Monday in July. Until then it was top secret.

"So you know what this means, May?"

May shook her head no.

"I'm going to be your boss."

May gazed out the train window, not at all the response that Grace had anticipated. She stared at May's dejected profile and waited for some kind of reply. This was a moment that she'd planned for since they were children. May, of all people, should know what it meant to her. Their target age had always been thirty, a year with May's favorite number three in it. May was going to be a famous artist and Grace was going to be a boss, of what or who didn't matter, she just wanted to be in charge, any position that would make her father proud. May's lack of support was probably about her own failure, goals never being something she cared about setting, landing wherever circumstance blew her.

Finally, Grace turned toward the window herself. They'd left beautiful Alexandria behind them and entered an unchanging landscape of yellow-white sand beneath a sky of endless turquoise. Everything had disappeared. There was nothing out there, miles and miles of nothing.

▲▲▲

When Jason was sure May was asleep, he grabbed Grace's arm and pulled her near. "Did you see her? When we left her alone in front of the train station? Spitting, for Christ's sake! Sitting on a piece of luggage and spitting that god damn Lifesaver juice on the sidewalk!"

May woke up. Jason backed away from Grace and looked out the window. There was nothing to see but the train's dark shadow as it skimmed the flat ground. He couldn't even see the Nile River, which ran just alongside the railroad track. There were only its bordering sandstone cliffs and the tips of an occasional felucca sail. With nothing to do, he found himself staring at Grace's red sundress. The way she was seated left a good portion of her bare back turned toward him so he could trace the fabric as it dipped across her bony shoulders down to her waist. He traveled up and down her skeletal spine like a train himself, dependent on the single track.

His wife wore a tan cotton dress with drawings of Minnie and Mickey Mouse in various poses. Carved wooden elephants, tigers and giraffes were strung on her necklace, and tiny ceramic parrots dangled from her ears. She was a god-damned walking menagerie.

When had she started dressing like this? Even the black dress she'd worn to Susan's funeral had ducks flying across its front. She had not dressed like that when they were dating, but some time shortly after their marriage, it began with one pair of Miss Piggy slippers. On every special occasion thereafter, friends started to send animal patterned blouses, skirts, purses, jewelry, nightgowns and underwear.

The caftan-clad strangers who sat near him in the passenger car stared at May's bizarre outfit, as well as one Egyptian fellow in a smartly-tailored suit and expensive boots. For the entire ride, he chain-smoked long brown cigarettes that smelled like burning rubber; and though he read a January copy of *GQ Magazine*, his thoughts seemed to hover in the smoke that lingered over Jason's head.

"Blow your filthy air somewhere else, bubba," he said.

The stranger took another long pull on his cigarette.

May turned to see to whom he was talking, then abruptly slid down in her seat. "It's the man from the courtyard," she whispered. "The one with the brown cigarettes."

"Stop it!" He tugged his arm away from her grasp. "I don't want to hear another word about that courtyard or your giant cat. Understand?"

He turned again toward the man, ready to fight him if necessary, wanting to fight. But the dark-skinned Egyptian nodded to him, then stubbed the cigarette against the bottom of his fancy boot until the smoke extinguished.

At last the train approached the outskirts of Cairo, and the scenery slowly changed. Dirty smoke billowed from the quarry at Muquattam Hills. Single-story mud brick homes with sugar cane roofs and dovecotes, large pottery structures built to house pigeons, were scattered in the desolate landscape. Nubian women in robes as black as their skin balanced large water vessels on their heads. They stood still as the train rushed past them, looking just like the postcard images they'd seen in the Sidi Gebir Station. Date palm plantations appeared sporadically.

"Not a single olive grove," May said. "I thought this country would be filled with them."

"These Egyptians must not know how to spit!" Grace joked.

May smiled. But Jason glared at Grace. What was she thinking? Just the suggestion might cause his wife to start spitting again. He couldn't wait to get off the train before May would do something weird, and away from that cocky Egyptian whose mere presence made him uncomfortable.

Finally, the noise of the city took over. Open spaces filled with gray-brown shops and apartment buildings. Modern hotels and ornate minarets towered above winding narrow alleyways, filled with stacks of merchandise piled as high as the top of doorways. People were everywhere: crossing through traffic, pinning laundry to third-story balconies, and hanging onto the outside of city buses.

Jason stepped off the train ahead of May and Grace into the brown haze that permeated Cairo. The streets were hot and crowded; the air reeked of stagnant water, rotting garbage, plucked chickens that hung upside down in the warm breeze of the butcher's window, and rancid grease in the street vendors' cooking pits.

"*Ah lan wasahlan,*" welcome, the dirty-faced children shouted to the people with luggage.

"Where?" a young boy said proudly in English. He had the same toothy grin as the young waifs they'd just left in Alexandria, but he wore shoes instead of sandals and a white button-down shirt with tan pants instead of a gellabeya.

"*Uray yib*," near, the boy said when Jason told him the Nile Hotel. He put his fingers to his mouth and whistled. Five children ran over and ducked under the luggage straps as he loaded them down, reserving the lightest bag for his own shoulder.

"Let's go," Jason said.

"But it's six blocks!" Grace pointed to the city map of Cairo in her *Frommer's Guide.* Her face was slightly flushed and the heat provoked her perfume: cinnamon.

He smiled at her. "The walk will do us good."

The combination of wine and the lull of the rolling train had made him drowsy. But now he also felt carefree. Watching the young boys zigzag in front of him, straining under the weight of the luggage, made him laugh he felt so light. Everything seemed different in Egypt, so far from home.

They walked through a city in transition, old and new coexisting. Ladies in fashionable suits with dark silk blouses stood next to men in skull caps and gellabeyas. Dazzling structures such as the new Ramses Hilton loomed over the one-room dwellings of Bouloq, Cairo's poorest residential area directly across from the Mahattat Ramses train station. TV antennas sprouted from every sun-dried, mud-brick roof, while goats and donkeys obeyed the same traffic signals as the automobiles on congested streets.

Amid such turmoil, the screech of tires and a blaring horn barely caught his attention. When he finally did look, Jason saw May sprawled on her back in the street, her knees bent awkwardly in opposite directions. He and Grace reached her at the same time. A man waved his short arms in front of him as though swatting at a swarm of bees and yelled in Arabic as he walked from the sidewalk into the street and then back again to show what May must have done. And then he hit the hood of his turquoise Honda.

Jason helped his wife stand while Grace brushed the dirt from May's dress.

"I'm okay," she said, only she wouldn't look at them. "Did you see him?"

"Who?" Jason said.

"The animal in that truck."

He looked where she did and saw a camouflage-painted military truck turn the corner.

"What animal?"

"Just like the cat in my dream."

"You almost get run over for that!"

"But it could have been the cat Richard told me about, the one that showed up at his dig."

"I told you I didn't want to hear another word about your cat, and I really don't want to hear anything more about Richard either."

Everyone in the street began to honk their horns. The young porters, who had dropped the luggage when they rushed toward May, pulled her back to the sidewalk.

"I can't watch after you every second!" He let go of May's arm.

"Who asked you to?"

"Your mystery friends from the courtyard, that's who!"

"Come on." Grace put her arms around both of them. "All this negative energy isn't doing either one of you any good."

"Shut up, Grace," he said.

"Here." Grace took off her crystal necklace and offered it to May. "It will work like a tuning fork on your energy field and make you vibrate at the earth's same frequency. Puts you in harmony with the universe."

"Leave me alone," May said.

No one said a word as they re-formed their caravan, single-file behind the young boys. This time Jason positioned himself last, keeping his distance behind the two women, watching each, irritated by May's suddenly over-cautious steps, equally annoyed by Grace's self-assured prance. Grace put back on her precious crystal necklace and for a moment, gazing at the short wispy locks at the nape of her neck, so soft and childlike, he almost forgot it was the lunatic Grace, who for the past eleven years had put him down with her rich girl disapproval of his grammar or his manners or his politics or whatever. And now there was this religious thing. One single weekend in Taos convinced this River Roads Catholic conservative not only of crystal power, but pyramid power, parallel realities, altered states of consciousness and a universe made of vibrations. Since Taos, it had become even harder to tolerate May's best friend. There was the religious babbling, the half-hour each day she chanted, and the twenty-four-hour fast each Friday to cleanse her bony body of toxins and evil.

From that moment on, he made sure they kept busy. There was no idle time, no opportunities for Grace to enlighten them. He made them join every tour group available. The first took them northwest of the city to the Camel Market, where herders from the Sudan sold their livestock. The second tour was to Babel Louk, a market of hundreds of small stands that sold fruits, nuts, seeds, baked goods, vegetables, sides of beef and live chickens, which could be slaughtered while the customer waited. The third went to the Spice Market, where sweet aromas of sandalwood and myrrh incense, perfumes, soaps and scented candles permeated the air. On their fourth tour, at the Covered Bazaar, Jason purchased a small tapestry from a craftsman who demonstrated his artistic skill as he sat cross-legged in front of his wares.

He signed them up for rides across the Nile on high-mast feluccas and tours of the Great Pyramids. He took them to the Egyptian Museum three times.

The ocher-colored museum was as chaotic as the ancient city streets surrounding it. Centuries-old masterpieces were crammed into every corner. Though the rooms were numbered, it was difficult to follow the sequence. Stairways bypassed entire floors, and certain rooms seemed impossible to access. Grace found a notation in the back of her museum guide book explaining that the revenue from the tour of the King Tut Exhibit through the United States would be used for the much-needed reorganization of the Cairo Museum.

He signed them up for the museum tour. The guide read hieroglyphics from inscribed stone tablets and showed them the sculptured faces of gods, pharaohs, queens, nobles, royal scribes and high priests. Along the front of the museum's second floor they viewed a display of sacred animal mummies. Enclosed in elaborately decorated coffins were the remains of fish, crocodiles, baboons, dogs and cats.

"Just as a person wakes from a dream or unconsciousness, my ancestors believed that preservation of the body could mean awakening from death to life again, or rather afterlife. This is why the art of mummification was perfected," the guide said.

The tour group shuffled down the hallway until they stood beside a human mummy, the image of a man's face skillfully painted on the exterior casing. On nearby shelves were alabaster vessels, fluted marble dishes, cups, weapons, maps, musical instruments, jewelry and toys that had been buried with the deceased.

"Many times the pharaohs had their advisors, wives and soldiers enter into death with them in order to be of service in the afterlife." Everyone laughed when the soft-spoken guide asked the women of the group if they would agree to such a request from their husbands.

The closer the final days of their vacation drew, the more Grace and Jason purchased: brass candlesticks, a copper plate, an alabaster vase, embroidered dresses and shirts, leather wallets and purses, a wooden box with mother-of-pearl inlay, and a basket made from palm fronds. Grace went on more tours, Jason roamed the markets of Khan do Khalili and El Ghuriyyah, but May spent those last days at the Cairo Museum in the room with the coffins.

She took her sketchpad and drew the caskets, the ornate patterns, the mysterious hieroglyphics, the gold-painted death masks, the portraits of baboons, crocodiles and scarab beetles. But she always returned to the sketches at the front of the book — the ones she'd made in Alexandria of the courtyard, with the two American women, the Asian, the Egyptian in his shroud of smoke. And more disturbing than these drawings was the glimpse she'd caught of Jason late one afternoon as she turned the corner near the museum, exchanging papers with this very Egyptian stranger. What reason could he possibly have to exchange anything with this man? Not even a "hello" made sense.

She sat in the museum near a statue of Anubis, the jackal-headed guardian of the dead, and fell asleep with her head against his stone shoulder, comforted to have a god so accessible. It seemed that modern man was no longer a descendant of the Divine; that somehow, through the millennia the ancestry had been diluted. Gods were locked away in exhibition rooms like this one, no longer a part of everyday life.

When the museum closed she strolled the narrow streets of Old Cairo, in the ever-present mass of people whose proximity forced her to take small steps and walk in rhythm to an unheard beat. Sights and sounds conflicted where the old and new collided. Somehow, the calls to prayer from the ancient minarets could be heard over the incessant noise of the traffic.

Unlike Houston, the past was always present in Cairo. It put time out of sequence. A piece of history was everywhere. Just knowing that massive pyramids with pitted blocks of stone stood close by as they had for thousands of years made the ancient past seem less far away, the recent past like yesterday, and Susan still within reach.

Each afternoon, she returned to the Nile Hotel looking less like a tourist. Swathed in layers of Egyptian cotton, her hair covered by a hand-woven band of colorful silk, she wore silver arm bands and 18-karat bangle bracelets, a necklace made of turquoise, and sandals that echoed the soft patter of the three camels who had followed her from Pompey's Pillar.

At night, in the solitude of the hotel room, the constant noise from the street blew in through the open windows and wrapped around her as she slept. She never felt alone.

She boarded the plane back to Houston in a golden dress that swished when she moved, rows of beads draped around her throat, and camel earrings. As reluctant to return home as she had first departed from it, she began to think of the trip as more of a success than it was. In the same way those goofy smiling vacation photos never really show anything, May's gyppie stomach and the kind doctor who came to the hotel with his family became an adventure in retrospect. Even her continual dwelling on the large cat, her recurring dreams, and her unending speculation over the courtyard meetings between the Americans, the Asian, and the Egyptian, Jason's whereabouts, and her doubting whether she had truly seen him exchanging paper with that same Egyptian, seemed easier to face than the return home, where there would be no escape in the shiny buildings, the fluorescent lights of the grocery, the faces of neighbors, co-workers, friends. No escape in the room with dolls on the canopy bed, folded socks that collected dust in the drawer, and unused schoolbooks stacked on the shelves. The very process of returning was painful, for it promised something that couldn't be done: a return to the way things had been. She wanted Saturday morning cartoons. After-school homework. Weekends at the beach house. Dance recitals. PTA meetings. Combing Susan's hair. The past had slipped away, leaving her in jangling Egyptian jewelry and a present cloaked in Egyptian cotton. The thought of home felt more foreign than the exotic country she was leaving.

During the crossing, over the black water, she drifted into the same dream. This time, there was a second cat.

As large as the black one, this cat was transparent at first, ghostly, though the closer it swam to shore the more opaque it grew. White, pure white as a marble statue, it stepped from the water's edge and sat down near the dark figure she had seen before — a female, who paced, clad in a long flowing gown. She was slender and shapely.

And had the head of cat.

Chapter Twelve

May followed in Jason's wake, through clusters of people at Houston's Intercontinental Airport who hugged and kissed and carried small flower bouquets wrapped in green paper, all with the same pink ribbon. Jason's luggage was checked at Customs. A heavy-set woman with a faint mustache sifted through his folded clothes, unscrewed cologne and medicine bottles and unzipped inner linings in his bags while a guard behind her watched perfunctorily.

"We knew you'd get caught," Grace said, loud enough so that the supervisor looked at them.

"Shut up, Grace," Jason said.

May touched her husband's hand and then his forehead. He felt cool and damp. He'd been unusually quiet for the last three days, and he never did tell her where he'd been their last night in Cairo.

"It's those horrible brown cigarettes you've started smoking! They're making you sick," May said.

"Shut up, May," Jason said.

The surly look on his face did not go away for another five days. May could still see it when he ate, when he slept, even when he smiled.

Only after she made an appointment with psychiatrist Dr. Claudia Somners did the lines across his brow and at the corners of his mouth soften.

"Those dreams are keeping me awake every night," she told him. "And don't get mad, but I keep seeing that sneaky Egyptian from the garden and the train, the one who smoked those same awful cigarettes you've taken up."

But it was so much more than not getting enough sleep, or possible glimpses of that Egyptian tailing her. It was hearing the yellow school bus pick up the neighbor's children; finding packages of Oreo cookies and Nestle's Crunch bars she'd hidden all through the house; the photos of Susan she'd tucked into her skirt pockets, rolled up in her sleeves, stuck in her socks, pinned to her bras; the burden of enduring all those expectant faces, even the check-out man at the corner Stop 'N Go, who'd hoped she would return from vacation a happier person; and it was finding Susan's bedroom as quiet as the day she'd left it, the pink and yellow wallpaper too cheery. Everything was too bright, everybody too bold, unlike Egypt where the veil of dust had toned it all down.

On the second Monday after their return from Egypt, she stood in front of a huge fish aquarium in a reception room and waited for her appointment with the psychiatrist. A variety of fish circled the tank, all in the same direction, traveling at different speeds, lazily dodging each other. When she put her hand against the glass, they stopped, faced her.

"How unusual," said a woman who wore no shoes. A yellow pencil just above her right ear poked out through her short graying hair. "They never just stop swimming like that."

"I'm told I have a way with animals."

She and the woman looked through the glass at the fish. Their colors were electric, little neon signs suspended in a sea of bubbles. In the greenery beneath them were miniature objects: a treasure chest, a painted coffin, a golden chariot. On the back wall of the tank was an illustration of the Giza pyramids and a temple with the relief of a large cat over its entrance.

"I'm Claudia," the woman said.

"You've been to Egypt?"

"No." Claudia laughed. "New York. I went to the King Tut Exhibit and picked up these things in the museum gift shop. Something a little different for my fish to look at."

She looked again at the relief of the large cat over the temple entrance.

"It's coming to Texas, you know," Claudia said.

"Who?" May said, louder than she'd intended.

"The King Tut Exhibit."

She followed the barefoot woman into another room and sat on one of two identical couches, a glass top table in front of it. Beneath the table was an area rug like the exotic weavings in Cairo's Bazaar. Miscellaneous ashtrays and Kleenex boxes were everywhere, and the walls were filled, floor to ceiling, with books of complicated title. She looked instead at the photographs scattered among the books like punctuation marks between abstruse sentences.

It was obvious the photos were of Claudia Somners' family. The growth of a daughter and son could be traced from one shelf to another. Both children resembled their mother — light complexions, stocky builds and the same pronounced jaw. Their progression seemed miraculous, as if growth were predictable. Unstoppable.

Then images of young Susan appeared in the frames. Then the large cats. Then the woman with the head of a cat. It was bad enough that the dreams were every night, now they started to intrude on the day. Hour after hour, like the doubt about an iron that hadn't been turned off or a back door that hadn't been latched, they were distracting.

"Tell me why you're here," Claudia said.

The fifty-minute session went by too quickly. She talked about things she had not planned to: the dusty back road that led to Gullcrest, Texas, and how her father and mother had first served up their own recipe for fried chicken in a ten-table restaurant there. She told Claudia how Southern Foods, Inc., bought them out when she was just twelve years old and eventually opened up Family Fried Chicken franchises throughout the state. It was a cash plus stock purchase.

"So you're the 'family' behind Family Fried Chicken."

"That's just it, no family. My parents were killed by lightning the same year of the purchase."

"How awful."

"Third cousins on my mother's side raised me, but I never felt like part of their home. She even did my laundry separate from theirs."

"Do you stay in touch with them?"

"They stay in touch with me." She looked at the photos of Claudia's children again and frowned. "Jason and Grace are my only family now that Susan's gone."

"Tell me about Susan."

She said everything about her child that came to mind. Claudia left her couch to sit beside May, held her hand as one story after another spilled out with no concern for sequence.

"You're so young to have gone through so much heartbreak," Claudia said.

They were scheduling an appointment for the following Monday when she mentioned the dream. There was only enough time to tell the therapist that after having the same dream every night, she woke up at three o'clock.

"Something must be waking you. An alarm in the neighborhood, or the newspaper boy? Something scheduled."

"I don't think so. The first time I had this dream I was in a plane on my way to Egypt."

Claudia's pronounced jaw moved forward as she rubbed one shoeless foot against the other. She told her to think about it during the week to see if there wasn't a logical explanation. "Or see if three o'clock means anything special to you. Or the number three maybe. Make a list."

"That will be easy. Three's my favorite number."

▲▲▲

A skyline full of morning clouds raced behind her as she drove to work. Ahead of her, the downtown glass buildings were still in sunlight, fragile and transparent in the summer heat. They reflected forty million square feet of empty offices throughout all of Houston, just one reminder of the economic crisis. The stress of lost fortunes, the realities of bankruptcy and the three billion dollars in unpaid loans showed in telltale signs of damage throughout the city that went without repair. Boarded buildings, uncut lawns, blank billboards perched along the freeways. "For Sale" signs were posted everywhere and on everything.

She missed the illusion of permanence that was Egypt. Even the sun-dried, clay brick homes and the cardboard box lean-tos with their blankets of dust seemed indestructible compared to the glass towers of the city in front of her now.

When the rain clouds caught up with her she recited her usual prayer: "Blessed be He, Lord of the Universe, have mercy on this '64 Mustang."

Some mornings she had to say the prayer just to get the car started. After the seventeenth rescue tow, Jason insisted she sell it, but it had been her parents' car. And besides, the prayer worked; the wiper blades scratched back and forth across the windshield well enough to almost provide a clear view.

She pulled the turquoise heap into the undercover parking lot just as the sudden onset of thunder and lightning made her wish she were home, under the covers, curled up with her three sweet cats. There was no escaping her parents' extraordinary death; every thunderstorm brought it back. Every booming clap and every blinding white light was a reminder that such a horrible thing had surely happened to her family. Every echoing retreat offered the question: was there a reason?

Walking into *Houston Harbinger*'s reception area on the thirty-third floor didn't help her mood. It was just as gloomy inside as outside: soft gray walls, gray slate flooring, dark gray furniture, light gray overstuffed pillows, a gray telephone with gray notepad paper beside it, even. The sofa, in light blue wool, was the only patch of clear sky.

"Everyone thought I was crazy when I said that bitch was going to be our next publisher, but here's the proof." The magazine's receptionist, Maggie McKnight, waved the memo at May that had been passed out that morning announcing Grace's promotion.

Maggie sat behind a counter of dark gray formica, in front of a light gray computer keyboard. "Oh, May. I'm sorry. I always forget that you and Grace are friends."

"We've been friends forever," she said, now knowing even forever had limitations.

Maggie frowned.

May headed to her work area, where she picked up a calendar so she could mark the date with a big fat "X": the day Grace became publisher. But the book fell open to August 3, her birthday, the start of a decade with her favorite number — three. She'd looked at that date so many times since the beginning of the year, the spine of the calendar naturally opened to it. A black and white lithograph depicted six men in a canoe with three large ships in the background. On a dock, a lady dressed in a long flowing robe and crown stood taller than the man beside her. A priest kneeled with outstretched arms, a crucifix in his right hand.

The cut-line under the picture: "Christopher Columbus says

goodbye to Queen Isabella and King Ferdinand before leaving on his voyage of discovery. August 3, 1492. Palos, Spain."

"Grace has called a meeting. Five minutes. Conference room," said an out-of-breath woman. "Oh, and I'm Grace's new secretary." Her red hair was disheveled, and her cotton blouse was not tucked in the back. There was no way of knowing if this was her usual appearance.

Though the meeting had been called without any notice, not a single person was absent. In fact, there was one new face among the magazine's directors, managers and editors. Grace swept in, introduced herself, though it wasn't necessary, and told the group her intention as the new publisher was to pull the magazine from the lowest circulation in its history to the highest within the next seven months.

"You'll want to blame the magazine's troubles on the economy," Grace said. "But the problem is all of you. You've been insulated behind your closed doors, your predictable routines, your guaranteed salary increases, while I've been out there. Selling. On commission." The magazine had new owners. By the October issue, they were to have a new format, new design and new way of working with one another. Grace extended her arm toward the stranger.

"This is Beth Fields."

May wanted to scream. Beth Fields, who you never stopped talking about the entire time we were in Egypt? Your new friend Beth Fields, who would have an opinion about everything we saw and said and ate every day of our vacation? The sudden pain in her stomach made her feel certain she was coming down with gyppie tummy again. She groped in her skirt pocket for a roll of Lifesavers while the dark-haired intruder, rather than meet everyone's inquisitive looks, stared into an oversized leather bag that teetered precariously on her lap.

"I've hired Beth as an outside design consultant," Grace said.

But I'm the art director.

"We work as a team. Your combined efforts will bring a better result. So, for now, plan on a staff meeting every Monday morning at eight-thirty a.m. That's it, thank you."

She thought of Dr. Claudia Somners' kind face and the plans she'd made just that morning to see her every Monday for therapy. "But I have an appointment on Monday mornings," she said.

Grace's movement toward the door was unaffected. "Then change it."

Grace heard the murmur from the conference room as she walked down the long gray hallway to her new office. Her first meeting had been conducted exactly as she imagined her father would have. How many meetings as a child had she begged to attend with him? There was never a time. Instead she listened to his muffled conversations through the closed library door at their house, never hearing distinct words, only the tone and clip of his discourse, which she practiced in her room in front of the mirror. She was never welcome at his skyscraper office downtown; she knew his secretaries only as voices on the phone. He conducted all of his work from home on a private line that she could never get access to, and his thick briefcase remained locked at all times with a key that she to this day had never found. He'd made business seem alluring, something she was determined to be part of one day. She played the role of understudy, absorbing every clue and nuance in an effort to emulate him, knowing that one day he would recognize himself in her success and be proud.

Inside her new office, she raised the chrome-plated mini-blinds, stared complacently at her own reflection in the glass and tried to see his image. She saw the busy intersection below instead. An obese man in a folding chair sat with a cigar box in his lap and a mangy brown Rottweiler by his side. He was as much a fixture to that corner as the stoplight. She'd passed him many times, tossed change into the cardboard container. "God bless you," he'd say. And she would feel blessed, blessed to be who she was and to have the fate that was hers.

At the conference in Taos she'd learned that her life was not happenstance. And since stepping onto The Path there had been immediate rewards: renewed energy, a glowing complexion, increased creativity, even improved eyesight; everything the leaders of the seminar said she might experience, and more. There was her promotion, her salary increase and the unlikely events that led her to an incredible deal on a new condo.

She felt sorry for the old man and his filthy dog. What choices had they made to end up in such doom? "'O know, O Lord, that a man's life is not his own; it is not for a man to direct his steps.' Jeremiah," she said.

Then she thought again of her prosperous father and all those years of locked drawers and doors and briefcases and whispered conversations and withheld information and weighty intonations and wondered, just what was so secretive about the banking industry anyway?

Chapter Thirteen

With the money May received quarterly from Family Fried Chicken, Inc., she and Jason could have afforded a nice house in just about any suburb. But she wanted to live where she had with her parents, The Heights, one of Houston's oldest, near downtown. Of course, their small wood-framed house was long gone, replaced by a U Wash & Fold; even the rock garden, where she and her mom had planted flowers, was gone. No trace of tulip, rose or crocus anywhere. But there were many homes in the area, still standing, in need of a family.

She'd picked out a two-story, yellow-brick one with an open porch across its front. Though it was large enough to house four families, every inch of it had a purpose when Susan was alive. It had been a happy home, transformed into a golden-brick kingdom by Susan, who chased fairies through the hallways. Now it was just too big, and too drafty. Even in the middle of summer, she roamed around in it wearing knitted-woolen sweaters and Jason's old argyle knee-highs.

After the first day with Grace as her new publisher, the house looked even larger that night, as if empty rooms had attached themselves to the sides while she was gone. There was a note on the tiled kitchen counter:

Will be home late.

J.

She couldn't remember when Jason had started using just his initial, but since she saw less of him every day, this condensed version of his name seemed appropriate. She imagined if he ever left her, it would be in this same manner. "Won't be home. Ever. J."

He hadn't always been the type to disappear just when you needed him most. When did it start? Susan's funeral? He'd sat in the courtyard, leaving her to face all those sad faces alone. A few months later, when she was sick with the flu, suddenly he had meetings after work every night. He went fishing the weekend May was going to receive an art director's award. The first night of their trip in Alexandria he was gone for hours, and as the trip dragged on, the more time he spent away from her. She still saw the brief moment on the street corner in Cairo — Jason accepting papers from that Egyptian in the expensive boots. Had she really seen that? Or was she lonesome and looking for him then, as she was now?

Ben, Jerry and Blue Bell, her three pet cats, gathered around her. "I wish we were in Egypt," she said. "In the noise and the crowds. Never alone."

Blue Bell jumped to the counter and rubbed his gray head against her hand. Ben and Jerry brushed her ankles in an endless circle.

That next morning, she couldn't find Blue Bell. She searched each room and called outside for him. She shook a box of Cat Chow, then opened and closed the kitchen screen door, hoping its squeak might get his attention. After an hour, she finally found him in the back of her closet, curled around himself, sick.

She threw on some clothes, bundled the cat in a bath towel and rushed him to Southbury Animal Hospital within fifteen minutes. She held him, the pads of his paws warm on her forearm, while a large bird with an emerald green crown and saffron yellow underside, from a hanging cage in the corner of the waiting room emitted horrible squawks that sounded like human coughing.

"What's the matter with my favorite kitty?" Dr. John Benston's assistant, Shelly, lifted the cat's head to look in his eyes, but Blue Bell wouldn't look away from the coughing parrot.

"What's wrong with that bird?" May said.

"The macaw?" Shelly laughed. "Nothing!" The parrot had belonged to a client, a nice old man with a horrible smoker's cough that had finally killed him the month before. He'd willed the pet to the veterinarians. "But the pitiful thing has taken to imitating his owner in his absence," she said. "You know how animals are."

"Pitiful," May said.

"Pitiful," the macaw squawked.

Dr. Benston reported a high temperature and dehydration. He drew blood for testing and suggested they keep Blue Bell overnight. He held the cat close to his face and rubbed its ears. May left reluctantly; it was all too familiar, illness out of nowhere, just like Susan's leukemia. One day she was in Macy's dressing room helping her daughter try on blue jeans, the next day helping her into a hospital gown. Susan's cough had been so small; it was barely there.

She called her office from the vet's reception area to let them know she'd be late and while waiting on the phone, caught a glimpse of herself in the full-length mirror across the room. She was dressed in a T-shirt imprinted with lions and tigers, a green belt that looked like a snake, a pair of fish-print shorts and her Miss Piggy house slippers. She stared down at them as she told Grace about Blue Bell.

"Poor May. Why do all these bad things keep happening to you?"

"I wish I knew," she said, recognizing the Taos influence in Grace's question; it was as subtle as an accent.

The parrot noisily cracked seeds in its powerful curved beak.

▲▲▲

Blue Bell's blood tests revealed feline leukemia, a highly contagious and common disease among cats. Though Jason told May from the beginning their cat would not recover, she insisted on trying to save him with medication and blood transfusions. When he was home, she fed him baby aspirin and Interferon; since he wouldn't eat, she fed him through an eye dropper. She massaged his body and cleaned his fur with a damp cloth when he stopped grooming himself. At night she slept with him to keep him warm, but he didn't get better. She dreamt of Bast's cats, begrudging their healthy bodies and hearty spirit. She thought of the cat from Richard's dig and wondered, if it were to get sick, who would take care of it? The Friday before her thirtieth birthday, Blue Bell died.

Chapter Fourteen

Jason came home a little after midnight. Too much scotch made the kitchen floor buckle beneath him. He moved slowly, his shoes tucked securely against his body, opened the refrigerator door and stared into the cool white air, refreshing even at that hour of the night. The shelves were packed with fat-free cereal boxes, sugar-free juice bottles, glasses of water that bulged with dried-out curling carrots and browning celery sticks, stacks of Diet Cokes, Diet Dr. Peppers and Diet 7-Ups. Five partially eaten Lo-Cal Lean Meals from the second shelf tumbled out onto the floor. He left them. May probably wouldn't even pick them up for days, she'd become so messy.

He stumbled upstairs and stood in front of their slightly opened bedroom door. Two dark shapes clustered around May as she slept. One was burrowed in her hair on the pillow, the other snuggled against her throat, like sentries.

Then he saw a third shape at her feet. Two yellow circles flashed at him. Blue Bell's eyes? Impossible.

He decided to sleep in the guest bedroom. Fully dressed, he flopped on the bedspread without taking off his clothes, and shut his eyes. Darkness. Then the room started to spin. Susan called out. He stood and walked right into the wall, having forgotten he was in the guest room and not his own. He must have slept without realizing it, but now, fully awake, he could still hear his daughter. Down the stairs, to the hall, he saw the back door was open. Had he forgotten to shut it when he came home? Lean Meals were strewn across the kitchen floor. Had someone broken into their refrigerator? What a disappointment for them. He tried to remember coming home, how he'd ended up in the guest bedroom. Through the sound of katydids and night whispers, he heard Susan's soft voice again. Calling out a single word.

But it was May's voice, outside in their yard. She paced back and forth, barefoot, dressed only in that old cotton nightgown. Bent at the waist, she kept saying something. A name? Was she calling one of their pets? No. Both cats were in the kitchen window next to him, watching her as he did. She roamed the yard looking under azaleas, checking behind potted ferns, separating hawthorn branches, even taking the lid off of the bar-b-que. Just how crazy do you plan to get, May?

It was just like the night before they left for Egypt, when he found her on the beach, that ratty old gown making her look like a ghost in the moonlight. Another night of sleep ruined by another one of her night strolls. He didn't know if he wanted to coax her back inside or scream at her. The sour taste of scotch from the night before started backing up in his throat. He turned around and trudged back to the guest bedroom.

Let her therapist handle it. He needed to sleep. He had his own problems, his own pain.

▲▲▲

That night May had dreamed she sat on the sand with both the black and white cats next to a gold shield inscribed with ornate symbols. They watched the cat-headed woman pace. With each step, she shook an object that looked like an egg beater. It produced a sound that combined a pleasant bass note with an imposing ring. She glided to the music she made, her movements reflected in her golden-colored gown and her long whiskers. Her eyes were Nile green, her skin bronzed from the sun, her jaw pronounced.

She spoke simultaneously in Arabic and English. "I have lost one of my cats," she said. "There are three. You rode Madee, the black one, and that is Miss Takbal next to you. It is Hader who is gone. He is as large as these two, only his fur is gray and he has yellow eyes."

"I've lost Blue Bell," May said. "He's gray with yellow eyes too!"

"No," the woman shook her head, her whiskers wavering. "Your cat died, my obstinate feline has run away." She threw the musical instrument at the sand. "All to retrieve his stupid stolen collar. Vain cat! And when there is so much work to be done."

Now, in the light of day, May couldn't explain why she'd gone to the back yard to look for this lost cat Hader. At the time it had made sense: find the cat, end the dreams, get some sleep. But there was no sense to be made of anything any longer. Moments before the *Harbinger*'s Monday morning meeting, she reached the psychiatrist by phone.

"Dreams are a healthy way of dealing with unresolved issues," Claudia told her.

"But this is no ordinary dream, is it? Night after night the same, and it's getting so complicated."

"There's always a logical explanation, May. You've probably latched on to the memory of that gray cat from your daughter's funeral. You know, a symbol, so you don't have to think of the enormity, the meaning of the funeral itself. We'll figure it out."

In the silence that followed, she stared out the office window and tried to loosen her grip on the phone receiver. Clouds drifted by: dinosaurs, sheep, a dog's head and a jumping horse. She and Susan had always seen animals.

"I know what you're thinking," she said to Claudia. "I'm the one who has lost my gray cat with yellow eyes. Blue Bell. And the giant cat is the one that appeared at Richard's dig. I'm the one who takes refuge by the ocean. The beach house in Gullcrest. And I'm the one who has had something stolen. My Susan. And you, Claudia, are the one on the shoreline with your pronounced jaw speaking psychological lingo as I bob around in my sea of uncertainty." She laughed so she wouldn't cry.

"That's a pretty good start!" Claudia also laughed.

She went to the meeting that morning thinking of nothing but sleep. The kind of still sleep that leaves deep imprints from the sheets on your face and shoulders, and your hair permanently creased at right angles; sleep without dreams. She was as listless as Grace was enthusiastic.

"I am the luckiest person!" Grace began the meeting. "It's just as if my parents knew when they named me that I truly would be graced."

Several fellow workers rolled their eyes, and a few others dropped their foreheads in their hands.

Grace circled the conference table in her dark blue pinstriped suit, masculine, something her father would have worn. Like the second hand on a watch face, it took her exactly one revolution to tell them about her cousin's archeological discovery in Egypt. Her aunt, Charlotte Sutton, had heard from her son Richard just the night before, that the dig had surpassed everyone's wildest dreams. Unfortunately, that was all he was permitted to say. The Egyptian government refused any press about the discovery until they completed their own analyses of the artifacts. Famed geologists, archaeologists and sedimentologists with state-of-the-art electron-scanning microscopes were being flown to Cairo. They had requested two weeks with the antiquities before going public with their findings. Aunt Charlotte had phoned Grace only to let her know about Richard's welcome home party on August 21.

May smiled at the thought of Richard's return. Maybe she could go to the party?

Grace stopped circling and tossed her blonde straight hair over one shoulder. "But I pushed Auntie for more info, and she was so proud she just had to tell me that the government has agreed to ship the find to Houston for its first public showing at the Museum of Natural Science! My cousin will get international acclaim, and if I plan it right, *Houston Harbinger* will get the exclusive interview!

"It's exactly the kind of story we need to introduce the magazine's new format in October. I can't wait to tell Beth about this change. We'll scoop everyone!" She raised her arms to either side of her, lifting the blue pinstriped jacket just enough to reveal a bare midriff.

"You mean in place of the story that we've already done?" Tom Salagaz, a copywriter, asked.

She dropped her arms with such force they made a thud when they hit her sides. She stared at him, a look that May knew too well.

He squirmed in his seat, causing a succession of tiny squeaks from the chair.

"It's not that much time, Grace, to start all over and have it out by October," May said.

"Is that my problem?" Grace said. "We have to guarantee this first issue sells. Everyone will be doing the Columbus Anniversary thing, anyway. You should have thought of that from the start."

They were to begin research immediately. Grace delegated the work, giving May her assignment last.

"Find out about Zagazig, the city nearest to Richard's dig site. We need a design motif that will reflect its ancient past. I want to know what those people wore, what they ate, what they drank, what their homes looked like, which gods they worshiped — all of it."

"Your cousin's dig took place outside of Zagazig?" It was Tom again.

"You have a problem with that too?" Grace said.

"No problem, I just happened to read an article last week about these soldiers in Zagazig who captured a mutant animal of some sort."

"Mutant, like in Ninja turtle?" Grace laughed.

"Like in house cat," Tom said, "but the size of a lion or tiger."

"What?" May said, louder than she had intended.

Tom's look of concern for her brought an irritated one from Grace.

"What magazine? I need to know the magazine." May stood.

Tom stared at his pencil. "*People's Choice.*"

"That trash rag?" Grace laughed again.

"I was in line at the grocery store. It's not as if I have a subscription."

"Anything else you'd like to contribute, Tom?" Grace waited a few moments while a few of the editors chuckled. "Okay then, everyone be sure to wish May a happy birthday, and don't you dare forget about the party I've planned for her Friday evening at my new condo."

May's co-workers expressed their birthday greetings. A few sang off-tune, some threw wadded balls of paper at her, and others hugged her as they left the conference room. When only she and Grace remained, she shut the door.

"I've looked everywhere for news of Richard's cat," May said. "I wrote to him through the University. I mean, at the time he mentioned the cat to me, I was only interested in the black one, but now I know it's the gray one that's missing."

"What are you talking about?" Grace gathered papers.

"The cats in my dreams. The dreams I started having on our trip."

"We all had strange dreams on that trip, I think it was the food."

"Come on, Grace. Even you must admit it's more than strange to dream of a giant cat and then have one turn up at Richard's site."

"Now, suddenly, you've stopped believing in coincidence?"

"And then stranger still for me to see the cat, in Cairo, in the truck. I wasn't sure it had really been Richard's cat, but now there's no doubting it."

"What are you doing, May? Looking for things to get upset about? Don't you have enough problems?"

She watched Grace slip papers into a brand new leather briefcase with a lock on the front. "About my birthday. I just don't feel like a party."

"But this is your thirtieth. A decade of your lucky threes, for heaven's sakes!"

"It's Blue Bell's dying, on top of 'all my other problems.'"

"Sarcasm, May? You can't pull it off." Grace strode into the hallway ahead of her. "You may not feel like a party, but it's what you need." She navigated the long carpeted corridor, unsteady on the pinstriped high-heel shoes that matched her new suit.

▲▲▲

On her way to the downtown library, May thought of about a zillion sarcastic things to say to Grace. She was still thinking of them as she lugged an armful of books on ancient Egypt over to one of the reading tables. They had the musty odor of shelved tomes, the same earthy smell of the tombs in Egypt, the air of antiquity. She remembered the vast desert and the endless expanse of empty sky that had made her believe she understood eternity, and then the abrupt change from hard-packed earth to fertile greenery at the Nile's edge. One step in the land of miracles made such a difference.

She turned one glossy page of the largest book, and saw a photo of a bronze-colored statue. Was she dreaming? Before her was the same figure she'd been seeing nightly for the past six weeks. Slender and graceful in her tight-fitted gown, was the woman with the head of a cat. She held a golden shield in her left hand and a musical instrument that looked like an eggbeater in her right. At the statue's feet were three bronze cats. Under the photo the cutline: From the ancient city of Bubastis (modern day Zagazig). Temple of Bast. Bast, the moon goddess.

"Bast?" she said.

"Sshhh!" An old man crusty with city grime sat at the other end of the reading table with an open book in front of him and his eyes closed.

She took deep breaths, trying to get her heart to slow down before daring to look at the photograph again. The earthy smell she'd welcomed assaulted her now. She watched the dozing derelict. Maybe it wasn't the air of antiquity after all.

She wanted to take the book and run, run outside, into the moving traffic, into a bus, into the largest eighteen-wheeler ever built. Instead she read on, of the names of gods and goddesses, their relationships to one another and their symbolic meanings. The cat was Bast's animal symbol because it could see in the dark, just as Bast could see at night when she turned into the moon.

She studied the photos of amulets discovered near the Temple of Bast. There were bronze cat statues with golden hoops through their ears, silver charms shaped like the crescent moon, finger rings engraved with the image of a cat, vessels with inlaid cat designs, and cat silhouette pendants of blue porcelain or turquoise. Hundreds of cat carcasses were swaddled in tattered fabric, others in sandalwood caskets, their portraits faded on the exterior casings, the sacred eye of Horus decorating their chests.

"Are you all right?"

She looked up from the book. Everything had a ghostly double-image. She tried to focus on the woman in front of her.

"The library is closing."

She checked the large clock on the wall. She'd been reading for six hours. "I had no idea."

The woman closed the book in front of May and looked at its cover. "Nothing more thrilling than being lost in a good book."

"I am lost," she said.

"I'm sorry?"

Nothing looked solid any longer. She was afraid what was in her mind had found a means of escape. Her inside had spilled out, took on a form of its own. Like the ka looking for its own mummified body, her thoughts came back to her.

"A good night's sleep is all I need." She gathered as many books as she could hold and took her place in the check-out line.

▲▲▲

During their emergency afternoon session the following day, Claudia's yellow pencil continuously scratched against the paper pad as May told her what she'd found at the library.

"I'm crazy."

"No," Claudia said, the pencil finally stopping.

"I've taken the step."

"What step?"

"One step, like in the desert. Soil to sand. You believe there's this whole big schism, but it's just a fine line. Sane to crazy, just like that." The weight of her long curly hair pulled her down. With each moment, she slumped farther into the tan couch until she had to prop her head up by resting it on the sofa's arm.

"You probably learned about Goddess Bast while you were in Egypt. You may have seen a picture or a statue of her and just forgotten," Claudia said.

"D.D. Dodd. There was this woman on the beach, in Alexandria. Wouldn't stop talking about what she'd seen on her tours. Went on and on about the gods and goddesses. Maybe she mentioned Bast?"

Claudia grabbed hold of the intricately woven carpet with her bare toes. "In your dream, why must the cat always save you?"

"You mean why can't I save myself?"

The therapist arched both eyebrows and stuck the pencil back in its nesting spot above her right ear, the fleshy-pink eraser tip stuck out like a tiny tongue.

"That would certainly be the nineties' kind of thing to do." She struggled to an upright position on the couch. "But it's a dream." She said these words loudly, distinctly. "I can't control it."

"But you are your dreams, May. Every ocean, every grain of sand, every cat, every cat-headed woman is you. You are in control."

"You say my dream, but you mean my life. You sound like New Age Grace. As if I can change things just through my thinking." She stood, paced on the multi-colored rug. "Please don't say for every action a reaction. It's how the universe works. It works regardless of what I want."

"So who works it?"

She sank back down on the couch, the weight of her body making it impossible to stand for one more second.

"I used to think God," she said, "but that would mean He planned Susan's dying."

"So who works it?"

She couldn't answer; there was a pain in her chest.

"Goddess Bast?" Claudia said.

She felt short of breath, but managed to pick up her purse and leave without even one last glance at the woman she'd hoped would save her.

In the elevator on the way to her car, she took off her shoe. Inside in a plastic sleeve that had clouded with age was a small photograph of Susan. When she shook the picture to get a clearer view of her little girl's face, a sheet of paper stuck behind the photo fell out. It was the list she'd worked on for Claudia. Written at the top of the paper was the number three with the following words under it:

My birthday - August 3
May - three letters
CAT - three letters
Ben Jerry Blue Bell

Chapter Fifteen

THE RAIN-SOAKED FREEWAYS were at a standstill the Friday night of May's birthday party. Car after car lined up in the evening dusk, with Grace already running late to pick up the new silk dress she planned to wear. Using the back streets, driving her red Mercedes coupe faster than usual to make up time, she hit a slippery curve in the road just as an animal darted in front her. Her brakes squealed, the car slid sideways. It came to a stop under a dark canopy of wet leafy limbs. Facing the direction from which she'd just come, she flung her arms in front of her face, braced to see oncoming traffic. The road was empty, but for a black-and-white-spotted cat.

Rain tapped against the windshield. The digital clock on the dash changed numbers. Six-thirty-one. Six-thirty-two. Six-thirty-three. She looked at the clock. The cat. The clock. Six-thirty-four. Even when a spot of dirty white fur moved in and out at the animal's belly, she sat, unable to move, unable to pull away from a memory of May's father, of all people. She knew she should at least back the car onto the side of the road, or turn it around in the proper direction, but all she could think of was Dillon Justice, as twelve-year-old May had described him:

a small-framed man with large ears, tip-toeing into May's bedroom, blocking the light from the hallway as he stood by the foot of her bed. And he'd just watch you sleep? she had asked. Only until he saw my chest move up and down or heard my breathing was normal, May had answered. Why? Mom said he just worried about me sometimes. Grace had spent the next three weeks as still as she could be when she was in her own bed, barely breathing for as long as she could, before she fell asleep. But her father never came to check on her. No one came.

A tremendous bolt of lightning froze the image of the injured animal in front of her. At last she pulled the car onto a bed of damp pine needles on the shoulder of the road and grabbed an old issue of the *Harbinger* from the back seat. With the magazine spread above her head, she tried to sidestep the deep puddles of rain, but her shoes were sopping wet and her clothes soaked by the time she reached the cat. She wrapped the wet magazine around it and carried it back to the car, where she placed it on the passenger's side floor mat.

Vague memories of a sign that had pictures of dogs and cats and birds on it led her north, then east, then in a circle and then north again. By the time she reached the veterinarian's office she was chilled, angry, inconvenienced, and out of time to pick up her dress from the alteration shop.

Her new secretary, Sharon James, answered the phone when she called her own home from the vet's waiting room.

"Did everyone show? The caterer? The florist? The bartender?" At least everything there was running according to schedule. She began to tell her why she'd be late. "No, it's too long a story. I'll be there before the guests."

But many of the guests had already arrived when she got home. They all talked about the cat she had rescued from certain death. By the time she changed her clothes and joined the party, she was a heroine.

When everyone complimented her on the rescue, she laughed.

When they condemned the horrible person who had run over the poor animal and left it, she nodded without correcting them. The very accident she'd caused had been misinterpreted to her benefit: typical of how life had changed since stepping onto God's Path in Taos.

"Don't say it was nothing," Jason said. "Not many people would have stopped on a rainy night like this to help another person, much less an animal."

"Never would have figured you for an animal lover," Tom Salagaz said.

"I must admit I surprised myself," she said, still looking at Jason, wishing Tom would just once drop the inquisitive copywriter routine. "I think my trip to Egypt, all that talk about the venerable cat, must have had an influence."

When a few more people with cocktails in hand gathered, she repeated what the guide in the Mosque of Abul Abbas had said about the history of the Egyptian cat. She entertained them for a long stretch with stories from the trip, careful to stop while they were still anxious to hear more. She took a long sip of scotch from Jason's glass even though it was Friday, her day to purge poisonous toxins and evil from her body by fasting. Certainly a little drink at the end of the workweek was allowed.

▲▲▲

May couldn't think of a single reason to be at her own birthday party. Dressed in yards of layered Egyptian cotton imprinted with golden camels, she'd been able to slip through the evening practically unnoticed. She listened to Grace from a far corner of the living room through a veil of cigarette smoke that swirled above the table lamps and clung to the ceiling lights, straining to recall just where in Egypt they'd heard these stories. None of it sounded familiar. There was too much to keep track of lately, even the simplest details had become monumental efforts: names, phone numbers, word spellings, how to get to places she'd been a hundred times before, remembering if she had brushed her teeth, put on underwear. Life seemed as uncontrollable now as it had been when she was young, after her parents had been killed. If growing older didn't make things better, more manageable at the least, what was the point?

"Happy birthday, May."

It was Beth Fields. Grace's new friend, Beth Fields. The outside design consultant, Beth Fields. The person she was expected to work with, Beth Fields.

The same large leather bag that accompanied Beth to her first meeting at the *Harbinger* was slung over her shoulder now at the party, the weight of it pulling on her so that she stood crooked. She held a frozen margarita in one hand and a gift-wrapped box in the other. "This business has put us in an awkward position. Hope it won't keep us from becoming friends."

"Grace has put us in this awkward position," she said. She accepted the gift with no intention of opening it, but after several minutes of Beth just standing there, not moving, not saying a word, she didn't know what else to do. She unwrapped the paper.

"What did your husband give you?" Beth said.

"A journal covered in turquoise fabric that's embossed with cat silhouettes. The paper pages inside are handmade with deckle edges."

"A blank book?"

It did seem like an odd gift for such a significant birthday. Although at the time she'd received it she thought it appropriate, another mirror, another dreadful reminder of herself: nothing more than a blank inside wrapped up in some animal print fabric.

She lifted the lid off the box Beth had given her. Inside, placed on white cotton batting, was a small turquoise pendant shaped like a cat.

"It's an amulet," she said.

"What?" Beth said.

"In honor of the Goddess Bast." She thought of the library books filled with images like this very one in front of her now.

"Grace told me you were a cat person. Hope you like it."

"I love it."

"And what about this party that I gave you?" Grace threw her skinny arms around her, catching her long-sleeved sweater on May's parrot earring. "Do you love it too, May?"

"Thanks for going to all this trouble, Grace." She disengaged from the silver threads of Grace's sleeve.

"You haven't seen the upstairs." Grace pulled on her with one arm, on Beth with the other. When they passed Jason on the way to the stairway, she let May's arm drop to grab his.

She showed them her bedroom last, decorated in shades of white and furnished with dark mahogany. Pussy willows filled a vase on top of an antique dresser and an arrangement of white silk papyrus, the ancient flower of Egypt, was on a marble table near the window. The same satin material that draped the windows in three tiers also covered the bed where at least fifteen pillows were stacked, all in varying shapes and sizes. Sewn to the center pillow was a gold leaf cross encrusted with tiny pearls.

Meticulously arranged on the corner of the bed was a red silk nightgown. Its shiny folds blinked on and off like a neon sign from the slow turn of a lighted ceiling fan directly above.

Beth looked at May, then at the nightgown and tried to hide a smile.

Though she smiled back, Grace's sexy negligee only made her think of her own tattered gown with the missing satin ribbon. She squeezed Jason's left hand, their signal that meant it was time to leave. He paid no attention. He watched Grace intently.

▲▲▲

That night when she sat near the ocean and stroked Madee's black fur, she wore the turquoise pendant Beth had given her for her birthday.

"Hader believes he is handsome in the turquoise collar," Goddess Bast told her. "He wears it like jewelry! The other two do not insist on collars, only this vain one." She licked the back of her hand and rubbed it against her whiskers, then straightened each fold of her golden gown. "Three worlds. Three cats. That is how it is." She licked the back of her other hand and rubbed it across the top of her right ear.

May found herself looking for the lost cat everywhere, no longer certain of which came first: her dream of the giant feline, or the discovery of one outside of Zagazig. She spent hours in the *Harbinger*'s research department and nights at the downtown library searching for articles about the mutant cat just in case it and Hader were one and the same. She couldn't wait until Richard came home from the student dig; he would tell her all about the Egyptian cat. She entered notes in the turquoise journal Jason had given to her for her birthday; everything had become so mixed up, writing it all down at least kept it in chronological order. And besides, it gave the useless blank book a purpose.

Chapter Sixteen

Lou's Five and Dime Variety was located in The Village, a six-block-square area of retail shops and small office buildings in an older section of Houston. May had met Lou Schultz, the owner of the store his grandfather had founded, three years before while hunting down heart-shaped name tags for a Valentine's party the *Harbinger* was giving.

As art director, public relations parties had somehow ended up as one of her responsibilities. These parties brought on impossible missions with never enough time.

Once for a gala with a rodeo theme, she had to round up ten cowboys with horses and gear, a country western band, bar-b-que and beer for four hundred, an ice sculpture of a bucking bronco, forty blooming cacti for centerpieces, ten silver belt buckles engraved with the magazine logo for door prizes, three hundred cow chips for a chip-throwing contest and one lively, but as friendly as possible, bull — all in thirteen days.

The guests' invitations were tucked into the leather bands of cowboy hats with silk linings. All this was easy compared to finding a facility to host the event. Luckily, this had been during a time in Houston when anything was attainable; it was just a matter of money.

The hotel she contracted with had been the location for many pleasure-boat conventions. It had easy access from the street to transport shiny, new Boston Whalers and Chris Crafts into the Grand Ballroom, or in this case, two thousand pounds of shiny flank, hoof and horn.

The party was fairly successful until a handful of advertising executives, primed with their own tequila, lassoed a waitress and tied her to a keg of beer. They mounted three unattended horses, then galloped into the main lobby where they tossed cow chips into the crystalline, turquoise-blue water of the indoor fountain. The hotel management forced an abrupt ending.

A lot had changed since then. Budgets were cut to practically nothing, while everyone still demanded the same grandeur. During this struggle to meet these expectations without the money, she had stumbled across the glory of Lou's Five & Dime Variety in The Village. Filled with every imaginable trinket and party favor in the world, the store was just what she needed. The miniature umbrellas with their toothpick spokes were in aisle one, place card holders and candy cigarettes in aisle four. Decorative plates, cups, party horns and higher priced items could be found in aisles seven, eight and nine. It was all there and affordable.

Lou had teased her when they first met. "Art director for the *Harbinger*, as in host of that legendary party with a rodeo theme?" Their friendship had started with a good laugh. She came to rely not only on his supplies, but also on his sound advice and fatherly manner. At seventy-eight years old, he maneuvered through his overflowing store with agility and gracefully squeezed into aisles barely wider than he. Lou knew his inventory as well as he knew all the back roads of his hometown Houston, and he could locate any item in the store as quickly as he could offer his opinion on any subject. A modern-day philosopher is how he liked to think of himself, the dime-store variety, he would joke, but nonetheless a thoughtful man.

She and Lou shared a common interest: jigsaw puzzles. Over the years, they'd given each other many, always trying to surpass the other in degree of difficulty. But she was the better at putting the puzzles together, returning with Polaroid proof of the finished product in record time. She was so good, Lou had stopped giving her the box top that showed the completed picture.

"Happy Birthday, hot shot!" He handed her a large plastic bag with thousands of cardboard pieces tumbling about inside. "Let's see if you can have it finished by this time next year!"

She held the bag out in front of her, shook its contents. "I missed you at my birthday party."

"Party?"

"Grace told me you couldn't come."

Lou shrugged. "Didn't know about it."

The bell on the front door to his store rang. Two noisy young girls entered, their hair still wet from a swim at the community pool down the street. There were ambiguous shapes on their clothes from the wet swimsuits they wore underneath. Susan, too, had insisted on wearing her suit at all times under everything: school clothes, Sunday school outfits, Girl Scout uniforms, just in case a swimming opportunity came along. These two looked just a little bit older than her daughter would have been.

"Girls! Girls!" Lou said. He stepped onto a wooden ladder that slid along a wall of shelves holding squatty glass containers filled with candy. Holding on to the ladder's worn rungs, he soared to where the children stood. The sudden sight of his large body hovering overhead made them quiet down.

He took the lid off the nearest glass jar and pulled out two twisted sticks of cherry licorice. Bending considerably, he handed one to each of the surprised children.

"What's the problem?" he asked.

"It's the moon!" the one with freckles said.

"Is not!" The taller one argued that the faint disk in the sky couldn't be the moon because it wasn't night. Her hair beginning to dry in odd clumps, she insisted it was an alien aircraft.

"Aliens!" Lou said. He climbed down the ladder and handed May a third piece of licorice that she had not seen him get. "Let's go outside and take a look."

The two girls flitted around Lou like little bees at their hive.

May and Grace had imagined some pretty incredible stories the summers they spent in Grace's L-shaped swimming pool. They threw pennies that would turn into diamonds or bombs or even babies before they settled on the pool's bottom. The Spanish-speaking maid was a Russian spy on Saturday, by Sunday a murderer who poisoned their peanut butter and jelly sandwiches. The Jamaican gardener cast voodoo trances on children in order to make mulch out of them.

The best days were when Richard showed up and their archaeological digs brought forth all kinds of treasures from the garage. He was so handsome, even as a kid, and made everything an adventure. She and Grace both had crushes on him; they made up quite a few stories that he starred in, without his ever knowing. Grace's stories had their roots in true adversities such as murder, disease and betrayal, while she imagined genies in a bottle, elves, fairies, and probably even alien spacecraft.

Now May turned strangers enjoying a pretty courtyard into deceptive rendezvous. A dream of giant cats into reality, and a tourist who happened to look like Jason into a man on a street corner concealing papers. And any nicely dressed, dark foreigner became the man from Egypt, his horrible cigarettes stinking up Houston, everywhere.

"What a relief, it's just the moon," Lou told her when he came back inside his store.

She stood near the plate glass window, chewed on the licorice and watched the pale circle slip in and out of wispy clouds. "It's Goddess Bast."

"Who, dear?"

She turned away from the moon and looked into her friend's gentle eyes. "Did I tell you Blue Bell died?"

Lou took her in his arms. "You've had so much happen in so short a time. I'm sorry." He smelled spicy, like his scented candles in aisle three.

"I have to go. Thanks for the jigsaw."

"Stay awhile."

"Can't. I have a meeting with our new design consultant, Beth Fields." She scrunched up her face. "Grace's big idea."

▲▲▲

Fields Studios was just a few blocks from Lou's Five & Dime. The offices, like the shops in The Village, were small, individually-owned, and only offered a number of parking spaces equal to their width. May preferred the smallness and clutter of this neighborhood area; too many retail centers had sprung up around Houston during the growth years. Miles of parking lots girding air-conditioned malls where people passed each other anonymously in stale air covered what once were the rice fields, meadows and hunting grounds that her father had reminisced about.

She missed the tired small buildings that some of these centers replaced, and wished for a law requiring every new structure to feature a plaque that described what it once had been. As did the sign at the city limits of Glen Rose, Texas: Welcome to Glen Rose. Home of the Dinosaur. To pass through the area unaware of the giant creatures that left their footprints in the Glen Rose dirt millions of years before would be a loss.

Office buildings should post in their lobbies all the companies that had come and gone during the years; and homes should have brass-plated plaques at the front door listing all the residents who ever lived and died within. Every new structure would have drawings or a photograph of the old building it replaced.

She stood in front of Fields Studios and looked for signs of what that building might have been. Wedged between a Japanese restaurant and an office supply store, it was seven parking spaces wide, two stories high. She walked through the front door, guessing antique shop or restaurant. The interior was bathed in soft white light from a skylight that made the full two stories of the reception area glow. It was painted lavender. She gazed up into the leafy branches of a row of trees against one wall.

"They're chinaberries," the receptionist told her. "Trash-iest tree in Texas! Most folks just pull them right out of their yards. I'm Linda."

She followed Linda down a peach-colored hall to an interior courtyard glassed in on all sides. They passed a variety of plants in large terra cotta pots.

"Corn cockle," Linda said. "Yarrow. Dayflower. Dandelions."

"But they're all weeds," May said.

"Beth grows them," Linda said, as though they had just shared a secret. She opened the door to a courtyard full of thistle, clover, goldenrod and more chinaberry trees.

Beth sat in the shade with a layout pad on her lap and her feet in a turquoise pond. She looked different from the other two times May had seen her; she now looked Egyptian, dark and compact, with leathery skin and spirited brown eyes. Like the fellahin, her mouth was wide and her wrists and ankles thick. The large leather bag that she carried to the first meeting at the *Harbinger* and again to May's birthday party was collapsed by her side, its contents spilled out on the brick.

"Your office is beautiful."

"Thanks, I live here too. Upstairs. A bunch of Italian brothers sank a fortune in this place before it went belly-up with hundreds of other restaurants in this city. I do work for the bank that got stuck with the note, so they're leasing it to me cheap. Want one?" Beth held up a glass of white wine.

"No, thanks." She looked around the courtyard and imagined tables with red checkerboard cloths and single white candles.

"It's practically happy hour. Have one."

She accepted the crystal glass, also left over from the restaurant? "I really appreciate the gift you gave me." She held the turquoise pendant away from her neck so Beth could see she wore it. "It was very generous of you, especially since we don't even know each other."

"I'm hoping that will change."

She liked Beth's direct manner. By the third glass of wine she could hardly believe how much she enjoyed Grace's new friend, Beth Fields. She was everything Grace had said: unafraid, unconventional, unaffected and unusually funny. At moments, she even considered talking to her about Susan. Instead they talked about art, movies, men and the difficulties of growing weeds.

"I have to plant them according to the cycles of the moon," Beth told her. "I use the Farmer's Almanac to determine the right times."

"The moon?"

"Oh, sure! The moon's gravitational pull controls lots of things, even our menstrual cycles!"

"No."

"There's more murders on a night with a full moon, too. Just check any police record. And I'll tell you something else. It isn't a man in the moon! It's a woman. I always see a woman's face."

"Goddess Bast," she said, then wished she hadn't.

"Who?"

"An Egyptian legend."

"Something you learned about while you and your husband and Grace were traveling?"

"Yes. And, strangely, something I dream about."

"Why strange? The things we learn seep into our lives on many levels. I think dreams are terribly important."

"This one is recurring, though. And it gets more involved each time I have it, and I'm getting all mixed up about what I learn in the dream and what I saw on the trip and what I'm learning from the research for the magazine article."

"When I was taking a French class with the Baritz School, all of a sudden French words started popping up in my everyday conversation. It was like I couldn't stop myself. I'd go to the gas station and say, check *mon pétrole, s'il vous plaît.* It was weird."

"My dream has an Egyptian goddess whose cats wear jewelry and run away from home."

"Hey, you're an artist. We're creative people. Lots of artists I know paint their dreams. If they stopped having interesting ones, they'd be out of material!"

May liked the idea of having an artist friend, like those she'd lost touch with from the University of Iowa. And there was nothing subtle about Beth. She said what she thought. Her features were hard, almost masculine, and the black eyeliner on the top and bottom of her lids was bold. There was something even attractive about the short stray hairs that would not conform to the shape of her eyebrows.

"You know, you almost look Egyptian, Beth."

"I look like my father. He was born in Israel." She said it in three syllables: Is-ra-el.

But Beth wouldn't talk any more of her family. She changed the subject quickly, and the rest of the evening they talked about Egypt, the sights May had seen and the things she'd bought, until there wasn't any time left to talk about the redesign of the *Harbinger*. They made lunch plans for the following day with a promise to stick to the subject.

On her way home, she dropped off a slightly drunk Beth at a neighborhood restaurant called Backalley's. Beth struggled out of the Mustang's bucket seat. May felt concerned as she watched her wobble up the stairs to the front door. Was she meeting someone? How would she get home without a car?

When she reached her own home, Jason had already eaten. He was settled in front of the television, the volume turned up too loud.

"I think I've made a new friend," she said. She waited for him to ask who, so she could see the expression on his face when she told him it was Beth Fields, of all people.

"That's nice." He didn't look up from the legal-size papers filled with columns of numbers: the reduced budget for the department of mammals at the zoo. "I won't be home tomorrow night."

She stood in front of the open refrigerator and ate her dinner. A carrot stick. A slug of cranberry juice. Forkfuls of cold shrimp egg-foo yung and a dried-out blueberry muffin left over from the weekend. Ben and Jerry stood on the tile countertop, waiting their certain turn at bits of baby shrimp.

▲▲▲

The next day, Beth walked to the car with her hands pressed against her eyes. "I feel like there's something in my head trying to get out."

"Then good thing I'm driving," May said.

"I never drive."

"How'd you get home from Backalley's last night?"

"Oh, May, we have to go back there. I need to know if I made a fool of myself."

When they reached the green scalloped canopy at the restaurant's front door, Beth grabbed her arm and drew her near. "Wait till you see Arturo, the bartender!"

They stepped inside. An amiable-looking man behind the bar suddenly turned toward Beth and smiled a warm, familiar smile that made others take notice. Then again, people would have looked at Beth regardless of the smile. There was something about her, a kind of recklessness that was magnetic.

"He smiled," Beth said. "I must not have been too obnoxious." Her large leather bag hit a skinny-legged woman beside them.

"Sorry," May said, when Beth didn't notice.

A waitress dressed in jeans and a T-shirt showed them to a table. "Drinks, ladies?"

"Iced tea, please."

"She'll have the house white wine," Beth said. "Give me Tequila Gold on the rocks. With salt. And put an olive in it."

An olive. She thought of her failed attempt with Grace to grow their own olive tree at St. Mary's, then imagined planting one with Beth. She could see its small limbs, strong and twisted, its leaves dark and shiny. Beth would know just how to take care of it; they would plant it according to the cycles of the moon.

"Remember I told you about my dream?"

Beth nodded, but watched Arturo mix drinks.

"There's more. I think I'm imagining things."

"Imagination is good, I always imagine things about Arturo."

"But this borders on paranoid. I keep seeing these people I thought I saw in Egypt. First this scary-looking Egyptian, and this morning on my way to pick you up, I'm sitting at a traffic light and I look into the cab next to me and see this Asian we shared a cab with on the way to our hotel."

"You see a cab, an Asian, of course you'd think of that same one."

"Maybe, but the Egyptian smokes these long brown cigarettes."

"Yeah, they're popular now, even here in the States. You were gone a long time, you're just going through your own kind of re-acclimation. Don't worry about it."

With their lunch menus unopened, they discussed the redesign of the *Harbinger.* Beth sketched their ideas on an 11 x 14 graphics pad that she'd pulled from her purse. They decided Houston's poor economic climate called for a conservative format — the look for the past four years was too flamboyant to work now.

Beth leaned back in her chair. Four plastic yellow swords, that had pierced the olives in each of her four drinks, protruded from the top of her head in all directions. She'd stuck them in her hair at random, but when she leaned toward the table again the little daggers fell against each other. They touched to form the outline of two perfect cat ears. Beth's face grew bronze-colored, her long nose flattened, and long dark whiskers sprouted around her mouth.

"Do you know where Hader is?" Goddess Bast asked.

"What!"

"Do you know what time it is?" Beth repeated.

May tried to swallow. She wiped her forehead with a turquoise napkin, looked at her watch. Three o'clock, exactly, but it couldn't be. She watched the secondhand. It didn't move. "Excuse me," she said, and headed for the ladies' room.

Beth followed, dragging her large purse behind her, and stood nearby as May splashed cold water on her own face.

"You okay?"

"Just not used to wine at lunch, I guess." She kept her head down, weight on her elbows, and clung to a shiny white basin. Beth laughed. At her? When she looked up, she saw Beth pointing at her own image in the large mirror.

"Look!" Beth pointed to the fancy yellow swords in her own dark hair and then started to laugh.

A pear-shaped woman came into the bathroom.

"Do you know the time?" Beth asked as the woman shut herself in one of the stalls. "Please," Beth added after a few moments of silence.

"One fifty-eight," came the answer from behind the door. They heard the toilet paper spin in its holder.

Now they both laughed.

"I'm supposed to have a two-thirty meeting with Grace."

"Call that bitch and cancel. Take the day off! Tell her you ate something bad at lunch and you have to go home."

"I need to let her know I'll be late." May saw a phone on the wall. "You have a quarter?"

Beth fumbled in her large purse for the change.

Just as she was about to press the last digit of her call, the pear-shape flushed. May hung up. "Why do they put telephones near toilets?"

When two more women walked into the restroom, Beth backed up against the mirror, sat on the edge of one of the washbasins and pulled two of the plastic swords from her hair. She held a dagger in each hand and addressed the closed stall doors.

"Ladies, my friend needs to make a call. Please, hold your flushes until I say so." Beth pointed one of the swords at her with the authority of a maestro and moved it in rhythm to her words. "Make your call."

"It's May. Yes, I know. Can you put me through to her? Thanks." She turned toward Beth. "I'm on hold."

Beth swayed a little, unblinking.

"What do you want now, May?" Grace said when she answered the phone.

"What happened to 'hello'?"

"I'm busy. Not all of us have time for leisurely lunches."

She looked at Beth. "It was a working lunch with Beth."

"So what do you want?"

"I must have eaten something that didn't agree with me. I can't make it back to the office."

Beth made a studied "O" with her mouth.

"And Beth?" Grace said. "Did she eat something that didn't agree with her also?"

"Beth's okay."

Beth's eyes widened.

"Fine, May. Go home." Grace hung up.

She hung up.

After they returned to their table, she asked Beth why she'd called Grace a bitch.

"Don't take offense, I know you two are life-long friends and all, but I don't like Grace."

"But Grace talked about you all through Egypt! She told us you were very close."

"You're kidding!"

"All we heard every day was my new best friend Beth Fields would do this, and my new best friend Beth Fields would feel that, and my new best friend Beth Fields says it this way."

"No. I can't handle all that religious stuff she's into. And she's so preachy with it. Really, Grace and I hardly have a thing in common. I mean the woman actually reads the last chapter of a novel first. And she doesn't even like foreign films."

Beth ate cheese enchiladas and beef tacos al carbon while May had green salad, oil and vinegar on the side.

"And this thing with her dad is too weird," Beth said.

"Gerald Sutton?" Just saying his name brought on the same unease May had felt as a child whenever he was around. He was a cold fish of a man, unsmiling, holed away in that smoke-filled library where the phone had a different ring from the others in the house. "What a selfish man. I don't think he even likes Grace."

"She's desperate for his attention."

"Hello, gorgeous," Arturo said. He had that just-got-out-of-the-shower look, clean-shaven and a little flushed in the cheeks. His straight brown hair, pulled into a tight low ponytail, slipped over his shoulder as he bent to kiss Beth on the cheek.

"Meet my new best friend, May Worth," Beth said and then smiled at her.

Arturo shook her hand. "Astros and Cardinals Saturday night. Want to go?" he said to Beth.

"Sure."

As he walked away from the table, Beth pointed and mouthed the words: cute butt.

"You guys serious?"

"With Arturo? He's only a 1Q," Beth said.

"You mean his IQ?" She stabbed at a round red tomato with her fork.

"Ha! In a way, but no. Like in one question."

"I don't understand."

"Okay, let's say Arturo is sitting here having lunch with me. So he says, How was your morning? And I say, Rotten. Then he says, I had a rotten morning too. When I got to the restaurant the ice machine was broken and there was water all over the place and then the big order didn't come in and then the new waitress didn't show and then and then and then. Understand? One question."

She shook her head no.

"Now with a 2Q man it goes like this: How was your morning? I say, Rotten. Then he actually asks a second question, What happened? And I say, On my way to a meeting I was run over by a semi. And he says, Those guys really piss me off. Just yesterday I had one try to squeeze me out of my lane on 610, almost put a dent in my front bumper, but I showed him and then and then and then. Understand?"

Beth had a crooked smile, cunning, not the kind that looked sneaky. May felt her face attempt to mimic it.

"And what does a 3Q man say?"

"Never met one!" Beth laughed, well, more like a cackle. She cut her enchiladas and smiled at several people who looked at her, then bent her head to catch the strings of cheese in her mouth. "Look! There's that giant cat!"

May spun around in her chair, knocking her salad plate to the floor. Was it the black, the white or the lost cat Hader who had come into the restaurant? "Where?"

Beth pointed to the ceiling-mounted television above the bar, a crowd of people dressed in gellabeyas, skull caps and veils on the screen. Many of them held a photograph of a dark gray cat stapled on to a stick. They waved it over their heads. A man with a microphone said something, and then the network broadcaster came back on the air.

"I saw the story earlier," Beth told her. "This enormous cat was discovered somewhere in Egypt."

A waiter rushed over, picked up the plate and lettuce, and mopped the salad dressing from the wooden floor.

"Near Zagazig, where the dig took place," she said.

"What were all those people doing?"

"The cat's an unknown mix of breeds. Some of the Egyptian people believe it's descended from the lion they've seen in ancient drawings."

May had seen the illustrations in her research books on Egypt. A large lion with no mane pictured on a pharaoh's hunting barge, another accompanying a pharaoh's chariot into battle. "But those were lions.

Female lions. And they were tan colored."

"Yeah, that's what they thought, until now anyway. This cat's become a celebrity over there. Some of them even think he's a reincarnation," Beth said. "They've started to call him Pharaoh's Friend."

They can call him whatever they want; May knew it was Hader. Stalking her. First in her dreams, then on the street in Cairo, the magazine articles and now television. How much closer was he planning to get?

"Would you care for more salad?" the waiter asked.

May shook her head.

The printed gray elephants on her cotton skirt grabbed the tails of those in front of them. Young calves darted merrily between the anvil-shaped hooves of their parents, protected by them, unaware of danger.

Chapter Seventeen

That next Thursday when Grace stood at the Worths' front door, a misdirected wind that had blown into the city brought with it the suggestion of crisp fallen leaves, golden and red underfoot. Though it was August, one of Houston's hottest months, it was this cool breeze that swirled her purple skirt as Jason opened the door.

"Hope you don't mind my just dropping in?" The red bath towel in her arms was in motion. A furry black head poked through the folds of one end, and a white cast through the other.

He invited her inside. It was difficult to handle the squirming cat while maneuvering through the clutter of May's dusty knick-knacks. On every table, desk, and shelf, crystal giraffes teetered on delicate legs; carved deer grazed in family groupings; and stone frogs, turtles, cats and ducks stared at her.

Jason scratched the top of the animal's head. "This must be The Hit-And-Run Cat."

"I thought with Blue Bell dying and since this one did appear right before May's birthday party, he just seemed destined to end up as hers. What do you think?"

His hand brushed her breast as he reached for the cat. He spread the red towel between them on the couch and laid the injured animal on top.

At times like this she could understand why May had married him. At times he could be caring, as he'd been with their little guide in Egypt. Sounds of busy Cairo, the boy's laughter, the jingle of the precious coins he'd kept in the pocket of his gellabeya, surrounded her again.

"You're so full of shit, Grace," he said. "You're dumping this cat. Don't turn it into some grand gesture."

She felt warm; suddenly her perfume smelled too strong. She stood. "Fine, I can't stand the smelly thing! No one claimed it at the vet's, so I took it home. The thing has growled at me for four days, and this morning it peed on the rug I brought back from Egypt."

She felt his smug stare all over her. His smirk widened as his gaze moved from her eyes to her breasts.

"So how are you handling Susan's death?" she asked.

She stared at him now.

He walked over to a desk and shuffled through unopened mail, his back toward her. Then he picked up a basket and threw it. She ducked.

"Look at this! May's got them all over our house!"

The basket's contents spilled out: an orange plastic ball and two ballet slippers. The ball had Blue Bell's name printed on it, partly obliterated by teeth marks. The small slippers, worn at the toes, were bound together by their own pink laces.

He pointed to the hallway table where Blue Bell's water bowl overflowed with little girl's ribbons. On a shelf above, the cat's turquoise collar was draped across a snapshot of Susan. He grabbed her arm and pulled her to the coat rack where three balls of string encased a polka-dot umbrella, and a child's knitted sweater had metal rabies tags attached to one of the buttons. He pushed her toward the dining table where Blue Bell's dish was on Susan's placemat, an unopened box of animal crackers next to a clown spoon. On the serving table were photos of Susan and Blue Bell. In front of the photos were worn crayons, a jar with baby teeth in it, a hairbrush imprinted with Blue Bell's name, and a shriveled, dead garden snake laid out on white batting in a small cardboard box.

Shrines. Everywhere.

Jason paced like a cutout target in a carnival's shooting booth, back and forth, his pigeon-toed swagger stiff with anger. Then he stopped, picked up the glass bottle of teeth and gently shook it.

"I'm sorry," she said.

He put the Hit-And-Run Cat in a guest bedroom upstairs. When he came back they went to the kitchen, where he poured a glass of cabernet for her, and a scotch for himself — probably not his first that afternoon. She sat on a wicker stool at the tiled counter. He leaned on the counter beside her and after every sip, moved his drink closer and closer to its edge.

"I don't know how much longer I can take this," he said. "I'm living with a crazy person."

"I'd offer to help, but I don't think May even likes me anymore," she said.

He filled his glass again. "The other night I found her out in the yard looking behind the bushes calling for something."

"One of your cats?"

"No, that would make sense." He took a long swig and set the glass down on the uneven tile so that a good part of it hung over the counter's edge.

Ben and Jerry raced into the kitchen through a cat door. Once inside they must have smelled the Hit-And-Run Cat. They circled, crossed paths, tails down, backs flat, until they picked up the trail of the intruder in the living room. She watched them track the scent as far as the stairs. Jason smiled and touched the back of her hand with his. "They suspect something," he said.

The kitchen was a dusky orange, streaked with the last rays of daylight. It was quiet, except for the tick of a Roman numeral clock above the oven. He ran his finger along the inside of her arm. She let him. Then she pushed his glass off the counter. It hit the floor, shattered.

"Jesus Christ!" he yelled. The yellow booze spread quickly. Bits of broken glass and ice cubes floated toward his alligator boots.

The phone rang.

"Jesus Christ!" he yelled and stepped over the growing puddle to answer it.

Two "okays" and three "yeses" later he slammed the phone down.

"It was May. I could barely understand what she was saying, those goddamned Lifesavers!" He grabbed a roll of paper towels and started to clean up the glass. "Why the hell does she buy the green ones anyway? Why doesn't she just buy the flavors she likes? They come like that, don't they? All cherry! All orange! All lemon! But no, I find green Lifesavers everywhere. In drawers, melted in the ashtrays in our car, stuck to our laundry. I sit on them, I step on them, I goddamn sleep on them!"

The kitchen faucet dripped into a pan that was filled with greasy water.

"May's having dinner with Beth Fields," he said. "What's going on with them? I thought Beth was your friend."

She looked at the pieces of glass at her feet. "So did I."

He went upstairs to get the Hit-And-Run Cat situated with kitty litter, food and water. She walked to the breakfast room, where a jigsaw puzzle was on the table. The outside edge almost complete, it was an outdoor scene, but of what? Thousands of pieces in a plastic bag with a tie at the top were in a nearby chair. She looked for the box top to see what the puzzle was going to be.

"No picture," he said as he came back into the room.

"Then how does she do it?"

He shrugged. "I need to check on a baby chimp at the zoo. You want to come?"

▲▲▲

Grace stood beside Jason at the zoo's side entrance in front of a wrought-iron gate. He'd forgotten his keys, something he must have done frequently because he'd hidden a spare set behind a loose brick in the wall.

She followed him down dark winding sidewalks alive with unfamiliar noises, to the building where the baby chimp was kept. Handling the ape as tenderly as he had the Hit-And-Run Cat that afternoon, he checked the animal's temperature and fed it formula from a bottle. The room smelled like sour milk and was dark, except for the small circle of yellow light from the lamp over the chimp's cage. Things unseen scurried around them as the animal sucked his meal down, gripping one of Jason's fingers.

"When we're done I need to look for one of my guards. Cutbacks have me down to two, and I don't trust the idiot on duty tonight."

"Can't you just page him?" She poked at the small phone-like device attached to his belt.

"What did I just say? Why would I want to tip him off by calling first?"

She followed him around the grounds looking for a security man named Dugacy. The night air was moist, and within a short time she was damp with perspiration. Her silk blouse clung to her. She pulled the fabric away from her body and billowed it with air, but it only settled flush against her skin again.

When they came upon a habitat that was completely torn up, he stopped. "This used to be for the ocelots, but I'm in charge of redoing it for the Bengal tigers we just bought." He insisted she follow him through piles of gravel and board and over a makeshift bridge so he could show her. The bridge, just a plank the workmen used, passed over a twenty-foot-wide safety gully that separated the pedestrians' area from the animals'. He crossed first, his heavy stride leaving the board in motion. She stood immobile in his wake, moving up and down in her purple heels, peering into the deep at dark objects floating beneath her. Crocodiles? Alligators? Her feet wouldn't move.

"Come on!" he said.

Dizzy from the bouncing, she couldn't answer.

"You need my help?"

She moved only her eyes. He stood on solid ground, his handsome features distinct even in the dim light, and his smile one of delight, not sarcasm. She looked behind her, the distance exactly the same no matter which way she went.

"What is it, Grace?"

The movement of the plank began to settle down. If she held her balance long enough, she could shuffle to safety, keeping both feet in contact with the bridge at all times.

"Well?"

"Shut up, Jason!" She laughed, though she wasn't sure why.

He stepped forward and stomped on the end of the board. It bounced her up. Then down. She threw her hands out and widened her stance. She screamed when one heel slipped. He grabbed her and pulled her safely to the other side. His arm wrapped around her waist and he slipped his fingers between her skirt band and blouse.

"You idiot!" She pushed away from him. "I could have fallen!"

He held her tightly.

"I can see through your blouse," he said. "Two dark circles." She stepped backwards but he stayed close. Holding her, he bent forward and placed his mouth over her right breast and sucked through the silky fabric.

"What are you doing?" She stepped back again.

"I don't know, I don't know anything anymore. This just feels good."

"Leave me alone." His tongue circled her nipple. Pungent animal smells mixed with the sweet fragrance of nearby honeysuckle. He brought his face close to hers; she felt his breath. He seemed lost in her, his sadness gone as he massaged the small of her back. She gave in to the attention, the affection.

One foot behind the other, they moved backward, together, until she felt the sharp edges of the cave's rocky entrance. He undid the top button of her skirt and then the next. It dropped into the dirt at her feet. A cloud of dust floated into the black open space behind them. He undressed her, swept her hair to the top of her head.

The night air felt cold as it wrapped around her naked body. And it was quiet. No city noises. No animal noises. No critical voices. She closed her eyes.

Moving back, pushing down. She felt the soft, short hairs of the ocelots beneath her in the dirt. It was damp. She opened her eyes. It was dark. She lay on her back just inside the cave. He stood over her, his boots pressed against the inside of her thighs, so that her legs were spread open. The sky behind him was velvet black, as black as the inside of the cave, but stars scattered a pattern of light all around him.

The moon was positioned just behind his head so she could only see its glow.

"You have a halo," she whispered.

He knelt, unzipped his pants, and she felt him push inside her.

▲▲▲

When May came home at ten o'clock that evening, she was surprised to find Grace's red Mercedes coupe there. Except for a single light at the back door, the house was dark. A note in the kitchen explained the Hit-And-Run Cat, and as always, was signed just with a "J." Beside the note was a lipstick-marked glass, a small amount of red wine in it.

Ben and Jerry scurried ahead of her as she turned on lights and headed toward the guest bedroom. She held the injured cat, talked to it, petted it while the other two circled and sniffed. Once the animals were used to one another, she brought the Hit-And-Run Cat downstairs and placed it on a soft cushion by the table, where she worked on the jigsaw puzzle Lou Schultz had given her. Never thinking to move Jerry, who'd settled down right in the center of the puzzle, she periodically raised a paw or his tail or slipped her hand under his belly to retrieve whatever pieces she wanted.

She'd put together enough of the puzzle to see a dragon-shaped cloud in the left-hand corner of the illustration when her stomach started to ache. The smell of Grace's perfume was everywhere: on the Hit-And-Run Cat, May's hands, even the towels in the downstairs bathroom.

At eleven-thirty she stood in front of the refrigerator. Nothing looked real in its white chilly light; the fruit had a waxy glow, and a dried-up piece of cherry pie on a blue dessert dish looked like the Styrofoam food that came with Susan's play kitchen.

There were large gaps where she could see clear to the back wall of the refrigerator; it made her shiver. She searched the cabinets for filler, things that would look soft and edible. She loaded the shelves with bags of pinto beans and shell pasta, baking potatoes and onions, a loaf of bread, sacks of sugar and flour, misshapen Tupperware. She stuffed checkered dishtowels into the spaces, yellow and orange sponges, and a roll of Scott towels. She shut the door and headed for the package of Oreos hidden behind the embroidered pillow in the living room.

Ten cookies later, she sifted through a barrage of advertisements, catalogues and bills and found a hand-addressed envelope to herself from the Baritz School of Language. She ate one more cookie before opening it.

August 10, 1992

Dear Ms. Worth:

The Arabic names for which you requested research are not names, but words. Provided below is their translation at no charge. Please let us know if we can be of any more service to you.

Madee: Past
Hader: Present
Misstakbal: Future

In none of May's research had she found the names of Goddess Bast's cats, only in her dreams.

At midnight, she put the Hit-And-Run Cat back in the guest bedroom and left the house. Grace's red Mercedes coupe parked at the end of the sidewalk grew smaller and smaller in her rearview mirror.

Beth showed no surprise at all when May walked into Backalley's. She simply moved her large leather bag from the stool to the floor so May could sit down.

"Arturo's not here tonight," Beth said.

"I need a friend," May said.

"Lou Anne, bring me another one," Beth yelled.

"I'm having a really bad night, well, bad year, actually," May said.

"How could you be having a bad night? You just left here! We had dinner together, we had fun!"

"That was over two hours ago."

"Look at that cutie." Beth nodded toward a muscular man in dark green gym sweats and black high-top sneakers.

Smudged black mascara encircled Beth's left eye, and five yellow swords were stuck in her hair. It had been a mistake to come. How could she expect Beth to understand all those things that had led to this moment: the tombs in Egypt, the unending desert, the silver crescent amulets, the cat-shaped charms, the dream, the giant cats, Goddess Bast, Pharaoh's Friend, the Hit-And-Run Cat in her guest bedroom, and Grace's red car still parked in front of her home.

"So?" Beth leaned forward. "I'm listening."

The story came out like a gush of wind. She felt empty, exhausted and embarrassed after telling it.

"Wow, when you told me you were having strange dreams I had no idea you meant this strange. But, May, dreams are just dreams," Beth said.

"I don't know Arabic! How could I have made up the names of her cats?"

"Okay, don't get upset, just think about it. Why has this goddess come to you?"

"Because I've just lost Blue Bell, she knows I understand how desperate she is to find Hader. Well, you know him as Pharaoh's Friend."

Beth leaned closer, her expression soft. "It's the Lateral Joker."

"What?"

Beth started a story that May sensed she'd told many times about an evening with friends during her years at the Rhode Island School of Design. While passing the hashish, they decided to do away with the unpleasant notion that everything was evaluated on an up and down basis: Heaven and Hell, penthouse and basement, top of the list and dregs at the bottom, high moods, low moods, scaling the ladder of success, falling from grace and so on. The true movement of the universe was from side to side: waves rolled to shore to recede again, trees swayed in the wind, a bird returned to its nest, and the great pendulum of time swung back and forth.

"The universe moves from side to side!" Beth stood and did a little hula dance. "We also decided there wasn't a God, or a Satan. Just the Lateral Joker. Well, that's what we named him anyway. See, he moves with the universe slipping around between us." She lifted her chin toward the brass light fixture above the bar and put her hands together. "It's when we have our reverent faces turned toward heaven that he's able to sneak up from the side and stick his holy elbow in our ribs. He's not good or evil, just a prankster!"

She had started to slur her words with the beginning of the story; now some of them were barely recognizable. "Just get through the night, May. Things always look better in the morning. Or different at least."

How had their conversation turned out to be so different than what she'd expected? Nothing was predictable any longer.

"Lou Anne, another drink," Beth said, "and see that really handsome guy in the sweats and black high-tops?"

"Want to send him a drink?" the skinny waitress said.

"No, send him this." Beth moved up and down. Then, like a magic trick, from under the tablecloth came her pink silk panties. She brandished them over her head and dropped them onto Lou Anne's brown serving tray.

May left the table.

"Lighten up, May. It's the only way to survive!" Beth said as the restaurant door closed.

Chapter Eighteen

Grace didn't sleep that night. The smells of the zoo, of the ocelots' cave, of Jason, wouldn't go away. The odors had burrowed in her lungs and nostrils so that every breath was laden with regret.

At two o'clock she showered and washed her hair a second time. At two-thirty she changed the bed linens. At three she heard an animal howl. *Arooo.* Mournful and portentous, the cry took her to every dark window of the two-story condo, but it was quiet outside, no creatures. *Arooo roooo rooo.* She checked the guest bedroom on the slightest chance that the Hit-And-Run Cat had returned, then every closet, under each bed, in the clothes dryer, even in the dishwasher. She secured her bedroom door with the alabaster planter she'd bought in Cairo and waited under the bed covers for morning.

It came with a jolt and a jingle.

"Get out of that bed!" the 93Q Radio D.J. said. "And just listen to this." His mike picked up noises like screeching monkeys. She shut off the radio.

Groggy and irritable, she hugged a pillow and hoped again for sleep, but memories of the night before rushed at her. The gamy scent of animals, a sour odor that brought a metallic taste to her mouth and turned her stomach. How could such a thing have happened? And with Jason, of all people?

Everything had come so easily since Taos, the start of her spiritual awakening. Her life was alive with miracles, and she had only to look at her successes to know she'd truly stepped onto the Path. She'd surrendered herself to the will of the universe. But Jason? She tried to make sense of it while showering, dressing, driving to the office. The morning heat distracted her. The touch of fall that had teased the city the day before was now a memory.

She leaned against the mirrored wall in the garage elevator, steadied herself for another day and took a deep breath. She grasped a fistful of her own hair and smelled it. She sniffed her hands, her jacket, her blouse collar. The doors opened and people crowded in. They pushed her toward the back wall. Briefcases knocked against her knees.

"What is that smell?" a man in a suit asked the person standing next to him.

"Oooooeeee!" another said.

Everyone snickered, yet sniffed at the air. When the doors opened she pushed her way out from the back, bumping right into a woman who was waiting to enter.

"Might wanna think twice 'bout comin' in here, ma'am," one of the occupants said.

▲▲▲

"What's that smell in the elevator?" Beth asked Maggie when she entered the *Harbinger*'s offices that same morning.

"Monkeys! I saw them in there," the receptionist said. "Stars of some new Hollywood movie. They had an interview in our building with 93Q Radio."

Beth sat down and pressed her fingers against her temples. "How do you interview a monkey?"

Maggie laughed. "Grace cancelled her meetings for today. Sorry, I tried to catch you before you left home."

She stared at the floor for a few moments, then reached into her large purse and pulled out a pair of dark sunglasses. She put them on, took her time getting up from the couch, groaned, and then groaned again when she had to push her entire body against the large glass entry door to open it. "Call me a cab, will you?"

She waited for the taxi in the lobby. Her sunglasses felt like a vise, and the weight of her shoulder bag pulled her to one side. The aspirin she'd taken at three that morning did nothing more than keep her from falling back asleep, bits and pieces of the night not letting her rest: May's story about a goddess, three giant cats, Egyptian soldiers, Pharaoh's Friend, a stolen collar, her own pink underpants moving through the tables on a serving tray.

A bright yellow taxi pulled up to the curb. Invisible waves of heat from the cement buffeted at her ankles on her way to the car.

"7909 Teasdale."

"Yes, I know. It's your office, but you also live upstairs."

She stared at the driver, then at his photo on the meter. Robert Leon.

"You don't remember me." He turned, reached over the seat and shook her hand. As they drove, he talked to her reflection in his rearview mirror.

"Last week, I picked you up from Backalley's one night. But don't worry," he turned again and flashed a lopsided, handsome smile at her, "I won't take it personally."

She turned her head and watched a bus pass by them. When he turned back around, she looked at him again. There was something familiar and gentle about his manner, the way his hands rested on the steering wheel, the easy way he glided in and out of traffic. His rose sport shirt looked nice against his summer tan and light brown hair.

"Coffee?" He raised a thermos first and then a stack of cups still inside their plastic sleeve.

"Thanks." She looked around the cab for clues about him; there was no telling anymore who people were by their professions. The Houston economy had mixed up everything. Last month an ex-Montessori school teacher served her lunch, Sunnyland Oil Company's ex-public relations man sold her a pair of shoes, and the ex-head of personnel for Texmac Computer bagged her groceries.

"You've got a nice place. I like your weeds," he laughed.

"You were in my home?"

"I helped you in, you'd had too much to drink."

Oh, great! Did he have a pair of her underpants too?

He drove without speaking.

She pressed her hands against her eyes to try and stop the throbbing. She remembered that night: Arturo had walked her out of the restaurant to a taxi. It was late. Who are you? she had demanded of the driver, then leaned her head back on the seat, having long ago learned the hard way not to close her eyes.

She remembered mercury lights that were warm overhead and buildings that tried to touch each other in the stars. Traffic signals suspended in colorful halos had flashed silent messages to the empty streets. Had the driver talked to her? No. The engine had hummed a low-pitched lullaby all the way home. Tree branches waved to her, bus benches opened their arms; the air was thick with communication, all things alive, joined together to thwart a past mistake that knew no boundaries. There was no out-growing or out-drinking it. It slept under her pillow.

"So how was your morning?" He glanced at her in his rearview mirror.

"Rotten."

"What happened?"

"I'm hung over. I rode up in an elevator that reeked from famous monkeys. My meeting got cancelled. And I feel lousy about the way I treated a friend last night."

"What will you do?"

She raised her sunglasses, staring at him.

"That was three questions," she said.

"Is there a limit?"

She smiled. They pulled in front of her studio.

▲▲▲

Grace soaked in her tub until she thought her skin would peel away. She oiled and perfumed herself and lit scented candles throughout her home. Tranquilizers that had helped her rest also brought on nightmares of being chased by zoo animals.

By Sunday evening she'd run out of every alcoholic beverage and sleeping aid she had in the house. It was three in the morning when she went to the all-night Walgreen's to pick up a refill on her prescription. The man at the register wore a tan clerk's jacket with a brown nametag: DUGACY. When he turned to ring up her purchase, she noticed he also wore the same kind of phone patch strapped to his belt that Jason did. Dugacy — she felt certain that was the name of the delinquent security guard that Jason had complained about at the zoo.

"Are you all right, ma'am?" the clerk asked her.

"It's nothing." She accepted the change he'd been trying to hand her. "Just a coincidence," she said, knowing there was no such thing in the universe.

Most of Houston moonlighted to make ends meet. Even the

Houston police patrolled private parties and stood guard in front of restaurants during their spare time. Why not a security guard from the zoo? But as she finally fell asleep at 4:30 that same morning, she wondered why, on a night off, would the Walgreen's clerk wear his Houston Zoo pager. Or, maybe, it wasn't his night off. Or, maybe, she was no different from May. She imagined Dugacy in a courtyard meeting with two old look-alikes in bad wigs petting two giant cats as an Asian taxi cab driver delivered a sneaky-looking Egyptian who sold them cigarettes.

The few fitful hours of rest she got made the first meeting Monday morning with May and Beth even that much more difficult. She tried not to see Jason's seductive smile every time she looked at May or hear his coaxing voice every time his wife spoke. She tried not to think of the tantalizing way he had undressed her in the ocelots' cave. She began to doubt her memories of the time they'd spent in Egypt; had she changed her loyalties even then?

She tried not to let her lack of sleep temper her critique of May's and Beth's work, but the words came out all wrong.

"These layouts are terrible," she said. "I expected better work from you, Beth."

"But not from me?" May said.

"You know that's not what I meant," Grace said, not wanting to address May at all. But when she looked at her, and then at Beth, she saw uneasiness between them. She thought of all the times she'd heard them on the phone together during business hours, chatting as if they'd known each other forever, making plans to shop or have dinner or lunch or see one of those tedious foreign films. They'd even started to look alike with their dark hair and dark complexions, more like sisters than May and she had ever looked. But now in her office, these two had nothing to say to one another.

"May, take Beth to the press check tonight. It will be good for her to meet the printers. Kind of like a trial run before the premiere October issue."

Still, neither of them said anything. They gathered their papers and left.

▲▲▲

The first call to let May know the press check had been delayed was at six in the evening. This was typical; few jobs were ever printed while the sun was still out. The second call was at seven-thirty, the third at ten. At eleven o'clock, May turned the phone off upstairs so Jason wouldn't be awakened and lay down on the couch in the living room and waited.

This wasn't how it used to be, before the city's economic problems. Printers had the means to soften the inconvenience of delays: hot tubs, video screens, sound systems and popcorn machines were installed in client waiting rooms. Many an expensive meal had been eaten while waiting for the color to come up or the plates to register, but now the wait was done alone at home, next to the telephone.

When the final call came it was two-thirty. She phoned Beth to let her know she was on her way.

An early morning fog had taken over the city, hovering above the roads and encircling the street lamps. Hardly any other people were out at that hour, all the homes dark except for an occasional porch light. She tapped on her horn in front of Beth's studio and listened to the sound echo all the way into the slumbering neighborhood nearby. She envied those who were snug under their cotton covers, safe in their sleep of pleasant dreams, dreams that were certainly not about giant cats and angry goddesses. At that moment, she wished she were anywhere else than about to face Beth. She was an idiot for having told her about Bast and the cats.

Beth opened the car door and plopped onto the front seat dressed in a pink nightgown, white terry cloth robe and slippers. She put her seat belt on and placed the large leather shoulder bag on her lap. "Well, the bastards should print at a decent hour," Beth said. "They'll just have to take me as I am."

They both started laughing. After a moment, Beth placed her hand on May's arm. "I'm sorry about the other night."

"Let's just forget it," she said.

When they were only a few blocks away from Primer's Printing, she asked if Beth had ever worked with Buster, the head pressman in charge that night whose name alone conjured up intimidating images. She feared the worst of the inevitable struggles that occur between the men who run the press and the artists who approve the initial print.

"Don't worry," Beth said. "Men with names like Buster are usually short and weigh less than we do. I know a photographer named Shorty, he's almost seven feet tall."

Buster was as big as the doorway in which he stood. A bright white glow behind him outlined his behemoth body with shafts of light that penetrated the early morning fog. The roar of printing presses inside seemed to come from deep inside his chest. When she and Beth approached, his arms spread like an archetypal monster.

"Wanted to make sure you gals got inside safe," he told them, placing a giant hand at the back of each of their necks. "Dangerous people out at this time of the morning."

It was an easy press check. And May felt comforted by Beth's apology. She returned home that morning hopeful of a silent, dreamless sleep.

"Why cats?" the goddess yelled. "Give me donkeys, lizards, pheasants — even dogs," she hissed and looked directly at the white cat, Miss Takbal, with this insult, "but who can control a cat?" Turning her back to May, she said softly, "Not even a goddess."

The cat cowered as Bast began to yell again. "Why did you tell Hader things of the future? Of things only you can see? You knew he would anguish over the turquoise collar!"

Miss Takbal flattened her tremendous body against the ground. Moments passed before Bast leaned over, her claws retracted, and licked the top of the cat's furry head affectionately. "Here I am, a goddess, asking a mortal for help."

"What's so awful about that?" May whispered to the black cat.

"Because mortals are foolish!" Bast shouted. "So concerned with themselves, only living for the present as if the past had nothing to do with them. That 'now is now, and then was then' nonsense is nothing more than the refusal to be responsible for one's actions. Your past is what you are made of. It shapes you individually and collectively, and it constitutes your future."

I would never let go of my past, May thought. How could I? Susan is my past.

Chapter Nineteen

Grace had disliked Tom Salagaz from the first day she met him. His small frame and tidy build made her feel like some gawky large bird whenever she was near him. She'd seen him demonstrate more creativity wooing Maggie McKnight, the receptionist, than in any of his copywriting. And he was doing a miserable job on his most recent assignment, a story about Houston women's private lives that depended on the response to a questionnaire sent out with the previous month's magazine.

She'd asked him about its progress. He took no responsibility, blaming the lack of replies on the questionnaire itself, saying it may have been too personal, the subscribers probably paranoid about their answers somehow being traced back. "Secret codes in the paper or something," he joked.

She herself had written the questionnaire with the help of her family therapist. Was his criticism aimed at her? "It's your article, your problem. You don't get paid to stand around bellyaching to management," she said.

The very next day she'd caught him and Maggie in her office.

"We thought you'd left for the airport!" Tom said.

"What are you doing in here?"

They both spoke at the same time, Maggie out with the louder answer. "We needed a few moments alone, sorry."

After they'd left, she inspected her room. The poster of Ranthka, a three-thousand-year-old channeler, had been unrolled and three books—*Understanding New Age, How to Survive in a World Out of Control,* and *A Course in Miracles*—removed from the shelf. The energy chimes, incense sticks, tarot cards, *Silver Angels* cassette tape, and the three small jars on her desk—Wishes, Dreams, and Star Dust—were just as she'd left them. She picked up the largest of her twelve crystals. Through its amber cast, the room broke into hundreds of distorted fragments. Her digital clock beeped. No more time to worry about what the Bard of the *Harbinger*, as she liked to call Tom, and his little busy-biddy receptionist were up to. She would find out eventually.

It hadn't taken much convincing to talk her Aunt Charlotte into letting her pick up Richard from the airport that Friday. The forty-five minute ride north had become increasingly traumatic for her nervous aunt. Twice, she'd been caught in rush hour traffic, three times in flash floods, and once she was stuck behind a group of people on horses and wagons who were part of the trail ride into Houston for the rodeo. Aunt Charlotte talked for months about the dust, billowing banners and flags, and the smell of manure she'd been forced to endure.

Grace pulled her car into the space she'd expected right in front of the airport entrance; people on the Path were immune to such mundane problems as parking spots. Though she barely recognized him, her cousin walked into Customs at the very moment she arrived at the gate. He had a full trim beard, unlike the scraggly one she'd last seen on him that June in Alexandria, and he was encircled by a white flowing robe.

His students, all a little scruffy from the long journey home, were nonetheless welcomed by loving parents and friends with open arms.

Richard looked happy to see a familiar face also, but she could tell he was surprised it was she instead of his mother.

The buzz of excitement about buried treasures could be heard in every conversation around them as they walked to the car. She kept her conversation with Richard on family gossip: their adolescent cousin had been arrested for car theft; their third cousin had given birth one afternoon in a Neiman-Marcus dressing room; and Richard's mother had a new career, hawking aroma-therapy door-to-door like some New Age Avon Lady, even in River Roads, ignoring Grace's mother's pleas to stay out of her neighborhood. But the moment they settled into her car, she turned on her tape recorder and started the interview.

"You don't waste any time," Richard laughed, but then added, "Actually, I can't stop talking about it anyway. The dig was incredible." He grew quiet and stared out of the Mercedes window.

She started the car and headed back toward the city, with a written list of no fewer than thirty questions on her lap. She asked about three of them, then waited for an answer. All she heard was blank tape winding through her recorder. She tapped her fingers on the steering wheel and tried not to say something she might regret.

It had been one week and one day since her night at the zoo with Jason—one week of sleepless, irritating evenings with maximum doses of Valium and sleeping pills prescribed by Dr. Williamson. Each night a repeat of the one before: *Aroo, Aroo,* the noise would wake her; she'd search her house for the Hit-And-Run Cat. Some nights she heard it in the kitchen, other nights scratching in the hall closet. Once she heard it howling at her window, the night before under her own bed.

Her chest felt tight and her neck began to ache. The drone of the tape winding on and on while Richard remained silent made her feel itchy all over.

"I almost forgot what they looked like," Richard suddenly said.

"What?"

"Clouds."

Then he spoke to her about the Egyptian weather. About the days that were identical to each other, cloudless with turquoise-blue skies and a hot, white sun.

"I was there!" she interrupted. "I know all about the boring weather. What I want to know about is the dig."

"But did you smell the wind?" he asked.

She turned away from him to keep her eye on the traffic as she entered the freeway.

"It blows from north to south," he said, "and teases the senses by carrying the smells of the ocean. But it's dry, filled only with the dirt it raises."

"So, why the get-up? You look like an Egyptian," she said about his loose-fitting robe and turban.

"My *gellabeya*? It's the most comfortable way to dress for the climate."

"Would you stop talking about the weather!"

"Well, you asked!" He laughed.

As annoying as it was, she wasn't surprised when he started yet another story about something other than the dig. She was used to his befuddled manner; he was the typical absent-minded professor. Though she was four years younger than he, she'd always completed his sentences when he got lost in a thought, and it was she who'd kept him informed of important family dates like birthdays and anniversaries. Everyone around him at one time or another had been called on to help him find misplaced keys or a wallet or whatever, which made him a favorite target of the Sutton family jokes. "Richard's always looking for something; if not a buried treasure then his own shoe," they teased. She didn't find him the least bit amusing at that moment. She drove a little slower to have more time for the interview before the rest of the family got hold of him.

"Before we talk about the dig, I must tell you about a most unusual cat, a cat the size of a lion with markings like a tiger, that lingered around our site," he said.

"I know all about that cat," she said.

"Oh, forgetful me. I did tell you and May about him when we dined in Alexandria."

"No, I mean I know about him from the newspapers. Haven't you read them?"

"No." He'd been so involved with the discovery, the artifacts, the students, government papers and then getting everyone back to the States, he hadn't had time to read anything. "Is the cat okay? I asked everyone about it."

"Well, it's only international news!" She told him how a huge group of people actually believed the cat was a descendant of the breed of feline that, up till then, had only been seen in paintings on tomb walls.

"But there are conflicting reports," she said. "I've also read he's just an unusual mix of two common breeds that aren't known to mate." She told him that an article in *Advertising Age* had credited Egypt's Internal Affairs with the whole controversy. "They're going to really play this thing up and then send the cat over here to help publicize the King Tut Exhibition that's touring."

"Send the cat to the United States?"

"Texas," she told him. "The Exhibit is going to be in Dallas next, but Texas A & M University has requested a look at the animal before he's shipped there."

"My cat? Here in Texas?" He shook his head in disbelief.

While they drove, the sun set in an ordinary sky of polluted orange dusk. The recorder beeped three times and shut off. It was an opportunity for her to remind him of the interview. She turned the tape over and at last, he started to tell the story.

"I couldn't have done it without my friend, Adob Ezula, who was working a dig just outside of El Maghra. When I got word to him of our unexpected discovery, he negotiated some kind of deal with his own sponsors so he could leave his site and come to ours. But I doubt he mentioned the six workers he took with him!" Richard laughed. "With his expertise and crew, we were able to dig quickly in the little time that was left of the summer program."

Besides the canopic jars, which they'd already found when he saw Grace in Alexandria, they had excavated pieces of obsidian and lapis lazuli bowls; small gold vases that looked like perfume bottles; the body of a harp, remarkably in one piece; and sections of a sistrum, a mystical musical instrument that was shaped something like an egg-beater. There were silver earrings shaped like cats; rings of amethyst, carnelian, jasper and gold with cat's faces engraved on them; and silver and gold amulets in the shape of a crescent moon.

"We also found a granite case that held the mummified bodies of twenty mice, fifteen rats, thirty lizards and four guinea fowl."

She remembered the intricate animal caskets in the Cairo Museum. "I thought each animal got its own casket."

"Usually," he said. "But these animals were most likely included in the *mastaba* as food or entertainment for a cherished pet that was buried with its owner, which brings me to our most incredible find — a large stone coffin."

He grew silent again. She could feel his thoughts drift back through the centuries, pulling him farther and farther away from the interview.

"Who was it?"

He just looked at her.

"In the coffin!"

"Oh," he said, like a comedian who'd almost forgotten the punch line. "We don't know."

"You didn't open it?"

"We've shipped it to Cairo to be X-rayed by an endoscope first. They may have to cut it open. Anyway, the government won't let the sarcophagus out of Egypt. But I'll tell you a fantastic secret. They're allowing a third of the find to go on display at the Museum of Natural Science. Right here! In Houston!"

"But I've based the *Harbinger*'s premiere issue on that coffin!"

"What? But how could you have even known about it?"

Now it was she who stared out of the car window.

"Ah, Mother," he said.

"Don't be angry with her, Richard."

"Mother Big Mouth."

"I made her tell me," she said. "And look at the trouble I'm in now with my lead story all about that casket!"

"Mother the Menace," he said.

Her grip tightened around the steering wheel as she thought of the revised preliminary magazine layouts she had approved just that morning featuring, as she had requested, the mysterious coffin.

"Isn't it a big enough story that our very own museum will be the first institution in the world to display the artifacts, coffin or not?" he said. "Probably the first institution in the world whose co-sponsoring of a student summer expedition actually ever paid off!"

His attempt to make her laugh only made her angrier. She stared ahead at the red taillights of the traffic in front of them and remembered Mr. Carlyle's pleased expression when she presented the idea. Without the stone coffin and only a measly one-third of the tomb enclosures being sent to Houston, the story just wasn't spectacular any longer. It was a flop.

"Will May be at my welcome home party?"

"Didn't invite her."

The moment she stopped the red Mercedes, the front door of a large white colonial house opened and a swarm of people rushed out of it. Richard turned toward her and smiled, a smile that only a relative who shares the same quirky family members and history is capable of understanding. He was pulled from the car and swallowed up by fat, fleshy arms, slapping hands and his mother's bright pink lipstick. She watched the crowd move in unison back toward the house, somehow avoiding the pink begonias that lined the winding sidewalk. Two of her young cousins grabbed hold of Richard's gellabeya and peeked underneath.

The welcome-home cake was shaped like a pyramid, and instead of party hats, everyone had put on the traditional black wig of ancient Egypt. Some of the guests had even gone to the trouble of finding crowns and coiled snakes for extra adornments. She watched her Aunt Charlotte dote over Richard, then checked the room for her own parents. Her younger sister, Lucy, stood in a corner of the dining room with one of her daughters tugging at her sleeve and the newest baby clasped in her arms. She saw the baby's chubby fingers reach for its mother's mouth. I'm just so proud, Lucy had crowed after giving birth. Proud? What did you do? You fucked, conceived, delivered. Are you proud of bowel movements too?

Lucy waved at her through the gold-colored party strea-mers draped from the chandelier. The dining table overflowed with food that she could not eat because it was Friday, her day to fast.

She left without waving back.

▲▲▲

As soon as Richard had a moment to himself, he called May.

"Come to my party. Grace forgot to invite you and I was really hoping you'd be here. You can even bring what's-his-name, your husband."

May laughed. "As a matter of fact, what's-his-name isn't even here." Hardly see him any more, comes home later and later, smells of perfume, slips into the shower no matter what hour it is, oblivious to the phone calls that are hang-ups whenever I answer, she thought.

"Then come alone! It's just family, and you're practically part of ours anyway."

"I'm on my way." Anything rather than stay in this big house alone, jumping at every noise, wondering which ghost made it — friend or foe, adult, child or large lost cat. To feel like part of a family again would be so comforting.

When May arrived everyone hugged her, those she knew and even those she didn't. She had on the same outfit she'd worn to her miserable birthday party, clothes she'd purchased in Cairo: yards of layered Egyptian cotton imprinted with golden camels, sterling snake arm bracelets, and of course, her turquoise cat charm that Beth had given to her. She fit right in, for once. The evening was a delightful mixture of conversation, food and even dance. Richard's mom had hired a group of local folk dancers for entertainment. By the end of the night everyone held hands and stumbled about while imitating the dancers' fancy footwork. Richard, who held May's hand, pulled her away from the line and into the back yard. They sat on a stone bench and caught their breath, the noise from inside the house gently filling the silence.

"Have you heard about your cat from the dig?"

"Grace just told me. It's all so fantastic, and to think that he's actually coming to Dallas."

"Will you go see him?"

"Yes, I feel responsible for him. I wish they'd left him alone, I tried my best to keep him in the desert."

Removing things from their place in the world has consequences: a seashell from the shore, a daughter from her mother. "I hope he isn't scared, so far away from home."

"Me too." Richard smiled at her. "Tell me about the dream you had before coming to Egypt. It was about a giant black cat, right? Not gray like mine?"

"Like yours?"

He laughed. "There's just something about this animal. I felt like I knew him, felt so close to him immediately, well, after the initial fear, that is."

"I feel like I know him, too. I dream about his family."

"Family? But he was always alone at the dig. What are you talking about?"

"Richard!" His mother stood at the screened back door. "Your cousins are leaving, come say goodbye."

"In a second."

When she left, he leaned close and kissed May on her lips. "I want to know more, I want to see you again, I want to know everything there is to know about you."

"No, you don't." She kissed him this time. "Believe me."

"Richard! We're leaving!" Someone stood at the door.

They went inside.

▲▲▲

The flow of cars in the street below Grace's office window was mesmerizing. Friday night. People with friends. People on dates. People celebrating the end of another work week while she hung on to it a little longer. She sat in her office with the door shut and the lights off and listened to the tape of her interview with Richard.

The light from the top of the Tranland Tower cut across the sky at regular intervals. Large vacant buildings spotted the landscape with dark shapes as imposing as the great pyramids, and the scream of an occasional siren joined by the steady toots and honks of the traffic reminded her of Cairo's busy streets. She wished she were just a sightseer again, with no more responsibility than deciding which restaurant to eat in. Everything had become complicated since returning to Houston. Sitting in the dark, her thoughts returned to Richard's welcome home party, and her parents' absence. But all those familiar faces made her think of two others that were missing: the Berry sisters. They were always in attendance at social events of that rank, their pictures appearing regularly in Shelby's Column. Remembering those past photos, their black-and-white frozen smiles and pasty complexions, made her think of May's drawings of the women in the Hotel Cecil's courtyard, and for one instant she remembered the two women who sat in front of them on the plane to Egypt. They had kept to themselves the entire trip, huddled over a book or magazine, perfect traveling companions, almost nonexistent. They had resembled the Berry sisters, but certainly not the Berry sisters. She would have recognized them immediately, though there had been many distractions — May's sulking, Jason's drinking. So much had changed since that trip. Her friendship with May was a disaster, her new friendship with Beth had come to a standstill, and her evening with Jason in the ocelot's cave was unthinkable. Yet she did think of it. Over and over. She could feel all those sleepless nights taking their toll; and now, learning she had built her first issue as publisher around a no-show coffin made her want to smash the tape recorder. What's a tomb without a coffin? What's a story without a hook?

She reached for the bottle of Valium on her desk and swallowed another blue pill, or was it two, while she listened to her own words play back, then Richard's. The interview went on continuously from beginning to end to beginning automatically. She listened with her head resting on the desk and prayed for an answer.

"*My* cat? Here in Texas?" Richard's voice said.

She turned the tape player off and her desk lamp on, made some hurried notes. The controversial cat, the internationally famous cat, the cat who first appeared at the site of the dig could save the story. And her.

There was no way of telling when she first heard the growling. It crept through her body like an icy chill, making her pull her legs up under herself on the seat without realizing it. Guttural animal sounds, like the previous eight nights, surrounded her. She peered into every dark corner of her office for sight of the Hit-And-Run Cat. It was real. She could hear it. She grabbed her purse and bottle of pills and ran for the front lobby doors, flipping on every light switch she passed.

The janitor ran after her. "What is it, miss? You okay?"

"Animals! Do you hear them? Growling!"

"Growling?" Dell stopped following her and laughed. "That be me, I'm afraid. Snoring. Didn't want to bother you in the office, so I sit out here for awhile waitin' for you to finish so I could clean."

"You?" But she didn't believe it.

"Musta fallen asleep while I waited. Sorry, wife tells me I have a mighty loud snore, never believed her."

▲▲▲

The moment Grace reached home she called Dr. Williamson for a prescription of stronger sleeping pills and a renewal on the Valium. He wouldn't give it to her without seeing her first. "What's there to see that you haven't already in the last ten years!" she told him. He insisted.

When they met in his fashionable suburban office on Saturday morning, a time that he rarely saw clients, she was taken aback by the way he scrutinized her. He smoked a cigarette, something she'd never actually seen him do, though he always smelled of tobacco. She caught a glimpse of herself in the large deco mirror on the wall behind his desk.

"Well, no wonder you're staring. I look awful." Her skin was splotchy, her hair stringy, and some crumbs from the powdered donut she'd eaten in the car on the way over were stuck to the corner of her mouth.

"You think I'm staring at you?"

She pulled a lipstick from her purse and smeared the red pepper color across her mouth. "I look like this because I haven't had enough sleep. I already told you that last night."

"You also told me about an animal that's been following you."

"Sounds ridiculous in the light of day," she laughed. The doctor didn't. His lax jowls and deep forehead creases made his seventy-year-old face look more worried than he might have been, but she didn't want to take the chance. She glanced at the clean white prescription pad on his desk and cursed herself for telling him about the animal noises, but she couldn't blame them all on a sleepy janitor. He would never understand the things that had happened to her since stepping on The Path. In all the years she'd known him, he'd never wavered from his Christian beliefs, his Freudian theories, or even his hairstyle. He could never understand the power of chanting. The force of universal consciousness. Karma. Miracles. And with no sleep and jagged nerves, she knew this moment was not the time to try and explain it to him.

"You were certain an animal was after you. You heard it outside your condo, then inside. You smelled it in the parking garage elevator and last night, in your office when you mistook a snoring janitor for it, you ran for your life."

"Yes, yes. But last night, after we spoke, I thought it all out just like you've taught me." She told him about the Hit-And-Run Cat and the little lie she'd told at May's birthday party. "While, in fact, I was the one who rescued it, I was also the one who ran over it. Obviously this little lie has been working on my conscience. It's really quite textbook that it would manifest itself in the form of animal noises and smells." She laughed.

Dr. Williamson walked to the front of his desk, just inches from her. "I agree." He crossed his arms on top of his silver belt buckle. "It is a little lie. Too little to cause this kind of trouble." When he puffed on the cigarette his eyes grew large momentarily. "Is there something else working on your conscience?"

She glanced again at the blank prescription pad behind him, knowing that if she were just able to get some sleep everything would be fine. The very thought of all the work still ahead of her necessary to change the magazine's lead story from the no-show coffin to the mysterious giant cat made her feel too tired to move. Too tired to even think up something other than the truth to tell Dr. Williamson.

She told him about Jason.

The doctor sat down beside her and put his arm around her shoulder.

I just have to get some sleep, she meant to say, but what came out of her mouth was sobbing gibberish.

"There, there," he said. "My, my."

She jerked away from him. "I really don't need your disapproval!"

He blew a gray cloud of smoke above her head, then went back to his desk, where he wrote out two prescriptions.

"Guilt is your noisy, smelly animal, dear. Tenacious in its stalking and treacherous when least expected." He handed her the pieces of white paper; one for Valium, the other for Peptomil. "After you fill these, you must go home and get some sleep. Sleep all day. Call on Monday to set up another appointment."

After filling the prescriptions, she took a double dose of the Valium and drove directly to the downtown library. There were fewer articles about the Egyptian cat than she'd hoped; the scientific community was holding back. Most of them believed that the animal was a hoax: "Just another unicorn with a single horn surgically implanted in the center of its head." Then she came across an article in *Cat's World*:

> "In 1812, Baron Georges Cuvier, one of the leading biologists of his time, reported there was not a single living mammal that

was unknown to science. With one-thousand, three-hundred and ninety species of amphibians, reptiles, birds and mammals already accounted for, he felt that if there were still creatures left to be discovered, they would either be ocean-dwellers or small insects hiding in the most remote waters and jungles.

"This announcement proved to be an embarrassment for Cuvier. A short six months later, one of his own colleagues discovered the Indian Tapir — a small pig-like animal with a long, flexible snout.

"By 1898 over twenty-one hundred species of animals had been discovered, and by 1970 over seventy thousand. Since 1900 an average of fifteen reptiles, two hundred and twenty mammals, and four hundred birds had been discovered every year.

"It is possible that the Egyptian feline may be just one of many discoveries this year."

The general public had responded with more interest to the Egyptian cat than the skeptical scientific community, who had obviously not learned from Cuvier's closed-mindedness. However, it was the Egyptian people themselves who were the most enthusiastic. They'd developed a fondness for the animal, and even though representatives from the Research Center of Dashur, the University of Aswan and the Cairo Zoo reported there was nothing, other than size, unusual about the feline, rumors were rampant.

The Egyptians called the cat "Pharaoh's Friend," not only because of his resemblance to the large animal so often shown on wall paintings as part of the pharaoh's hunting expeditions, but also because there was a sense of majesty about him, a look of nobility.

In a tabloid with the headline SNAKE IN HIGH COUNTRY OF TIBET GIVES BIRTH TO HUMAN BABY, was an article about

Pharaoh's Friend that not only verified he was from ancient lineage, but was in fact the very same cat that traveled alongside the pharaoh centuries ago. Unearthing the mastaba tomb had caused the animal to materialize from the past.

And from the *Cairo Times*, an article claimed Pharaoh's Friend to be the materialization of a mythical cat. Ajibba, the farming village nearest to where the animal was captured, had been blessed with good fortune, and even money, because of the cat's presence. The omda of the village, Teliah Motrinsh, was quoted: "This legendary cat brought our village prosperity for four years. Now Allah has decided to share him with the rest of the world. I invite all of you to come to Ajibba to see where it all began, 'Home of Pharaoh's Friend.'"

And share him we shall, Grace thought. Who needs a coffin for a lead story when you have a living, breathing legend? The universe was working its magic once again, the laws of cause and effect in action, and confirmation that no one on The Path moved autonomously.

Mr. Carlyle approved her idea to feature the famous cat in the article about the Rice University students' discovery. But when she told him she planned to bring the mysterious cat to the Museum's Grand Opening, he objected. His fingers immediately went to the top of his brow, where he flicked them through his gray hair. The expense, the liability, the logistics, Egypt's approval, the museum's approval, the upkeep, all was of great worry to him.

"You're not putting that four-hundred-and-twenty-pound animal in my backyard!" he said. "Honestly, Grace, you think you alone have enough influence to bring this celebrity cat all the way from Egypt to Texas?"

"But he's already on his way," she said, and Mr. Carlyle stopped laughing.

▲▲▲

Grace waited in her father's office at the downtown branch of First Security Bank for over an hour. Dressed in a blue silk suit, she'd toned down her makeup, put her hair in a braided twist, and done her nails in the clear lacquer that her father preferred.

"Are you sure he knows I'm here?"

Gerald Sutton's secretary, Monique Beaulier, gave her the same irritated and surprised look as when she first showed up unexpectedly that morning. "*Oui*, dear. But he has *monsieur* in his office."

She resented Monique's French accent as much as the patronizing "dear." Her father's perky assistant had lived in the States for over fifteen years, yet her speech was still thick with native words that made her lips pucker.

"More coffee, *cherie*?"

At last, the dark oak doors to her father's office opened. She'd expected to see two people, her father and the "monsieur" he'd been meeting with, but only Gerald stood in the doorway. He wasn't a handsome man, but striking. His height and confident demeanor and even the heavy creases at the sides of his mouth made a powerful presentation.

"What in the world are you doing here?" he asked.

"Mr. Sutton." A man close to Grace's age rushed toward her father and handed him a thick legal-size document. He was one of those young executive types with the chiseled chin, suspenders, polka-dot power tie, and silver cufflinks.

"Mr. Grant, have you met my oldest daughter?"

He held on to her hand a little too long after shaking it. "She's as lovely as I expected."

Gerald took a step back and looked at her. "Yes. She has her mother's cunning face, but unfortunately her father's chest." Monique laughed along with the two men.

Grace nearly pushed the ample-chested secretary out of her way as she stomped behind her father into his office.

"How could you embarrass me like that?"

"It was a joke." Gerald sat down in a Vittron chair behind his massive antique desk. "Have you waited all this time just to be angry with me?" He shuffled papers.

"You and Mother missed Richard's welcome home party."

"Well, I can't do anything right, can I?"

"I just meant that if you'd been there you would know all about his Egyptian dig, the success he had."

Gerald stopped the shuffling, leaned back in his chair.

She felt like a child again, when she was able to entertain him with stories of achievements, good school grades, perfect piano recitals. And just as that child learned to never make reference to her father's associates, an unknown group who called at strange hours of the night and sent packages to the house that required signatures, nor did she then. But she knew if the famous cat were to make it to Houston, those associates would certainly be contacted.

He spent more than a half-hour with her, even telling Monique to hold his calls.

"It's true," he said, "I didn't attend Texas A & M, but I have a few associates there." He stood, so she did. As they walked toward the office door he even put his arm around her. "Don't worry about this. I can get your famous cat to Houston for the exhibit."

She began to think the Egyptian people were correct in believing Pharaoh's Friend was mythical, for he was already working his magic. She felt so happy she stepped to her father's side to hug him. Her shoe bumped a Zero Halliburton case on the Persian carpet beside the door.

Before leaving she asked Monique who had been in her father's office before her.

"You're trying to get me in trouble, *jeune fille*?"

She was about to push for the information when she caught sight of an Asian man entering the hallway to Gerald's private conference room. By the time she reached the corner, he was gone. She stood in the hallway and sniffed the air. Was it lime? The same scent as the Asian who shared their cab in Alexandria.

"Something wrong?" It was the young suspendered executive, Mr. Grant, again.

"No," she said. "Who's meeting with my father?"

"Don't know his name, but they've been behind closed doors for two days now, sending out for meals, and, oh, those rich biddies joined them yesterday."

"Pardon me?"

"You know, those silver-haired ladies who back every fundraiser in this town."

"The Berry sisters?"

"How about dinner some night, or a drink?"

"Pardon me?"

"Mr. Sutton tells me you haven't dated in a while."

"My social life is none of your business."

She left. Once again, a fleeting glorious moment with her father had been ruined. How dare he talk about her with a fledgling? And why did the mere mention of the Berry sisters immediately make her shoulders tense? She sensed something was terribly wrong, but then caught herself behaving as ridiculously as May again. Of course he could have business with the sisters; after all, he was probably on many of the same committees they were. So they're meeting behind closed doors; it's not as if they're having secret conversations in a courtyard in a foreign country. All old ladies look alike. May's the one who had her turning strangers' faces into familiar ones. And yet, she couldn't stop wondering if the stranger in her father's office might not be that very man with the Halliburton case they'd shared a taxi with.

She went back to her office, and within fifteen minutes received a call from the dean of Texas A & M University. He chatted with Gerald Sutton's daughter as if they were old friends while he told her about the deluge of letters already received from concerned citizens around the world. All kinds of rumors circulated about the tests his colleagues planned for Friend — the media having shortened the cat's name from Pharaoh's Friend to this. He admitted not knowing what he was getting into when the school had asked the Egyptian government for a look at the star feline before sending him to Dallas to promote the King Tut Exhibit. Protestors from Greenpeace, the ASPCA, PETA and the Cousteau Society had marched non-stop in front of the administration building for over a week. There was a rumor the university had killed the cat to gain information from an autopsy.

"Can you imagine?" Dean Whitaker said. "Our university that turns out this country's leading veterinarians, accused of doing something so senseless."

The truth was that Friend would not arrive for another two weeks at the school in College Station, just one hundred miles outside of Houston.

"He's to stay with us from September first to the twenty-first. Then he'll be sent to Dallas for ten days to publicize the Tut Exhibit." She heard a voice in the background say something, then Dean Whitaker continued in a clipped, unnatural rhythm, as if he were reading his words. "We do not feel there is any harm in sending the cat to Houston for the week of the fourteenth." In a more spontaneous tone he added, "Besides, the sooner the public sees him after being with us, the sooner we can end this horrible PR the university is enduring."

Gerald Sutton's mysterious network had worked its far-reaching influence once again. It was confirmation that movement in the universe by one cat, no matter how small, or in this case large, could be felt throughout. She practically danced into her meeting with May and Beth.

"I just arranged for Pharaoh's Friend to come to Houston for the museum's opening night!"

May stood up. "No! You can't bring him here."

"What's the matter with you? This is wonderful news," Grace said.

"You have to change it! Right away."

"But May, this is just what we need for the article." Grace made grand sweeping gestures with one arm, then the other. "Think how we can play it: Is he a new breed? Is he a descendent of the pharaoh's cat? A zoologist's dream? A hoax? Or is he a materialization from the ancient past, formed from the very dust that my cousin's summer students stirred?"

"How could this be happening to me?" May plopped back down in her chair.

"To you?" she asked. But then she saw the comprehensive layouts on the conference room table. They were of the dig's coffin, the design she had approved on Friday. May and Beth had obviously worked all weekend. Headlines, reversed from tan-colored blocks, looked like ancient hieroglyphics cut from sandstone walls, and the delicate papyrus plant that had once grown in abundance along the Nile provided a subtle background pattern to the copy.

She held the layouts in her hand. "These look great," she laughed, "but the coffin's not coming to Houston. Friend is."

May looked dumbstruck, and Beth, as if something alive were flying around in her closed mouth. Their expressions did not change when Grace told them that in addition to changing the theme of the layout from the coffin to the giant cat, they were to design the museum's opening night invitation. An employee of the museum would show them the artifacts the Egyptian government had permitted for display.

"Is there a problem?"

It was Beth who answered, barely parting her lips. "Tell us about the invitation."

The museum's opening night would be black-tie. The guests would include socialites, patrons of the arts, symphony goers, opera buffs and Neiman Marcus shoppers.

"I want you to think up an invitation like the ones we used to do when this cow town had money," she told them.

May and Beth gathered their papers and stumbled out of the conference room. "With some enthusiasm?" she called after them.

As soon as the door shut, she phoned Jason and insisted he have lunch with her. "I have some news that will change your future."

"Can't you tell me over the phone?"

Grace was surprised by his reluctance. She'd assumed he would want to see her, talk about their night at the zoo. "This is important."

"Jesus Christ! You're pregnant!"

"You idiot! Just forget it!"

She hung up on him.

A few moments later he called back.

They met for lunch near the zoo at an outdoor cafe called Zinn's. She told him about the plans to bring Friend to Houston.

"As curator of mammals, you'll be in charge."

But Jason didn't react with the gratitude she'd expected.

"There'll be interviews and television cameras, and just think of the crowds Friend will draw. You'll be famous."

"Did you do all of this just for me?"

"What?"

"I'm afraid you might have misunderstood what happened between us the other night."

"I'm glad you brought it up. What did happen?"

"Nothing. Me drinking too much, me not being right since Susan died, me and May not getting along, much less touching."

"But, Jason, something did happen. You feel something for me, I know you do. I know it even started while we were on the trip."

"I'm sorry, Grace. It isn't so."

"I see, first May dumps me and now you?"

He checked his watch. "This is a wonderful opportunity you're giving me with Friend. I appreciate it. But don't let things get all mixed up in your head."

He let a few cars pass by him before he stepped into the street toward his parked Jeep. "I'll call the university and set things up. Don't worry about the plans," he said. "You should rest, you look really tired."

She finished her wine alone at the table with the lunch bill.

Chapter Twenty

May tossed the letter from the Baritz School of Language onto Dr. Claudia Somners' desk. She'd changed her mind about never seeing the therapist again, especially since Friend was now on his way to Houston and her life kept growing stranger by the day. It was too difficult to live a delusion alone. She was desperate for the comfort of this woman's logical explanations.

"Before I even knew Bast was Egyptian, she told me the names of her three cats. I wrote them down, phonetically, and sent them to Baritz to see if they could come up with an origin or translation. This is what I got back."

She pulled at her curly hair and bit her lip until she almost drew blood. Claudia read the letter. She read it again.

"You must have learned these words while you were in Egypt, just as you learned of the mutant cat and then started dreaming about him," Claudia said.

"No, you don't understand. If Miss Takbal's the future, and Madee's the past, then Hader is the only one who can enter the present to carry souls into the afterlife. It's like, his job."

Claudia got up from the chair behind the desk and motioned for her to sit down on the couch beside her. "I don't know what you're talking about."

"I read about it at the library when I was researching Bubastis for the magazine article. I even wrote it down." She pulled the turquoise journal from her purse, flipped through the pages and read:

"The venerable cat was their guide to the afterlife. The Egyptian word for cat, *mau*, also meant seer, in the clairvoyant sense. The cat's ability to see in the dark, sense danger and always find its way home made it an excellent guide through the frightening territory of death and time for recently departed souls, or *kas*. This type of transference, known as 'metempsychosis' or 'transmigration,' is the passing of the soul at death into another body, either human or animal."

Claudia took the journal from her and read the passage again. "I must admit that all these coincidences are remarkable. And now this mutant cat is not only on his way to Houston, but you are directly involved with its publicity, and Jason in charge of its care. It really is strange."

"You're missing the point! Without Hader, Susan's without a guide."

Claudia slid off her shoes and tucked her legs beneath her on the couch. "You're talking about an ancient belief. Transmigration of souls to an afterlife."

"The first time I felt it was at the funeral. I held her little body, and kissed her, and I knew that wasn't my baby any longer. Her spirit was gone, only I didn't know where it had gone. I tried to imagine a reception of angels opening their wings, welcoming her to their kingdom. I tried to imagine my mom and dad embracing her, Fluffy running circles around their happy little gathering. I even tried to imagine God, in whatever form I could conjure up — Jesus, a sunrise, a field of violets, anything that might receive her, but nothing felt true.

Not until I dreamed about Bast and read about her cats was I able to locate my daughter. She's waiting on Hader to take her. She's in limbo."

Claudia's raised eyebrows, the slant of the psychiatrist's head, the worried brow — it was all too easily interpreted. You're the one in limbo, May. You're the one who's lost. You're the one without belief.

"Maybe religious beliefs don't change with time, like technology or fashion." May took the journal back, flipped through it and read again. "Our past is what shapes us, it's our history, it's what constitutes our future."

"Jung?"

"No! Goddess Bast!"

Claudia moved her jaw back and forth and pressed a tissue against her forehead. "Well, if Hader is unavailable to escort Susan to an afterlife, why can't Bast?"

"I told you, only Hader can enter the present."

"But Bast talks to you, May, and you're in the present."

She stood up. "Bast talks to me in a dream, which isn't the past, present or future!"

"Then why doesn't Bast talk to Hader while he's dreaming and make him come back?"

"She does! During every nap he takes, which is plenty." She threw the journal on the couch. "But Bast doesn't have any more control over him than anyone has with a cat!"

She felt warm and sweaty, her heart raced, and she knew she sounded crazy. She could tell Claudia didn't believe a word of it, as the therapist posed question after question to poke a hole, to let in the light of reason.

"Even going to Susan's grave is no comfort. It's just a reminder that she's no longer here with me and that I don't know where she went. And this hurts just as much as her dying."

"Recovering from loss doesn't mean forgetting, but it does mean letting go, May." Claudia reached for her hand. "You have to let go of Susan."

There was a knock on the door; the next client.

"Are you okay? Do you need to stay longer?"

"This is Miss Takbal's fault. She's the future, the only one who could have known Hader's collar was going to be taken." Though she tried not to say it, she added, "If only that cat had kept quiet."

Claudia wrote out a prescription for Zoloft, an anti-depressant. "I'm not a fan of Freud's," she said, walking her to the door, "but Freud was a great fan of archeology. He said the psychoanalyst, like the archeologist in his excavations, must uncover layer after layer of the patient's psyche before coming to the deepest, most valuable treasures." She hugged her. "We'll get to the bottom of this, and when we do we'll find the best treasure of all. It will be you, May."

When she pulled away from her, the yellow pencil over Claudia's ear fell to the carpet, the lead point stuck exactly in the middle of a circular design so that the shadow it cast worked like a sundial: three o'clock.

"I almost forgot." May reached into her purse, pulled out a piece of paper and handed it to the therapist as she left.

THREE
CAT - three letters
GOD - three letters
May Grace Beth
May Grace Jason
Ben Jerry Blue Bell
Madee Hader Miss Takbal
Past Present Future
Right Middle Left

Height Width Depth
Beginning Middle End
Mother Father Child
Father Son Holy Ghost
Creation Revelation Redemption

▲▲▲

Back in her office, May stared at her calendar that always opened to the same page: her birth date with the lithograph of Christopher Columbus about to depart on his "Voyage of Discovery." How many times in the last year had she looked at this illustration? Could it be the three ships that bobbed in the ocean were her giant cats? Queen Isabella, Bast? She stood near the water in a flowing gown just as Bast appeared, wearing a crown that tapered to two jeweled points, much like the goddess' cat ears. Even her favorite number loomed at the top of the page. Three o'clock. Three cats. Three worlds. All tossed together like some sort of psychological salad. She wondered if her dream was nothing more than a voyage of self-discovery.

Chapter Twenty-One

May guessed Janet Brandt was only in her forties, but her flowered dress, horned-rimmed glasses and rubber-soled shoes made her look as old as some of the relics on display in the Museum of Natural Science. Her brown hair, mixed with strands of gray, spilled over her shoulders, separated and frayed like a worn shawl. From her didactic tone, May also guessed that she and Beth were getting the same introductory speech she delivered to visiting classrooms of children.

On their way to the exhibition hall, they followed Janet beneath a tremendous reconstruction of a Brontosaurus dinosaur — a three-story network of bones.

"Hard to believe that creatures of such magnitude didn't make it while our minuscule common spider not only survived, but has remained virtually unchanged for some three hundred million years," Janet said.

May thought of Hader. A sound, a shadow, a looming giant skeleton, everything reminded her of the goddess' cat. She wondered how much the animal had changed with time. Had the burden of carrying souls into the afterlife increased his size and strength?

She remembered the summer evening Blue Bell met up with an armadillo. She'd left Susan in the back yard to finish an ice cream cone that was melting faster than she could eat it. Blue Bell licked up every messy drip of praline crunch until the armadillo stumbled out from under the azaleas just a few feet from them. The poor cat puffed out to as large an image as possible, but it was no match for the bony armor of this intruder. Blue Bell scurried up the closest tree, praline crunch or not. At the time, she and Susan laughed. Now she couldn't help but think of how easily her dear pet had deserted her child. There was no telling what kind of formidable adversaries might challenge the path to afterlife; it would take a very special guide.

Beth tugged on her sleeve to get her to move from under the dinosaur bones. They followed Janet through crowds of soft voices that circled displays, to double doors with a maroon velvet rope suspended in front of them. Janet slipped a security card into a slot just above a large brass handle. "Safer than keys," she said.

The room was small and windowless. May had assumed the treasures would be stored in a vault or at least under guard, but there they were, scattered all about. Some were on top of wooden crates, some on the silica gel packets they'd been shipped in, others on the carpeted floor next to the pedestals that would display them. Each artifact had a small white numbered tag. A cane chair, with a pair of white cotton gloves in the center of its seat, was in the middle of the room.

Janet told them the shipment had arrived at midnight. The Registrar of Collections had spent the entire evening unpacking the treasures and checking their numbers against the bill of lading she'd received from the Museum of Cairo the previous week. After recording the condition of each piece, she'd photographed them for insurance purposes. The Department of Exhibits needed only to put the artifacts on the displays they had specially designed.

As Janet talked, May strolled among the antiquities, almost right past the pedestal that held a turquoise necklace. Hader's stolen collar, just as the goddess had described it. Right there. Right in front of her. The stones, cut in graduated lengths, formed a sunburst pattern, and each piece, bordered in gold, had a small gold ball at its tip.

She plopped down on the cane chair, not even bothering to remove the white gloves.

Beth showed no surprise at all upon seeing the collar, just the same lopsided smile as always.

"So Grace said this would be a black-tie affair, right?" Beth asked.

"It's amazing you remember anything at all!"

"What was that for?"

"The collar! I mean the necklace! Look!"

Janet Brandt offered to get May a glass of water and left the room.

Beth sauntered back through the treasures to the necklace, the weight of her open leather shoulder bag making her walk as though she were drunk even at that moment. One of the items poking out from the purse would surely knock over a priceless artifact.

"It's Hader's stolen collar!"

Beth looked at her through squinted eyes, lashes thick with mascara. "The oversized cat from your dream?"

"Don't look at me like that! It's the reason he's coming to Houston."

Beth bounced a black drawing pencil between two fingers and kept looking at her with the same squint. "Pharaoh's Friend, not Hader, is coming to Houston for the grand opening of this exhibit."

"You don't know anything."

"I know that a dream is just a dream," Beth said.

The museum employee returned with two tall glasses of ice water. "I'll have to ask you to drink these by the door, not near the treasures."

"May, for your own good, you have to drop all this stuff," Beth said.

She walked away from Beth, but stopped abruptly again, this time in front of a pedestal displaying an object that looked like an egg beater. It was Bast's sistrum: the magical musical instrument, symbol of the afterlife.

While the museum worker sat at a chair by the door and filled out papers, she and Beth circled the artifacts in silence.

They sat down at opposite ends of the room, each with a sketch pad on her lap. Hours passed. Janet came and went a dozen times. Beth sketched away, sheet after sheet, but May sat beside the turquoise collar without moving.

At last, Beth walked over and sat on the dark carpet beside her. "Grace wants an invitation like the old days. That means sending something worth keeping."

May didn't take her eyes off the collar.

"Well, I'm not getting anywhere, and from the look of it, neither are you." Beth got up.

May stayed seated. "We'll send them this necklace."

"The necklace?"

"We're targeting the ladies, the ones who decide about attending affairs like this. Don't you think something arriving in a jeweler's box would get their attention?"

"I like this." Beth sat back down and began to sketch the turquoise artifact. "The card could say something like, 'Enclosed for your viewing pleasure, one small example of the timeless design of beauty. You are cordially invited to…"

"Not small," she said. "Same size as this one."

"No way," Beth said. "It's too big! Besides, the ladies on this guest list would never wear anything that wasn't real."

"Doesn't matter. The size alone will keep it from being thrown away."

"It will cost too much."

"I have a friend who owns a Five & Dime. He'll work it out."

She watched Beth sketch the design, but thought only of the gray cat. She could see his yellow eyes, his nostrils growing large and then small to take in her scent, searching for familiarity as she fastened one of the replica necklaces around his neck. She would smile at him. He would turn on his powerful hind legs, leap into the air and go back to Bast.

But what if Hader could tell the collar was fake?

Rehearsing the moment again, she saw the collar, felt its weight, imagined the turquoise luster. She knew Lou Schultz could pull off the imitation. After all, if she couldn't tell the difference between a diamond and a cubic zirconia, surely a cat, mythical or not, could be fooled with turquoise.

"Let's work on it tomorrow and present it to Grace on Tuesday."

"How about Wednesday? I'd really like it if you went somewhere with me Tuesday," Beth said.

"Where?"

"Just plan to pick me up at noon."

▲▲▲

When they arrived at a large white building on Tuesday, she helped Beth carry her black portfolio inside.

"This room." Beth opened the door and then slammed it shut, just before a small chair flying through the air hit into it.

"What's in there?" May said.

"Children. They stay here until the court decides if it's safe to send them home or to foster parents. Sometimes they're here for a few days, sometimes for months." Beth put her ear against the wooden veneer, then slowly opened the door again. A teacher's aide had the upside-down chair in her hand.

"Sorry," she said. "That one caught me by surprise."

A room full of children sat at long plastic tables. They were of mixed ages, gender and color. The youngest looked to be about nine; the oldest, not quite fourteen.

"Tell her to get," a scrawny boy in a black leather jacket said. "We don't want no stupid art class."

May remained at the door's frame rather than venture into the room. "A classroom full of weeds," she said as she handed Beth the portfolio.

Beth pulled her inside, pointed to a chair towards the back of the room, then picked up a piece of chalk at the blackboard. With her back to the class, Beth started to draw. A few of the children got out of their chairs so they could see what she was doing.

"A cat," a small girl who wore long wool pants under a cotton dress said.

Beth kept drawing.

"Elephant," a child said, his arm in a sling.

"Get her out of here," the boy in the black leather jacket said again.

Beth kept drawing.

"It's a rhinoceros," a chubby boy said, bandages wrapped around his head.

Beth finished the drawing and stepped aside.

"Dinosaur! Dinosaur!" a bunch of them screamed.

Beth wrote the word "dinosaur" next to the drawing. "Anybody know what kind?"

"Brontosaurus?"

"Flintstone?"

Everyone laughed.

Beth wrote the word "triceratops." "So where do I find one?"

"There ain't no dinosaurs any more!" yelled a chocolate-colored child.

"No?" Beth said. "When did the last one exist?"

A variety of answers were shouted. Two thousand years ago. One jillion. Thirty hundred.

"Seventy million!" the teacher's aide said, then put her hand over her mouth.

Beth wrote the number seventy million on the board.

"What if I told you that natives of Africa, South America and Asia have all claimed to see this animal within our own century? They say he's seventy feet long and they even have a name for him: Chipekwe."

"Awesome," the black leather jacket said.

Beth drew a picture of a winged lizard with a long snout and razor-sharp teeth.

"The people who live in the swampy region of northwestern Rhodesia call this animal Kongamato. In 1889, when a scientist named Frank Melland showed them a drawing of a pterodactyl, also a creature that is believed to have been extinct for the past seventy million years, they all said it was Kongamato, alive and well.

"Who knows this animal?" Beth wrote the word "YETI." "This is what they call him in Tibet." Then she wrote the word "SASQUATCH." "This is what the Canadians call him."

No one said anything. The teacher's aide pressed her lips together, put both hands over her mouth this time.

"In Russia they call him Almas. Here in the United States, in Florida they call him Skunk Ape; in Missouri, Momo. Or maybe you know of him as the Abominable Snowman."

"Big Foot! Big Foot!" several children screamed.

Beth pulled a photograph out from her portfolio. It was grainy and spotted, but in the center was a dark shadowy figure shaped like a man with hairy edges. The aide held it up for everyone to see as she walked around the classroom.

"The first documented sighting of Big Foot was made near Mount

Everest by a British traveler named Frazer in 1820. Since then, there've been nearly one thousand sightings in the Northwestern United States and nearby regions of Canada alone. There's even a ten-thousand-dollar fine plus imprisonment if a person should ever harm one. And the United States government includes sketches of Big Foot in their training manual for soldiers going into the Pacific Northwest.

"But," Beth held out her arms, palms up, "no one believes the creature exists!"

"I do," said a child wearing an oversized yellow rain slicker.

Beth told them about the Loch Ness monster and a giant squid named Kraken before giving them their assignment. Over the next week they were to make up their own creature. They had to name it and give it a history. They were to tell the class what it ate, what its habits were, where it lived, what size it was and what it smelled like.

May reached in her shoe and pulled out a photo of Susan. Wrapped around it was a newspaper article about Hader that included a picture of him. He looked like an ordinary house cat, with nothing in the picture to compare his size against. But she could see Madee in his profile, Miss Takbal in the pose he struck, Bast's defiant glare in his eyes. He was so much more than an illusion.

Creatures built of cardboard boxes, paper, scraps of tin, old clothes, bottles and clay started to take shape around her. One child drew a horse with horns and a dinosaur tail; another created a webbed-footed robot with pinecone eyes and sharp teeth for fingertips. She walked past a caterpillar with machine guns mounted along its underside instead of feet, then pushed the newspaper photo of Hader into Beth's hand.

"This photo was taken by the UPI. It isn't some fuzzy image that's been enlarged a hundred times. He's not some creature that's only been spotted in some remote swamp by some forgotten tribe. Did you bring me here just to make fun of me?"

"No, I'm worried about you."

"Well, don't. Hader exists, he's on his way to Houston."

"Pharaoh's Friend exists, Pharaoh's Friend is on his way to Houston, May."

She left. Beth would have to find another ride home.

Chapter Twenty-Two

May and Beth presented the revised magazine designs and the invitation layout on Wednesday. To celebrate Grace's approval, Beth insisted May have dinner with her at the Japanese restaurant next to her studio.

"Only because I feel bad about leaving you stranded after your class the other day. I know your intentions were good, I'm just not myself lately." She would have accepted any invitation from anybody rather than go home to that dark, empty house again.

Since she wasn't an experienced sushi eater, she let Beth order for both of them. They started with California rolls, then tuna and salmon. But the more sake Beth drank, the more adventurous her selections grew. The meal ended with dishes of slimy-textured squid and sour-tasting octopus that she could barely look at, much less swallow. She wanted to leave.

"One more sake, one more story!" Beth said.

She listened to Beth with her car keys in hand, her purse strap over her shoulder, and arranged each fold of her skirt so its pattern of horses all galloped in the same direction. The story was about exchanging secrets with a friend.

"A secret so private the mere thought of telling it brought immediate regret," Beth whispered. "But you know the funny part? Months later we saw each other again, and after a lot of hem-hawing around we realized neither one of us could remember what the other one had told! We only remembered our own dreaded tale."

She didn't understand the point of the story or why Beth had insisted on telling it at that particular time. She just wanted to leave. She stood up, but Beth sat there, poking at fallen pieces of rice in her soy sauce with the end of a chopstick. Thick mascara, clumped on her eyelashes, made her eyes look dark and forlorn.

"I lost a baby," Beth said.

May didn't trust what she heard. She'd twisted Beth's words, her own sadness reshaping the world around her again.

"What?"

This time Beth spoke in a monotone with none of her usual embellishments. She told the story as if it were about someone else: a young girl still in high school who'd fallen in love with an older boy who played the bass guitar in a rock band on the weekends. He drove a green Triumph Spitfire, smoked Marlboro cigarettes and wore a faded blue-jean jacket. For two months following the one and only time they'd had sex together, the girl went to the temple every afternoon to pray she wasn't pregnant. Then, when there was no denying it, she went to the rabbi for help. He told her parents, who did not respond with the love and kindness he'd promised. They shipped her off to Amille, a small town in France, to stay with a friend of the mother's for her senior year and the duration of the pregnancy. Nobody was to know the truth — family, friends, teachers, schoolmates, not even her two younger sisters. From the moment her parents found out until three days later when they sent her away, the girl's mother kept herself shut in the bedroom. It was the father who fixed all the meals and took the two younger sisters to school. He continued to put braces on the tiny teeth of his clients at the office, pick the girls up after school, bathe them at night and read them stories at bedtime, all the while doing everything possible to avoid their older sister.

"You had a baby!"

"No, I lost a baby," Beth said. "When nothing else mattered but that tiny life inside of me, when there was no one else in the world I cared about, when the only reason I could think of to stay alive was to be a vessel for that little beating heart, it stopped." Beth bent over and pulled her large purse from the floor to her lap; it looked like a child cradled in her arms. "I don't know what I did wrong."

Beth was dry-eyed, but May was not. The printed horses on her skirt reared up, bucked and ruffled her hemline so that she had to hold it down. She wanted to throw her arms around Beth and share this terrible pain they had in common. This was why they had become friends so quickly, why she had felt as close to Beth as a sister. There was so much more to share, so much to tell her about her own lost child, Susan.

"Sorry I'm late." Arturo, the bartender from Backalley's, stood behind Beth and put his hands on her shoulders. Without looking back, she reached over her head and pulled him near.

"Get me out of here," Beth breathed in his ear. "I've become maudlin and my own conversation is boring me to death." She pushed a boat-shaped straw container that held a steaming white towel out of her way and left the table.

"Beth! Wait!" She followed her across the room. "I need to tell you something too."

"Look, I don't know what got me started on that old story. You've been wanting to go home, so why don't you."

"But we..."

"Go home, May." Beth turned and walked toward her studio next door. Arturo supported her, his arm around her waist.

Home was still the last place May wanted to go. It took too much courage to be in the house of too many rooms in this weepy frame of mind. She went to the office instead. By the time she reached her desk it was ten-thirty, but all the overhead lights were still on. Noise from a vacuum cleaner probably kept Grace from hearing her approach.

"What are you doing?"

Grace was so startled she banged the top of her head on the extension arm of the artist's lamp over May's desk. She was a spotlighted caricature of herself under the lamp, eyes too piercing, cheeks too hollow, lips too red. The dark low-cut blouse accentuated her long bony neck, delicate and white at the throat, making her look like one of the ibises they'd seen perched on the banks of the Nile scanning the water for prey. Her hand was on the turquoise journal.

"That was in my drawer!"

Grace closed the book, stared down at it, refused to meet her glare.

"How much have you read?" She grabbed the journal and clutched it to her chest.

"Enough."

The whooshing of the vacuum cleaner stopped, and in the sudden silence May could hear her own heart everywhere, in her ears and fingertips; her body twitched from the surge of it.

"I understand when Susan died you questioned, well, everything. But this goddess stuff and magical cats, it's, it's paganism."

"And your chimes and crystals and vibrating with the universe aren't?"

"I'm on God's Path. I don't know what you're on."

"God's Path? Funny how it works — whatever you want and God's will." She pushed Grace away from her desk. "You think a song on the radio is God singing to you. The morning headline is a message to you. The open parking spaces, the job promotion, never having to diet, all part of some big agreement between you and God."

"You can't just turn away from God, May, without turning toward Satan."

"Where are we? Back at St. Mary's?"

"Exactly. You've taken everything we learned and twisted it all up with this Egyptian legend of yours."

"Of mine? I didn't make it up." She started toward the front lobby.

"Think about it. You have three cats instead of the Holy Trinity, Bast instead of Jesus. But now, a savior that has asked for your help?"

She kept walking. Grace followed her.

"Oh, and the musical instrument your goddess carries, the instrument that's a symbol of the afterlife. It's the cross, May. The cross. Only it was resurrection, not transmigration, that occurred. Christian souls don't need any kind of escort into God's Kingdom, and certainly not from cats." Grace grabbed her hand and turned her around. "This lost cat isn't Hader, or Pharaoh's Friend, or Blue Bell or even Susan — it's you. You're the one who's lost. You're lost because you've turned away from God, and without God in your life, you're vulnerable to evil."

"When you've lost a daughter, when you've lost a part of yourself, when you've lost your future, then I'll let you talk to me about God."

"Your doubt is Satan's passage. The more doubt, the closer he comes. Can't you feel things getting out of control already?"

"You girls okay?" It was the janitor, Dell. He let go of the vacuum's handle, reached into his back pocket for a handkerchief and wiped his face.

May looked at Dell's worried expression and then at Grace's.

"Just a philosophical difference," Grace told him.

"Mighty loud for just that. You sure you okay, Miss May?"

"Thanks, Dell. Just a little upset."

Little upset, how about crazy! Absolutely out-of-my mind, fine-line-in-the-desert crazy to be listening to Grace. And yet, she made sense. Why else would the world have turned unfriendly, and her innermost sadness been reflected in everything and everywhere she looked?

God was omnipotent. It was a universe of cause and effect, a universe of reward and punishment after all.

She pushed on the heavy glass doors of the lobby and ran down the hallway to the elevator.

"It's blasphemy," Grace called out from the lobby doorway. " 'Fear God and keep His commandment, for this is the whole duty of man. For God will bring every deed into judgment, including every hidden thing, whether it be good or evil.' "

▲▲▲

Again May refused to go home to the chance of an empty house. She headed for the freeway, something she'd learned while attending college in Iowa. The flat two-lane highways winding through black-green farm fields, the night air pungent with the scent of earth and manure, the stars as fellow night travelers, always calmed her.

But a detour steered her off the freeway right into downtown Houston, through deserted night streets and black-windowed office buildings toward a different freeway entrance. She sat at a red light and searched her glove compartment for just the right cassette to accompany the ride. The light changed to green and back again before she found it: Beethoven's *Moonlight Sonata.* Ludwig could surely transform miles of empty parking lots into gentle Iowa cornfields. She pushed in the tape and lowered the windows in anticipation of the night air that would rush through the car and cleanse her.

There was a noise. The muffler? It grew louder. Please, not the engine. Blessed be He, Lord of the Universe, have mercy on this '64 Mustang. Louder, like a train roaring down upon her. She saw them in her rearview mirror. A group of at least forty people, their arms swinging low across their bodies, they leaned right, then left with each graceful stride. Spread across all four lanes of the city street, they moved quickly, fearless of the possibility of oncoming traffic.

The Urban Animals? She didn't know of anyone who'd actually seen them.

The clatter of their polyurethane wheels on the asphalt street grew louder. A yellow glow from overhead streetlights turned the skaters fluorescent as they glided beneath, so many different colors, alive and electric. Their rhythm was mesmerizing. Leaving, or even rolling up the windows, never crossed her mind until it was too late. They surrounded her, and circled the car with such speed she felt as though she were spinning amid their hoots and hollers and whistles. Strong lean bodies; purple-streaked hair; golden hoop earrings and wide, silver bracelets; feathered headbands; red and black skates with blue, purple and orange wheels; cut-off jeans; bare-chested men with leather armbands; young women in lacy red bras and pink Spandex pants; a leopard print cape; bows and tassels and ties; spiked hair, Mohawks and silver chains; wrist guards, knee guards all whirled around her. Better than any ride down the highway, it was sheer joyous energy.

Then, with no discernible command, they broke from the circle and vanished as quickly as they had appeared.

Sitting in the silence, the adrenaline pumped through her body.

"Devil worshippers!" She laughed at the stories she'd heard about them appearing at night to suck the blood of indigent street people.

A warm gust blew across her face. She turned toward the open window and saw huge, shiny black nostrils, moist and distended, while Grace's words burned in her ears: You turn from God, you turn toward evil.

She screamed.

"You okay, Miss?" A Houston policeman astride his horse leaned down to look in through her car window. Dressed in a short-sleeved blue shirt and black pants with a razor-sharp crease, he seemed unaware of the night heat. He touched his cap and flashed a handsome smile of teeth as bright as his silver badge.

"You've sat through a couple of green lights. Do you need assistance?"

When his horse took a few steps back, the young man leaned farther forward to keep his eye on her. He stroked the animal's shoulder the same way she petted the black cat, Madee, at the shore's edge while listening to the goddess. Smiling up at him, she felt a kinship.

"I'm fine." Then before she could stop herself she said, "Didn't you see them?"

"Who?"

She listened for the fading rumble of the Urban Animals' skates but heard nothing. It was unbelievable that he could have missed the whole thirty or forty of them. Even if buildings had blocked his view, he still should have heard their hooting and hollering.

"You didn't hear them?"

"Ma'am?"

"How could you have missed them?"

No longer smiling, he struck a pose in his saddle that caused the horse to bristle and toss its massive head high above the turquoise Mustang.

"Pigeons!" she said. "A flock of pigeons flew over my car."

She could feel the officer's stare as she pulled away from the intersection. So, Grace is right. First I dream up mythical cats, and now the Urban Animals.

▲▲▲

That night, the goddess looked different, more beautiful than ever. Her gold mesh gown sparkled with each movement. Her cat ears, pierced at the tips, were linked together by a thin gold chain. On each of her whiskers she had threaded tiny gold beads that floated near her face like a private galaxy. Black Kohl lines encircled her eyes, and the blue-green color of the Nile shaded her lids.

But even more than her appearance, there was something about her manner that was different: the way she pointed her toes with each step, shaking the musical sistrum, her golden shield nowhere in sight.

"Find Hader and send him home. Collar or not, I need him," she said. The white cat, Miss Takbal, swam to Bast and wrapped around her feet. When she leaned over to stroke it, a turquoise tear fell from the goddess' eye.

The sun appeared and turned the gray sky golden. Bast shimmered, radiant in the light, and smiled with a warmth that May had not seen before.

"It's my lover," Bast said. "Ra, the sun god."

"Gods don't have lovers! Gods don't have sex!"

Awake, she listened to Jason's breathing and wondered how they had ever drifted so far apart from one another.

Chapter Twenty-Three

"Boss, someone's looking for you."

Jason turned from the top of the scaffolding and looked across the habitat. In the pedestrian area on the other side of the safety moat stood Grace. From his perspective, she looked diminutive in her bright pink dress, its full skirt blocking her legs so all he could see were the pointed toes of her matching pink shoes poking out from underneath it. She reminded him of a doll of Susan's that used to dance up and down inside a glass dome, its floppy legs and ballerina slippers flying left and then right under a billowing skirt in rhythm to a sad little song. Strangely, the closer he got to Grace the more she resembled the doll. Her pallor was waxy, and she was wearing too much makeup.

"*Saeeda*," hello, Grace said in Arabic, as they had taken to greeting one another in Egypt.

He stared at her.

"Looks nice," she said in reference to the wooden-framed pyramid he and his workers had built as a prop in what used to be the ocelots' habitat. The space was to become Friend's temporary home. All reports of the famous cat indicated he was docile, but the zoo's board of directors insisted extra precautions be taken for insurance reasons. Stronger safety glass with wire mesh was installed in the door between the handler's room and the pen, the moat separating the public from the animal was made deeper and wider and covered with smooth cement, the fence on either side of the running area was reinforced with steel rods, and the lower ledges of simulated rock were removed from the back wall so there would be no chance of the cat's scaling it.

He walked to a bench in some nearby shade and sat down. She followed, sat beside him and placed her hand on his.

"We're in danger." Her expression was animated, doll-like again. Her eyes were too round, her cheeks too rosy. He pulled away from her and glanced at his watch.

"It's May." She fingered the crystal pendant at her throat.

"Jesus Christ, what has she done now?"

She pressed her hands to her chest.

"She's invoked Satan."

"What?"

She told him about May's journal. How May's sadness and doubt in God had made her vulnerable to evil. "Satan's not just a concept — he has a name, like you and I do, because he's real. He breathes. He feels. He thinks."

"A name. You mean like Lucifer? The Prince of Darkness? The Boogie Man?" He laughed.

"Pharaoh's Friend, Jason. It's Friend."

He stood to leave, but she grabbed one of his hands with both of hers.

"You don't understand the risk I'm taking. Discussing him, even mentioning his name gives him credence and draws him that much closer to me!"

He saw his workers watching them. They were too far away to hear what she said, but several of them mocked her gestures while the others snickered.

"'There is no truth in him. When he lies, he speaks his native language, for he is a liar and the father of lies.' John 8:44," she said.

"You're nuts." He walked away from her as quickly as he could and looked back at his crew.

She followed him.

"What happened that night in the ocelots' cave, this very cave we're standing in front of now, was Friend's doing. We're all under his influence because of May."

"That's the most ridiculous thing I've ever heard, even from you!"

The next day, Grace left ten messages for him to phone her. The day after that she was waiting for him in the parking lot when he arrived at the zoo, at the concession stand where he bought his lunch, at the Shell station where he stopped on his way home from work to get gasoline, and at the Heights Hotel bar where he went for drinks. For four days, wherever he went, she was. Each time she looked more wretched, ghastly. Her appearances started to feel like a haunting.

He was sick of her. Every glimpse reminded him of their night together. Her clammy body, her perfume that no amount of scrubbing could get rid of, the smell of his own vomit from all the scotch he'd had that night, and the bruise on his knee that was just starting to heal from the rock he'd knelt on while fucking her. He hated the sight of her, the smell of her, the very thought of her.

When she appeared one evening in front of his own home, he'd had enough.

"Jesus Christ! Stop this!"

"*In Shallah,*" if God wills it, she replied in Arabic. She started to cry. He grabbed her arm and pulled her around to a side of the garage that couldn't be seen from his house.

"Why don't you go pray or chant or fast or whatever it is you do to solve your problems? Friend will be in Houston on Tuesday, and

I have too much going on to have to bother with you popping up around every corner. Now, I told you I was sorry about what happened. You need to take responsibility for what we did, then let it drop."

"I know it sounds crazy! But this is a spiritual battle, not a physical one. We can keep the animal away from us simply by thinking it. Change our perception and we change our reality."

"I don't want to see you again! I don't want to hear you again! What do I have to do to get that through to you?"

"Just ask May," she answered. "Ask her about Pharaoh's Friend. Ask her about the turquoise journal."

His hands flew out at Grace before he could stop himself. He pushed her, sent her sprawling to the ground and her black high-heel shoe came off her left foot on impact.

Of all things, Grace had to say that. He didn't have to ask his wife anything. He already knew too much about her. He knew everything from her first lumbering shuffle in the morning directly to the scale in their bathroom, to that pathetic final sigh she made every night before going to sleep. He knew she brushed her teeth on the right side before the left. He knew every stupid animal-print outfit in her closet, where every cookie bag and candy box and Lifesaver roll were hidden. He knew she bit at her lower lip when she was nervous, that she never put enough ice cubes in his glass, never enough mayonnaise on his sandwich, that she hoarded her so-called big inheritance and that, somehow, before it's too late, a mother is supposed to know when her child is sick. That's how it worked on his family's farm, or out in the wild, or at the zoo. Always, it was the mother who nurtured and cared for the infants. It was instinct.

He walked toward the house and punched the fence post with his fist. The phone rang. It was the head of the veterinary school from Texas A & M calling to confirm final arrangements for Friend's journey.

Dr. Hirston was in charge of the team examining the cat. He'd been in touch by phone just about every day since the decision to send Friend to Houston. Their conversations had grown friendlier with frequency, and after a while, he felt like he knew the doctor well. Just from the sound of his voice he had an image of the veterinarian that felt so real he was sure he could recognize him. But it was Friend that he could not picture, even though he'd seen many photos of the cat. Each time he tried to envision the animal he felt confused, possibly from all the media hype. Even Dr. Hirston had told him they had not found anything mysterious. He and his team had done hair follicle tests, had taken blood and tissue samples, ran an EKG, electrocardiograph, stress test, and X-rayed the animal. Just as the Egyptian institutions had reported, the results indicated that Friend was simply a mixture, an unusual mixture, yet still just a mixture of two existing species of felines: *Felis silvestris lybica*, known as the African Wildcat, and *Felis chaus*, the Reed Cat.

Praising Friend's intelligence, Dr. Hirston had also told him about a complicated maze his team had set up in a room the size of a gymnasium. They'd made sure the cat was hungry so the dish of raw red fish and vitamins placed at the end of the maze would be a nice reward. From an observatory glass booth on a second landing, they electronically released the latch on his cage and watched in horror and wonder as the four-hundred-and-twenty-pound animal trotted directly to the door they'd just exited through. He stood on his back legs and pushed down on the door's lever with his front paws, allowing him to walk right into their own dining area. By the time the doctor and his associates scrambled down the flight of stairs with a loaded tranquilizer gun, Friend had also opened the door to a refrigerator. "He opened the damn refrigerator! Well, we didn't actually see him do this, someone could have left the door ajar, but I doubt it!" They found Friend munching on a Granny Smith apple and a leftover enchilada. He and the doctor had a good laugh about the number of times they hadn't believed cat owners who claimed their pets could open doors, drawers and window latches.

The following day the test was repeated, only this time all exit doors were locked. But rather than laboriously wend his way through the maze as they'd planned, Friend outsmarted them again. He leaped to the top ledge of the maze walls and simply crossed over to the last compartment to reach the food.

"I have it on video," the doctor told him. "We couldn't even get Friend to jump at all before that day, but it's just beautiful to watch. His takeoff was so powerful for a moment I thought he was going to fly right over the maze!"

Jason was quick to ask the doctor the exact height of the maze walls. The following day, he removed even more rock ledges from the back wall of Friend's future home.

Along with daily anecdotes, he and the doctor exchanged information about the cat's diet, antibiotics, vitamins, temperature readings, behavior, and habits. They had talked about the cat's troubled sleep patterns.

"How's Friend sleeping?" he asked now, on the phone, as he watched Grace through his kitchen window dust the dirt from her skirt and hobble toward her car holding one shoe.

"Whenever he naps, he's extremely active. We've tried hooking him up to record his REMs, but unless he's drugged he tears the wires off. And when he's drugged, we don't get true readings. Don't know what's going on with him. I'm afraid he's not getting enough rest."

"I'll be sure to keep an eye on that while he's here," he said, keeping an eye on Grace, willing her to start the ignition and leave already.

"You know, the way he tosses and turns in his sleep, if he were a man I'd say he had a guilty conscience!" Dr. Hirston laughed.

He watched Grace's red Mercedes finally pull away from the curb and race too quickly down the neighborhood street. He caught himself thinking of how his wife's dark hair used to smell like fresh sea water, and how sometimes her skin tasted salty and sweet at the same time, and how her laugh and their daughter's had sounded the same.

Chapter Twenty-Four

Maggie was the last person Grace wanted to see first thing every workday morning. But there was no avoiding her. No back door to slip through, no escaping the perky receptionist.

"I've got this entire office building buzzing with that questionnaire, Grace," Maggie said. "You know, I'm dating Tom, and the poor dear just wasn't getting the questionnaire responses he needed, so I've asked some of the women around here to help."

"Why, would I care that you're dating Tom?" Grace started to walk toward her office.

"Grace, fill one out. We all are," Maggie said.

Grace heard Mr. Carlyle's deep voice approaching. She waited, frowning at the scuffmarks on Maggie's shoes, until he was beside them.

"It would be fun to answer one of these. Thanks for your help, Maggie. I only wish Tom could have thought of it to help out."

"Just grab one." Maggie pointed to the light blue stack of papers on the table near the reception area couch.

Mr. Carlyle smiled approvingly.

Grace looked forward to answering the questions that she and Dr. Williamson had thought up, but once she read it again she had to admit that Tom, the *Harbinger* Bard, was right: the questions were very personal. Remembering his concern that women might not be answering in fear that their responses could be traced back to them, she held the form up to the window light to check for unseen marks, then laughed at herself. Even so, later that day she checked the office for more copies on the unusual blue paper, but couldn't find any. Finally, she filled in the same form she'd originally taken, waited until Maggie left and then dropped it into the clear, locked box in the reception area where at least twenty other questionnaires had been deposited.

The questions had stirred memories of childhood fantasies, disappointing first kisses, dishonest boyfriends, discarded relationships, and her disastrous surrender to Jason. But that evening with Jason weighed the heaviest. In every thought, every decision, every move she felt a constant crushing remorse that made her restless. Even with heavier doses of medication, sleep was almost impossible in the final days before Friend's arrival. She could feel the animal nearing like an approaching storm, causing errant whorls of wind in the oppressive air to kick up dust and swirl treetops and stir branches unnaturally.

She kept herself busy with work. The premiere issue of the *Harbinger* made it to the printer on time. The new design worked beautifully, and the exclusive interview with her cousin nestled into the one hundred and forty-four glossy pages like a treasure itself, just waiting for the reader's discovery. The museum officers and directors were ecstatic over the turquoise necklace invitation, and they'd received an overwhelming number of acceptances for the exhibition's opening night. The escalating controversy and interest in Friend had enabled her to line up the Channel 13 News crew to be on hand for the cat's scheduled arrival at the zoo on Tuesday.

Yet none of these successes mattered. She meditated, she chanted, she fasted, she even tried to get her father to cancel the cat's visit, but nothing could stop it from happening. Late into the night on Monday, she did menial tasks to fill the time: cleaned closets, organized drawers and arranged photo albums. She sifted through memorabilia from the Egyptian trip: travel stickers, hotel brochures, napkins, matches and maps and such, and found a small pamphlet the travel agent had enclosed initially with their airline tickets. On the front, in large red Arabic letters, were four words with their English pronunciation and translation in smaller black letters underneath:

MISR. MADEE, HADER, MISSTAKBAL.
Egypt. Past, Present, Future.

She'd found May's three cats, or rather, their origin. Proof that May had created this whole horrible situation, and a last chance to convince her that she could end it. Stop the belief and May could stop the nightmare she was about to bring on all of them.

The moment she saw May in the hallway at the office the next morning, she rushed to hand her the pamphlet, but May handed her something first. It was the front page of the *Houston Chronicle.* She pointed to a picture in the bottom right corner of two older attractive women. "River Roads Sisters Murdered."

"These are the two women from the plane to Egypt," May said.

May had drawn ridiculous hairdos on both of them in blue ballpoint ink. It took several minutes for her to recognize them.

"The two women in those horrible wigs who sat in front of us on the plane!" May said.

"These are the Berry sisters, May. Society. Blue bloods. Friends of my father's. They've never flown coach class in their lives. And never looking like this." She refused to let May's craziness control her. She ignored the sudden cramp in her stomach and grabbed the paper from May, folding the word "murder" out of sight, and tucked it under her arm. She handed May the travel pamphlet.

"This came with your tickets. Long before we even left for Egypt."

May lowered her head to read it, and her face disappeared behind a veil of curls, just as it had all those years ago when she sat across from her at the table at St. Mary's during lunchtime blessings.

"These are the names of Bast's three cats," May whispered.

She nodded. "You took pieces, just like your jigsaw puzzles, May, and created this whole thing. Now you have to stop it. You've put all of us close to you in danger. Can't you tell by how strangely everyone is behaving, that this isn't normal?"

Bursts of laughter interrupted their conversation. They walked down the hallway toward the sound to the employee's lounge, where everyone was just getting their morning coffee.

"I can't believe this!" Maggie laughed. Seated on top of the same counter as the coffee maker, she held a light blue piece of paper in front of her. "Listen to this one! 'Question: where was the most unusual location you have had sexual intercourse?'"

Everyone held still.

"And Grace has answered, 'In an ocelot's habitat at the zoo,"' Maggie said.

Whistling accompanied the laughter this time. Only Maggie didn't laugh. She dropped the paper to her lap at the sight of Grace and May standing in the doorway. The room full of snickering people followed Maggie's startled gaze and grew silent.

Grace watched May glance at the travel brochure she still held in her hand and then at each face in the room as they averted their eyes.

"I guess you want me to believe I've created you and Jason also?"

Grace waited until May had turned the corner and glared across the room at Maggie.

"May's the last person in the world I wanted to hurt," Grace heard her say to Tom.

"What does May have to do with it?" Tom said as he put his arm protectively around her.

"Cancel my appointments," Grace said as she raced down the hall past her office.

But you have messages," Sharon yelled. "And Friend arrived early!"

But she was already gone. All she could think of was getting to Jason to warn him the nightmare had begun.

On the way to the zoo, she saw May everywhere: standing on a street corner, in the car next to hers at the stop light, on billboards, on theatre marquees and posted on the sides of Metro buses. Every time bearing the same gloomy expression she'd last seen at the door of the employee's lounge.

She parked at the farthest point from the zoo's entrance, the only spot she could find, and rushed to the ticket gate. The hot sun worked its way through her red linen suit; perspiration beaded at her hairline and ran down her face and the back of her neck. She passed by the Channel 13 news van and pushed through the crowds until she saw Jason in front of a cage on wheels. A news reporter questioned him and another man while a cameraman filmed.

In the cage behind them was the dark gray cat. More imposing than she'd imagined, he was also more frightening. His yellow eyes did not reflect the typical lazy afternoon gaze of other large cats; his stare was intense. His gait was too lithe, his turns too deliberate, and the sway of his head too calculating. He was as large as a lion, but his markings were tiger-like, and his body was as sleek as a jaguar.

▲▲▲

From the crowd, May also watched as the reporter interviewed her husband. But she, too, could not keep her eyes off the large cat behind them as he paced off the moments, his rhythm like the heavy pendulum of a clock. Back and forth, the sideways movement of the universe, like Beth's Lateral Joker. All four hundred and twenty pounds. The camera crew moved closer to Jason as he spoke into a microphone, but she could tell by her husband's sudden change in posture that it would be the last question he would answer. He was a master at ending conversations, knowing just how to create dead ends, just how to make exits.

When the crowd broke into small families again, she started toward him, but stopped at the sight of Grace, her sunny-blonde hair, wet with perspiration, stuck to her face. She moved with quick bursts of emotion, engulfed by her red linen suit.

"Jason." Grace placed her hand on his forearm. "May knows."

The terrifying sound that followed ripped through the crowd like a thunderbolt. When Friend roared a second time, children cried and the crew turned the camera on again. The cat stopped pacing, the large pendulum suspended. He threw himself against the bars of the cage and clawed through the open spaces, his sound deafening. There was commotion all around, a melee of brightly colored baby strollers, swirling pink cotton candy and sneakers with runaway laces. This could not be the same cat she'd dreamed of night after night.

"What's wrong, Dr. Hirston?" Jason screamed to the other man. Friend threw himself against the bars of the cage again.

"Get these people out of here!" Jason shouted to his workers. He pushed Grace aside just as Friend reached out at her from between the bars with his claws fully extended. It took thirty seconds for the tranquilizing dart he shot into the side of the cat's neck to take effect.

They examined the subdued animal in the zoo's infirmary.

"What happened to you, boy?" The doctor took the cat's temperature, looked into his ears and eyes, studied each paw and between the pads, felt him, rubbed him and gently pried the cat's jaws open to look inside his mouth. He stuck his face right between Friend's jaws and inhaled. For one instant, Jason saw the cat's lip curl. He sprang forward, remembering the countless times he'd squirmed in his seat while watching circus performers in this same predicament, but Friend was merely yawning.

Dr. Hirston couldn't find anything wrong with the cat. He felt the outburst must have been caused by the extended trip in the confined space of his travel cage, the very one that he was shipped in from Egypt. They waited five hours for Friend to fully awaken, then observed as he investigated the new habitat. He seemed content, even playful. There were caves to explore, dead tree limbs to climb and water to splash in. The late afternoon turned his gray coat a rusty brown and his eyes a daffodil yellow. Prancing back and forth, he moved like the Egyptian wind, with varying intensity, but never ceasing. He took gentle steps that had the latent power of gale force. His ears, large and pointed, jutted forth from the top of his head like a crown. He was magnificent. It was obvious to Jason why the Egyptians had linked the cat to royalty.

Friend stretched into the air as if to box imaginary playmates, then suddenly dropped to all fours and stared directly at the doctor.

"This is the animal I've grown to know," Dr. Hirston said. It was time to say good-bye.

▲▲▲

May watched Grace catch up with Jason after he'd walked the doctor to his car. She hid behind a birdcage; they stood in the shade of a white and red concession stand. Too far away for her to hear them, their movements were their words: Grace's frenetic and grasping, Jason's imperceptible. Though his pose was a portrait of strength, his hands, pressed so firmly upon his hips, seemed as though they could barely support the weight of his own torso. For an instant she saw a trace of doubt in his confident face, an expression she'd seen once before in an artist's self-portrait, sorrow so private yet so consuming. Then everything changed. Grace stood still while Jason threw his arms violently into the air and cut at the space in front of her.

"You're fuckin' nuts!"

He screamed so loudly, the jay-sized birds fluttered from their branches inside the cage in front of May, sending loose feathers everywhere.

He tramped off, nearly running into one of the zoo's security guards. But then he turned and jabbed his finger into the guard's fat chest.

"You don't show for your late shift one more time and you're fired!" He pushed the man. "Understand, Dugacy?"

"May?"

The birds fluttered again and she turned. Richard stood in front of her. He'd shaved his beard, his skin was smooth, his expression happily mischievous, looking just like the boy she used to play with in Grace's backyard.

"I came to see my cat, but I'd much rather see you," Richard said.

"I saw him earlier. He was angry."

"I think he followed me all the way home from Egypt."

No. He's followed me, she thought.

"I wish they'd left him in the desert. I feel so responsible for his situation."

No. I'm responsible.

"I hope he's okay."

"He had a rough morning, I'm sure you'll see it on tonight's news."

"And are you okay, May?"

She stepped toward him, and her head fell against his shoulder as if it were a pillow, as if she'd done this a thousand times before. He held her, the old family quilt wrapped around them, its pattern of violets everywhere, comforting, his touch familiar.

"I'm sorry, Richard. I didn't return your calls."

"Not one of them. And there were many."

"I'm lost."

"That doesn't have to be a bad thing."

"It's awful, I'm doubting everything and everybody I've ever believed in."

"Maybe you have good reasons." He gently pushed her far enough away to look into her eyes, his grip tight on her shoulders. "Don't be afraid."

"You think this is about Jason, but it's so much more."

"Then tell me."

She wanted to, but couldn't. He wouldn't understand a doomed life, one that was predestined for loss after loss: her parents, Susan, Jason, Grace, Blue Bell, her beach house. Sometimes you can't deal with a new pain until you have come to understand an old one, Claudia had told her. Let go, she'd said. As if she had a choice.

"I haven't been sleeping, I just need some sleep."

He kissed her.

"I'm here, if you need me. Just call."

She walked away from him, relieved she hadn't said anything about Friend's true identity, the stolen collar, the imitation one, her plan to give it to the cat. It all seemed crazy in Richard's safe caress.

Chapter Twenty-Five

When Grace arrived home from the zoo, there was a cold moon burning a hole in the sky over her house. She ran from the garage canopy to a tree and then beneath her own front door awning, never allowing Goddess Bast a full view of her. Inside, she lowered her shades, went straight to her photo album, and tore to shreds every picture of Jason and May from their trip to Egypt.

She flushed the pieces down the toilet, over and over, as fragments of faces and friendship swirled in the water, then disappeared. She closed her eyes, saw claws grasp for her from the cage, felt the warm gush of the cat's roar. It smelled of decay, the breath of carrion.

She opened her eyes and reached for the medicine chest. She swallowed two blue pills and one yellow before noticing the blinking light on her answering machine.

"It's Dad. I've been trying to reach you all day, dammit, I need..." then a different voice, one with a heavy accent, Egyptian maybe. "Have you seen today's paper, Mssssss. Sutton? Your father's associates ran into a little trouble. Front page. Bottom right. If you want your dear daddy returned, then follow the directions I've left in your box."

She listened to the message again. Her father's associates. The Berry sisters. The murder in River Roads. She called his office, even though it was late. Monique answered his private line, obviously upset. Her saccharine tone failed to hide her agitation from not having seen or heard from Gerald all day. She called her mother, who'd also gotten no further in finding him than Monique. "Of course, the French Dip would tell me any lie Gerald asked her to," her mother said. "I wouldn't fret too much about his absence, dear, your father always turns up eventually."

Before her mother could start in on the many other times Gerald was not where he was supposed to have been, Grace hung up the phone and hurried to her mailbox, where she found a small envelope, her name hand-printed on it, the note inside.

> *Bring the turquoise necklace from the museum to Pharaoh's Friend's cage — 2:00 am tonight. I know you have access to it, and I will know if you contact the police.*

▲▲▲

"But Grace, this is crazy," Richard said.

"Crazy? No. We have to celebrate tonight. Tomorrow, after the opening, it will all be over. Everyone will have seen the artifacts, the newspapers will have taken their pictures, and you, cousin, will be old news. It will all be old news!"

"I don't even like champagne," he said, "and it doesn't like me!"

But she kept on until he finally agreed.

In his driveway, she gave the family honk (five short beeps followed by two long). On the back seat of her Mercedes was the wicker picnic basket she'd filled with appropriate things for their celebration.

Richard came out of his house no longer wearing the traditional flowing robe of Egypt but back in his urban clothing — faded blue jeans, a white cotton shirt, loafers. Flinging the car door open, he struck the ancient pose of a walking Egyptian by holding one arm bent in front of him, palm down, and his other arm bent behind him, palm up.

"Let's boogie!" he said.

His levity made her grip the steering wheel. She wanted to scream out that her father was in trouble. She wanted to pull him into the car and jam the hand-written instructions she'd found in her mailbox just a few short hours before into his smiling mouth. If only she could tell Richard, but he would panic, call all the wrong people in to help — whoever those people might be.

There were hundreds of people she considered calling: the police, the museum, the dean of Texas A & M, even people she thought might have a connection to her father's mysterious network, but she didn't know who to trust. The network might be who held her father now. She'd even called Beth Fields, of all people, and left some hysterical message. As if Beth would help her. She knew Beth wouldn't even care enough to call her back.

The night guard at the museum looked confused to find the two of them at the door at that late hour. Fortunately, Richard had become friendly with him over the last week when he'd worked late with the director of exhibits.

"It's like a dress rehearsal," he shouted through the thick glass door. The old man pulled a chain of keys off his leather belt, unlocked a metal panel in the wall and punched a series of buttons. After signing in and letting the guard check their basket, she left him some strawberries and bread. Richard opened the door to the exhibition room with his own access card and turned on the lights.

The turquoise necklace was spread on a pedestal, one of several displays whose glass covers had not yet been bolted in place.

"It's too bright in here." She shielded her eyes with the back of her hand.

He touched a switch on the wall and all the lights went off except for those directed at the artifacts. The pedestals, covered in dark carpet, disappeared so that the treasures looked as if they were floating. The low whir of the air conditioner kicked on, and the smell of fresh paint and drying solvents filled the space with the suggestion of embalming fluids and reverential spices. She felt the goddess everywhere: in the carnelian and jasper bracelet, the pieces of inlaid wooden chair embossed with bronze fittings, the copper dagger with the ivory handle. Worse than maneuvering through May's unhappy home where all her personal knickknacks crowded and shouted from every space, this was suffocating, as though she'd trespassed right into Bast's mouth and was being held between her pointed white cat teeth, moments away from being swallowed.

"It feels like a tomb." Richard walked between the displays, slightly bent at the waist, his hands feeling the air.

She set the picnic basket in the center of the room, arranged the food on a silver platter and opened the champagne. "To your show's success!"

"No, no. This is not my success." He touched his hand to his chest, then made a sweeping gesture with his glass of champagne to the artifacts that floated around them.

"To the glorious past," he said.

"Present!" she said.

He turned and looked at her, obviously confused, then he laughed.

"And to the future!" he said, and clinked his fluted glass against hers.

An unnerving chill ran down her spine as she sipped, knowing they had inadvertently toasted Bast's three magical cats. She felt swallowed whole, as though she were sliding down the goddess' gullet toward the large cavernous black hole where it would be too dark to see.

They drank and ate while he told long boring stories about each item in the room. Encouraging him, she smiled when he started to get silly and poured him more champagne when he felt dizzy. He reenacted the first time Friend came into their camp, reminding her that the cat was not yet a celebrity. He moved to a dark corner of the room. She moved toward the turquoise collar. He crept forward on all fours, then stood as himself, then pretended to be one of the students. A scream. A growl. He threw his new Timex watch just as he'd thrown his old one that night in the desert. She applauded. When he scampered off as the cat had, she replaced the turquoise collar with one of the invitation replicas.

She packed their things back into the wicker basket, haphazardly throwing in the dark green bottle without even corking it. Everything else was piled on top of it; loose strawberries in the bottom stained the lace napkins with bright pink spots. She retrieved the thrown wristwatch, pushed it into his hand, and pulled him toward the door. But just as they were leaving the room, he stopped.

"What?" she practically shouted.

"I can't believe I almost forgot what tonight is!"

"Tonight? Tonight's over." She grabbed his arm and pulled him through the door.

He shook loose from her.

"Tonight," he said, "the Nile will reach its highest point! Since June everyone's placed wagers on this measurement. They follow the newspaper reports more closely than the stock market."

He got that far-away look on his face again. She pulled on him as he put his arms out to his sides and did a grapevine dance step.

"I can see the celebration. The dancing. And then everyone will throw paper dolls into the Nile to show their gratitude for the annual flooding that keeps the land fertile. Well, now they throw dolls. In ancient Egypt they sacrificed young maidens."

Still holding the basket in one arm, she wrapped her other around him and steered him down the granite floor hallway.

He put his grinning face close to hers. "There'll be a sacrifice tonight," he said.

The night guard's brow furrowed as he watched the professor sign out. She kept her arm around him and started them toward the door.

"Not yet, Missy! Have to search your basket and purse." To Richard he said apologetically, "It's policy."

She placed everything on his desk. He poked through them.

"How were the strawberries?" she asked, her head reeling.

"Just fine."

"And the bread?" Her heart pounded.

"Fine. Thank you."

The guard returned her purse. He started to hand the basket to Richard, but gave it to her instead.

"Don't worry, I'm driving," she said over her shoulder as they headed toward the door again. She counted her steps. One. Two. Three.

"Hold it!" The old man was at their side.

Richard grinned at him. She couldn't breathe.

"Got a reading on the metal detector." He nodded at a red flashing light just above the exit.

This time the guard removed every item from her purse: a wallet; lipstick, "Red Pepper Red"; mascara, "Jet Black"; a compact with two different shades of brown eye shadow; a bottle of liquid foundation, Honey-Beige; a tortoise-shell powder compact; five Walgreen's pharmacy bottles with a myriad of colored capsules inside; a small, white leather Bible.

Then he removed every item from the basket. The stained pink napkins, the open champagne bottle, the heel of crusty bread, the cork, the foil cream cheese wrapper, the green plastic-mesh strawberry container, the fluted glasses, the champagne bucket, two silver butter knives, and the heavy silver platter with engraved initials in fancy looping calligraphy.

Her teeth clenched. Her nails dug into her palms. Richard swayed.

"Champagne doesn't like me," he said.

The guard responded with a sympathetic look, fidgeting with the brass buckle under his large belly. She tried not to look at his holstered gun as he picked up the platter with one hand and a butter knife with the other.

"These solid silver?" he asked.

"Given to me by my great aunt," she said, and prayed that Richard would come through just as he had a thousand times before with the predictable response.

He burst out in laughter and looked at her.

"Greaaaaaaat Auuuuuuunntt Ruuuuuuutheeeeee," they said in unison, pronouncing the vowels through their noses in the family tradition.

The guard smiled at them. "Well, they got this thing set pretty sensitive," he said, looking once again to the red light over the door. "This amount of silver could be enough to trigger it, though I don't remember it flashin' when y'all come in."

"You just never know," Richard said, his head wobbling.

"Guess I was so surprised that you were even here at this hour and all, I forgot to look at the reading." There was an unbearable moment of silence while the security officer removed his cap and stared at the metal detector. Then he put everything back in its place. She helped.

On the way to the car she couldn't feel her feet. She couldn't feel the basket in her hand. She couldn't feel Richard leaning against her. She couldn't feel the moist night air, the unevenness of the parking lot, or the sick feeling in her stomach. All she felt was the cold weight of turquoise and gold, heavy on her chest, pulling on her neck, underneath her high-collar blouse.

Chapter Twenty-Six

The same Tuesday that Friend arrived in Houston, Beth walked over to Lou's Five & Dime from her studio a few blocks away. She'd grown accustomed to dropping in on Lou while they worked on the museum invitation. She enjoyed their visits and even the short stroll over, but the store was closed when she arrived. On a chance that the back door might be open, she ran down a narrow alleyway, slapped at the old red brick on either side of her, and jumped through the open doorway into Lou's back office.

"Thought you'd come to rob this old man," he said after he caught his breath from the surprise of her sudden appearance.

"I have!" She smiled. "Of a turquoise and gold necklace."

He'd promised her one of the imitation necklaces if there were any extras. The invitation was a "keeper," as she called it, not to mention an impressive addition to her portfolio. While he went to the front of the store to get her one, she waited in the small dark space of his room where shelves were stacked ceiling-high with catalogues, telephone books from different cities, brochures, binders and boxes of all colors and sizes, paper and files and small notebooks with torn pieces of yellow paper sticking out from them. She pulled a catalogue from the nearest shelf and skimmed through it: Red Watering Can - $12.37 per carton/ twenty-four, with decorative floral - $12.98, Columbus, Ohio; Padded Satin Hangers - $3.50 set of six, $31.23 -ten set carton, Champaign, Illinois. It was comforting to think that each of the thousands of items on display in Lou's store had an origin. A home.

"It's by chance that you've caught me here," he said as he walked back into the room. "I've been closed all day for Yom Kippur. Just stopped in for a moment to pick up something."

"Yom Kippur?" The very mention of the holiday brought with it the sweet taste of Manischewitz wine, the aroma of freshly baked challah, the memory of a mosaic wall in the temple that depicted the twelve lost tribes of Israel, the dancing flame of the eternal light that made parts of the mosaic shimmer with flecks of gold, the smiling faces of cousins and friends whom she had not seen for a long time. She thought of her own family.

"The most holy day of the year," he said. "The Day of Atonement. I thought — well, excuse me, dear — but at one time I thought perhaps you were Jewish. Something I felt about you, but forgive a lonely old man who's always trying to make relatives out of everybody!"

She didn't say anything, still stuck in the memory of a time when she had felt part of a family, a lineage, a history. There were so few people in her life now. Intentionally, she had avoided one after another, the latest being Grace, though she'd been a hard one to shake. Oddly, May, a person she wished were a friend, she'd probably run off without trying. Why had she told May that pitiful story about the baby she'd lost so many years ago? And then, after telling it she felt too embarrassed to stay, even though May seemed desperate to tell her something. Everything was all out of whack. But Grace's phone call that afternoon was at the top of her list. The message Grace left, stranger than ever. Something about her father being in trouble and not knowing whom to call, and something about having done something horrible to May, and then something about all of them being dragged into a vortex of evil. She had considered calling her back till the vortex of evil language scared her off.

Lou reached for Beth's hand. The turquoise and gold settled into her palm like a creature bedding down for the night. Cool to the touch and substantial in weight, it was spectacular, imitation or not.

On the way out of his office, she picked up a small photo of a child in a simple brass frame from his desk. Perhaps it was the unexpected holiday memories, or maybe just knowing that the project was over and with it the opportunity to see Lou as often, but whatever the reason, she didn't want to leave.

"I'm so sorry you lost your daughter, Lou."

He rubbed the tarnished frame with his index finger. "But how did you know about my daughter?"

"You've talked about Susan often."

Lou shook his head, no. "This picture is of my daughter, Beth, the same name as yours, dear. Susan was May's daughter."

"May doesn't have a daughter."

"Yes, she did. She died just this year."

She plopped down with such force in Lou's swivel-cane chair that it rocked her back and forth.

"But she never told me. You never told me."

He shrugged his shoulders. "I assumed you knew."

He looked again at the small face in the photo and smiled back at it.

She stared at the worn wooden floor. "So much about May makes sense now. I would have been so much kinder if I'd known." She thought again how she'd told May about losing her baby. "I think she tried to tell me about Susan just the other night."

He offered to drive her home on his way back to the temple;

she asked to be dropped at Backalley's instead. In the car as they rode through the neighborhood, she caught frozen moments of life through the windows. A family at their dinner table. A woman at the kitchen sink. Cozy couches plump with pillows. A staircase with picture frames all the way up the wall. The soft blue cast from a television in an upstairs room. It all seemed the same, all the same window.

He talked as they drove. He talked about his daughter, May's daughter, May. He told her about a puzzle he'd given to May for her thirtieth birthday.

He'd asked an artist who owed him a favor to do an illustration of May that a specialty company then turned into a one-of-a-kind jigsaw. He never could have afforded such a customized gift otherwise. Since it was a favor, he didn't give any directions, was happy to accept whatever he got back, but he almost cried when he finally saw the drawing. It included Susan, who, at the time he'd supplied the photos, wasn't even sick yet. He'd considered not even giving May the gift.

"Timing. It doesn't always follow our plans," he said. "So what you do is listen to your heart, not the tick of some clock."

The world looked dismal when she left his car and walked into Backalley's. Even Lou's dime-store philosophy, as he himself called it and which she usually enjoyed, had put her on edge. Arturo, the bartender, had taken the night off and Lou Anne, the friendly waitress, had moved out of town for a better job.

"Strangers! Everyone's a stranger!" she said to the bartender she'd never seen before. She looked around the crowded room for people she might know and heard him and the two men he was serving whisper. When she turned back around, they stopped, all three wearing the same vacant expression. "And getting stranger by the minute."

She ordered the usual, and then had to explain what it was. She moved to a nearby table. By the time she'd finished her third drink, she'd befriended Lou Anne's replacement, Mary Lou, an elf-sized woman with a husky voice.

At ten o'clock, she watched the news on the TV behind the bar. The opening story was the interview with Jason and Dr. Hirston, followed by close-up footage of the lion-sized cat hurling himself against the bars of his cage. Then, like a made-for-TV western, in slow motion, Jason aimed a tranquilizing gun and shot the animal. This part played twice.

The tequila had kept her from thinking about May and her dead little sandy-haired girl all evening; now she could think of nothing but them. She saw mother and daughter, just as Lou had described them, on the violet-flowered quilt that May kept in the trunk of her Mustang, calling out names for the various cloud shapes that floated overhead.

She looked up at a brown stain in the bar's white ceiling tile and tried to see a dog or bear in its shape. Soulful tones of a cantor wafted from the TV through the noisy room. A rabbi, dressed in white flowing robes, held a torah, also draped in white but embroidered with intricate gold designs.

At the table next to her, a brunette with the odd squint of someone adjusting to contact lenses mimicked the cantor's rocking movements and voice. She ignored her, listened to the familiar hymn, watched on the television a Jewish family prepare a lavish meal to break their twenty-four-hour fast of atonement. The sight of matzo ball soup, gefilte fish and baked chicken reminded her that except for the olives in her drinks, she also had not eaten that day — had fasted without knowing it.

"Would you mind holding it down?" she said to the woman who continued to wail. "It's the Day of Atonement," she told Mary Lou.

The waitress lit a cigarette.

"Ten days ago, on Rosh Hashanah, the Jewish New Year, God opened three books." She placed three paper napkins on the table. "One held the names of the righteous, the second the names of the wicked, and the third was for those whose good deeds equaled their bad ones. But during the ten holy days between Rosh Hashanah and

Yom Kippur, Jews can change their destinies for the coming year by repenting, praying or doing good deeds."

"Who cares," the woman who'd been mocking the cantor said.

"Was I talking to you?"

"Ya'll know how God just loves to forgive His chosen people." The brunette flipped her lacquered bangs, and the three women sitting with her picked up her purse and walked her to the front register.

"God forgives," Beth said, mimicking the woman's squinty eyes, "it's people who don't, you bitch!"

The women left, whispering to one another, pushing their friend out the door.

"Doesn't matter who I'm with; lately, I can piss off anybody," she told Mary Lou, then grabbed her leather purse and turned it upside-down on the table.

"Hon, what are you doin'?" The waitress used both hands to try and contain the mess that was spilling out of the purse from falling onto the floor. But a brush and a day planner slipped over the edge.

Finally, the turquoise necklace appeared. She held it, felt its weight, watched it glisten and then laughed. "He's come for the stolen necklace."

"Who?" Mary Lou shoved layout pads, notebooks, a pink comb, a blue-gray kneaded eraser, a soft brown spotted banana, a wallet and a Sony TV Remote back into the bag, along with the drooping ash from the tip of her cigarette.

"If I'd only known that May had lost her child, I would have been more understanding about the goddess and the magical cats and, well, everything."

"Magical what?"

She grabbed the purse and walked toward the door, even though her day planner and a few other belongings were still on the floor.

"Where are you going?"

"Will you call me a cab? I need to do something."

"You don't need to do anything, hon, you've had way too much to drink."

"I need to do something for May."

"It's too late." Mary Lou pointed to the clock over the cash register.

Too late? She thought of what she'd told the waitress about Yom Kippur, the chance to change destiny by doing a good deed within the ten days. She bounced the turquoise necklace in her hand and laughed.

"I don't believe in that religious crap."

Chapter Twenty-Seven

When May got home that Tuesday after Friend's chaotic arrival at the zoo, she cried for more than an hour. This wasn't unusual. Crying for long periods had become as routine as doing the laundry or washing the dishes, just another necessary chore that made life more bearable.

Mostly she cried in the shower where it was private, and she could lock the door, avoiding the risk of Jason sneaking in to play one of his stupid pranks. Crying in the shower also saved her from facing the pathetic heap of soggy tissues afterward. It was painful enough to find torn shreds of Kleenex in every suit, pants and skirt pocket she owned.

That afternoon's crying ended differently than all the other times since Susan's dying, though. It brought a burst of energy instead of the usual hopelessness, the usual silence. She stormed through the halls, up and down the wooden stairs and in and out of the house with too many rooms, to try and wear it down. She turned on lights, threw sofa cushions, pillows, knocked hardcover books off their shelves, until finally she screamed.

Later, when cleaning up her mess, putting books back in place, she found several brown bags that smelled of shoe leather and were tied at the top with gold drawstrings, stuffed behind the photo albums. Inside them was cash, lots of cash. She counted around ten thousand dollars before getting too tired and angry to count the rest. There was also a note written in what looked like Arabic. She guessed the stash was meant for Jason's big escape from her. The note made no sense at all.

When Jason finally came home, he brought a small bouquet of wild flowers. Delicate purple, blue and yellow petals combined with the soft spray of fern put an end to any hope that what she had learned about Grace and him that day could somehow be denied. She stood on the opposite side of the kitchen island from him, feeling hot waves of rage lash out, moving the copper pots that dangled overhead.

She grabbed the flowers and threw them in his face.

"Some people grow closer after something horrible happens to them! Why didn't we? Why didn't we help each other?" she screamed.

He just stood there, as far away as ever, not even offering a word to hold on to. His silence made her scream, regurgitate words that tasted of blood, but she couldn't stop them. They kept coming, took up all the space in the room.

When he saw the brown bag on the chair near the counter, he grabbed it, went upstairs and slammed a door shut.

She continued to scream at him.

She cried. She stared into the refrigerator. She read the same paragraph of a magazine story over and over. She went to work on the jigsaw puzzle Lou Schultz had given to her.

Twelve animal-shaped clouds had already been put together: a dragon, turtle, giraffe, unicorn, squirrel, bird, cow, sea lion, dolphin, dog, goldfish, and bear. From the number of pieces left, there was probably only one more animal to complete.

It was a cat. Large and gray and powerful, it hovered just above the horizon, its tail curled high, one paw stretched toward the earth. Its eyes were kind, the way she imagined Hader would look, not like the feral animal she'd seen at the zoo that afternoon.

She studied the faces of all the other animals. Each wore a tender expression, but something about the cat was different. It was the only one looking toward the ground, his eyes focused directly beneath him at a field of wild flowers — the only part of the puzzle that she'd not completed. She worked intently. In the center of the flowers a woman and child sat on a violet-patterned quilt. The sandy-haired girl balanced on her toes and reached for the cat, her fingers almost touching its outstretched paw. The two tiny faces were Susan's and hers.

The phone rang.

"I know your plan."

"Beth?"

"The turquoise necklace." Beth's words were slurred.

"It's almost two in the morning."

"You had the necklaces made so you could give one to the cat."

"What?"

"I'm at the zoo!" She laughed hysterically. "Cabby thought I was nuts. Maybe I am!"

"The zoo?"

Beth babbled on about friendship and Lou Schultz and finding out about Susan dying.

"I'm taking the necklace to Friend for you. That was the plan. Right?"

"Okay, that was my plan, but not anymore. He's dangerous, Beth. Don't go near him!" Then she remembered the zoo was all locked up and besides, there was night security.

"You need to know all this stuff about goddesses and legends and whatever is happening because you're sad and trying to work out of it. I want to help, I want to show you it's not real."

She could use Jason's phone patch to contact the guard, but one glance up the darkened hallway steps only made her angry again.

"Stay where you are, Beth."

"I'm so sorry, May. I'm so sorry I wasn't a better friend."

"Don't move. I'm coming to get you."

▲▲▲

The driver of a red Mercedes coupe made a slow turn in front of the zoo entrance where the public phones were, then turned off the headlights and rolled to a stop a block away. Beth had just hung up from talking to May on the phone when she caught sight of the car, and then Grace. She trailed the dark skinny figure, hiding behind telephone poles, oak trees and garbage cans with the slogan "Don't mess with Texas" plastered across them.

She watched Grace feel along a brick wall behind a full azalea shrub, and seconds later unlock a gate and walk through it.

She followed her, the evening awash in tequila. Everything looked too perfect. Branches swayed too gracefully, stars shone too brightly, the air smelled too sweet.

Down winding sidewalks, past dark cages, she stopped when Grace did, in front of a habitat with a large pyramid in the middle. The quiet stirring of unseen animals made Beth uneasy. She watched as Grace stood there, not doing anything, barely moving. Was she waiting for someone? Time passed. Beth started to second-guess her plan, seeing the television footage of Friend play over and over, the pandemonium his unexpected outburst had caused. She remembered the caged animal's fierce roars resonant with conquest, his regal carriage. She decided to leave. Something grabbed hold of her arm.

"I took Jason's keys," May said, "but how did you unlock the gate? And what's Grace's car doing here?"

"Not just her car." Beth put her finger up to her mouth to let May know she needed to be quiet, then pointed at Grace. "I got this weird phone call from her, something about her dad being in trouble. Maybe I should have called her back?"

May peered into the darkness. A cold moon illuminated the tremendous pyramid. Cool Alexandria evenings, the smell of grilled pigeon from street-vendors' open pits, the call to prayer from the muezzins, the pleasant murmur of the River Nile, all came rushing back to her. She saw the Egyptian people — entire families who lived on the muddy lower ledges of the Nile, who drank, bathed and defecated into the magic water. She saw their scrawny livestock. But she saw no sign of Hader in the fabricated scenery.

Grace tossed her hair over one shoulder, stretched her long white neck like a fluffed-out egret and stalked away from the railing around the safety moat. Keeping their distance, May and Beth followed her around the concrete boulders to the habitat's back wall.

Grace unlocked the rear door to the handler's room with the same key she'd used at the zoo's side entrance. Yellow light poured out of the space.

"I don't want her anywhere near my cat!" May charged down the path. Limbs loomed overhead like dark creatures with feathered tails. Chirping crickets chased at her heels, while lightning bugs brightened her way. She pushed the door open.

Grace stumbled, then fell backwards. "We have to get out of here," Grace said.

May grabbed Grace's arm and looked through the viewing window. "What have you done to him?"

"He's not here. But how did you know about him?"

"He has to be here!"

"He said two o'clock, but he's not here!"

"Who said? What are you talking about?"

Grace pushed past her to get at the door, but May grabbed her again. Grace looked frantic, desperate, all bones — long and fragile.

Beth rushed inside, pulling the weighty door shut behind her as quickly as she could. "I just saw the cat! Out there! He's gotten out of his pen!"

Grace shot an angry look at Beth. "You're here too?"

"Did you let him out?"

"No!"

They listened for noises. Beth looked through the steel-enforced mesh window of the handler's door and tried the steel knob. It was locked.

"I have the key." Grace held it up.

"I'm not about to walk out in that habitat!" May said.

"Didn't you hear what I just said! The cat's not in there! He's outside." Beth ran her fingers over her eyes. "There has to be an alarm or something in here. Isn't there a phone?"

"Just patch phones," May said. "Like walkie-talkies. We'll have to hope the night guard finds us."

"He's not here. It's Dugacy's night," Grace said.

How could Grace know who was on duty that night? Then May saw all too clearly an image of Grace and Jason in the ocelot's cave, wrapped in each other's arms. This very habitat. How many times? Where else?

"The Berry sisters have been killed, my father's in danger, and I've had to steal the turquoise necklace from the museum to get him back." Grace handed May a folded note. She looked like the injured sparrow that Blue Bell had cornered last summer.

"It was the Berry sisters on the plane to Egypt with us, just as you thought, May. They were stealing antiquities," Grace said. "Only someone double-crossed somebody, and now my father's in trouble."

The room was small and smelled acrid from the combination of vitamins, urine and dung. She tried not to breathe as Grace spoke. Everything was so mixed up. She read the note.

"I don't understand, what would my father have to do with any of this?" Grace started to cry.

"He wants the necklace in exchange for your father?" May asked.

"You can read, can't you!"

"And you have it? The necklace?" May said.

The lever on the door to the room clicked once. Then it clicked again. May spun around in time to see the handle move. Beth bumped into her as she ran toward the handler's door.

"The key!" Grace dropped it.

May picked it up.

She scrambled through the door behind Grace and Beth into the outdoor habitat just as the enormous gray cat entered the small room behind them.

She backed into the dark space.

"He opened the damned door!" Beth yelled.

May screamed when Hader's large head suddenly filled the square space of the window, each whisker silhouetted by the yellow light. His tail slapped back and forth, his paws huge as he pressed against the glass.

She ran alongside Beth past the pyramid to the edge of the safety moat and stared into the black swirling water. Grace was already standing at this edge.

"Can we jump it?" Beth asked.

"No," May said, recalling useless facts about the zoo's safety features that she never thought she would actually need to know.

"Maybe the door locked behind us."

"No," May said, again remembering another safety feature.

She studied the dark gulf in front of them, the ancient papyrus flower made of painted plywood lining its edge. It looked miles wide at that moment, like the frightening ocean in her dreams, night after night that the black cat Madee would rescue her from.

"Can we swim it?" Grace asked.

"No," May said. "The pedestrian side is smooth so the animals can't get out." Not even Madee, she thought.

It was Grace who had them tear at the pyramid in hope of getting a piece of wood long enough to use as a plank to cross the moat. She pulled, pushed and jumped on the beams supporting the structure, but couldn't get the pieces of lumber to budge.

"Why don't you ask your goddess for help?" Grace said. "Or now do you understand what kind of cat you've conjured up?"

A faint orange light glowed in the darkened space behind Grace. Then it was gone, then it appeared again, grew closer. A man walked toward them, smoking a cigarette, the tip burning bright as he drew in on it.

"You're the man from the garden in Alexandria, the man on the train to Cairo. I knew I'd seen you, here, in the last week," May said.

"Who are you?" Beth asked.

"Evil," he said, then exhaled a cloud of smoke in her face and laughed. "And all this time you thought it was the little pussy cat to fear." He turned toward Grace. "Correct, Msssss. Sssssutton?" He ran the "s" of Ms. and the "s" of Sutton together into one long hissing sound, a snake talking.

"But how did you know about the cat?" May asked.

"Shut up, May," Grace said.

"Did you let my cat out?"

"Shut up, May! Where is my father?" Grace said.

"Where is my father, pleasssssse, ssssssir?" Again he hissed. Then he paced. "Such a good plan. All this time, all the way from Egypt, the artifacts were hidden in the bottom of the pussy's very own traveling cage. And stupid Teliah, of all people, the idiot *omda* from my village who has turned my home into such a tourist trap that I cannot conduct my business from there any longer, was the one who thought to put the treasures in the cage. But then somebody had to go and cut me out. Jaber al-Sabath, their leader, cut out of the money." He walked to the mobile cage that had been Friend's home since leaving Cairo, pulled out a small Beretta handgun wedged behind his belt, and tapped its barrel against the metal bottom of the cage. "My fortune, right here."

"We have nothing to do with this!" Beth said.

Jaber approached her. With each step, he sniffed at the air, turning his mouth in a deep frown. He touched the end of the gun to her forehead.

"I smell a Jew."

"But how did you know Beth is Jewish?"

"Shut up, May," Grace said.

Beth flattened her body against the sandstone rock, but there was nowhere to go. He struck the side of her face with the butt of the Beretta; she slid to the ground. When he kicked her head, her hand opened, the imitation turquoise necklace spilling out.

Jaber prodded it with the tip of his shoe, then picked the piece of jewelry up so its full length shimmered and shimmied, a mesmerizing dance in the moon's light, a dance that brought a twisted smile to his angular face.

Please believe this is the real necklace. May shut her eyes, willing it.

"This is bullshit," he said and let go of the trinket. It landed right back in Beth's open, unmoving hand.

"Where is my father?"

"I sold my own sister for a gold necklace that wasn't even worth a hundred dollars. It's remarkable the circles our lives make, once again lured by a necklace, as if this were my fate."

"You'll get your necklace when you tell me what you've done to my father."

"You spoiled Americans! You wouldn't be so brave if you knew real evil." Jaber laughed, a low guttural sound. "Not the kind you so stupidly attribute to the legendary cat, but the kind we humans do to one another."

He sprang forward, wrapped one arm around Grace so she couldn't move, and put the Beretta to her right ear. "You want this to be the last thing you hear?"

Grace was silent.

"God doesn't care about you and I care even less than that, Mssss. Sutton."

"I'm wearing it!" Grace said.

He tore her blouse open, jerked the necklace from her neck and then shot her.

Just like that. No warning, no preparation, no threat, and no noise, except for the smallest of pops, sounding as harmless as corn kernels in a microwave.

Grace fell to her knees and then folded up, compact, tidy, like a rented party chair. Jaber put the necklace around his own neck.

"How does it look, Mssss. Worth?"

May took tiny backward steps, not taking her eyes off the man who now pointed the gun at her, but she couldn't help but see the pool of blood taking shape around Grace, an escaping dark shadow.

"Your husband was such an easy mule," Jaber said. "Of course our timing was impeccable, his being all confused over your poor daughter's death, questioning life, wanting something to stop the pain. Money is such a reliable anesthetic, even the mere promise of it works. Jason took *Pharoni* through Customs for the smallest of rewards. Didn't even know what he carried was worthless, but he passed our test. Didn't take much to get him on board for this job. Let's see, how did he put it? He said, 'my wife clings to the money from that piddling trust fund of hers as if the dollars were pieces of her dead parents' flesh.'"

She felt everything inside of her flowing out, darkening the ground beneath her just as the blood under Grace did. Empty and unoccupied like the seashells she'd tried to return to the Gullcrest beach, she was out of place in her own body.

He stepped right over Grace as if she were just a puddle, something he didn't want to stain his boots, and walked toward her. "Are you putting it all together? Your big trip to Egypt was my planning, from the beginning. Well, I guess I do have to give Grace's daddy a little bit of credit, after all, he purchased the three student tickets without Richard ever knowing those students never existed. And when they canceled, it was just the tiniest of suggestions, one that his stupid daughter probably doesn't even remember, that put in her vacant head the idea of a trip to the foreign country."

An enormous light rushed toward them. Blinding and radiant, for a split second she hoped it was Ra, the sun god. Jaber threw himself on top of her, his force more than his weight flattening her against the ground of the habitat.

"Three o'clock," he said, his mouth against her ear.

Three o'clock? She tried to wake herself, as if from another of her dreams that had occurred at exactly this same hour.

"You move, you're dead," he said and got off her.

She heard Beth moan as the brilliant light overhead grew larger. Loose grains of sand and gravel and dirt lifted and swirled around them. She squinted to see through the debris, wiping away the man's sweat that still crawled along the top of her arm. He raised a black hood over his head, ran toward the back wall and waved to the hovering, whirling blades and light. He climbed on top of Hader's traveling cage and attached the three steel cables that dropped from above. When he jumped back down the whole cage tipped on one end at first, then righted itself and lifted as high as the highest boulder of the back wall of the habitat and flew away.

He cursed at the sky in Arabic. Then his lips became flat horizontal lines pressed tightly against one another as he removed the hood that had concealed his face. His gaze, turned inward, reflected a vast vacant landscape where no living being could survive.

"Now," he said, his voice raspy from screaming, "I have seen with my own eyes who has double-crossed me, but he did not see it was I who attached the cables. I'm so clever. I can hardly wait until he discovers how I have defeated his plan." He gently fingered the turquoise stones at his neck. "And on top of it all, I have my lovely bauble."

He pointed the gun at her and then stood there for what seemed an eternity, absorbed in thought, his eyes focused on nothing in particular, oblivious to her gasps for breath, her attempts to scramble to her feet.

"The poetry of it all is probably lost on you," he finally said, still not bothering to look at her, "but to end this whole thing right here in the very quarters of the miserable legendary cat that started it — why it's, what is that word?" He hesitated. The sound of breaking glass cut his silence.

The viewing window shattered into a fine spray of yellow shards that clung to Hader's gray fur. Like an approaching earthquake, his growl grew louder as he neared. Covered in pieces of broken window, he sparkled. Glass that slipped from his coat to the dirt floor made bell-like tinkles. He looked and even sounded like a magical cat.

"Oh, this is priceless," Jaber laughed. "You never give up, Msss. Worth? I mean, that wretched look of hope, though truly reminiscent of my sister Katia's face just before I sold her, is not enough to stop me, save me. And there's nothing here to save you, certainly not a cat. Why, I'm even the one who let him go, but now that he has come back," he aimed the Beretta at it.

She lunged at the thief's knees. He fell against the wooden pyramid, the gun knocked loose from his hold.

Hader's hind legs spread, his coat fluffed, his tail whipped from side to side. He lowered his head and sniffed at the air, a familiar routine that her own cats did before attacking lizards, cockroaches, snails.

"You think I'm afraid of you, pussy cat?" He brushed himself off and stood. The light from the broken window made the gold and turquoise flash at the base of Jaber's throat.

Hader flattened to a crouch. His tail whipped furious figure eights in the air as he shifted from one front paw to the other.

A police siren momentarily distracted the animal. Jaber reached for the gun and again the necklace flashed. Hader's back legs thrust him forward. His front claws swiped at the shiny collar, hurling it across the space.

Jaber pressed one hand against the darkening slash in his throat, reaching again for the gun with the other. He took quick, direct aim.

A loud shot pierced May's ears, sending jolts through her body, as the lightning must have felt to her parents in their last moments. Her eyes had shut so tightly she felt they would never open again, but then she thought of Grace and the shot that had put her down, how quiet it had been, no more than an airborne kiss. She opened her eyes just in time to see Jaber fall forward. His body was stiff, his knees locked, so the toes of his leather boots stuck straight into the soft dirt when he hit the ground.

May didn't move, didn't breathe, didn't think.

"This isn't a miracle that you have been saved, Ms. Worth. It's my choice."

Across the safety moat, standing in the pedestrian area, was a man with a gun in one hand and a shiny metal Halliburton briefcase on the ground beside him. The Asian.

"Strictly business," he said. "It's the reason for everything."

He left. He left her alone, alone in the habitat, alone with three bodies — two still, the other moaning — and one enormous animal approaching. The light behind Hader cast a shadow more than twice his size upon her, closer and closer until she could see his gray and black coat was in motion, like an Iowa cornfield in the night wind. Only there was no wind. He purred. Only cats that roar cannot purr. And he smelled of pancake syrup, Susan's sweet scent after a night of sleep. Only Susan wasn't asleep.

She had envisioned the moment so many times: the sleek animal sitting beside her on his back haunches, his head chest-level to her, his eyes warm yellow like dear Blue Bell's. But looking at him now she only saw herself, all of it a reflection. Everything she'd done, every interpretation she'd made, every dream just a puzzle piece.

"Beth," she said as loudly as she dared.

No answer.

"Grace."

Nothing. Nothing happened. Nothing moved. Not a tree limb, not even the cat's fur any longer. The moon was painted onto the sky, and the sky was a painted outdoor ceiling, no longer an endless black night stretching into forever. She searched Hader's eyes, unsure of where she stopped and he began, and she saw her wish to make her daughter's dying something tangible, something she might still be able to affect. Water lapping against the cement banks of the safety moat mocked the quiet currents of the River Nile. The smell of oil-based paint from the towering pyramid mixed with the scent of fresh-cut plywood that formed the rigid papyrus cutouts along the moat's edge. Nothing was what it appeared it to be.

"There's no such thing as a magical cat," she said, her attention on Grace instead of the animal.

The cat didn't move.

She grabbed Grace's torn blouse, wadded it and pressed it against the dark seeping hole. "Beth! You okay?" She dragged Grace's body over to Beth's, sat between them, holding one hand against the bloody blouse, the other on Beth's forehead. A siren's wail grew intrusive.

The cat didn't move.

Beth tried to sit up but fell over.

Two helicopters circled. Their cone-shaped lights scanned back and forth in jerky motions, the yellow beams everywhere; crossing paths in tree branches, joining deep within the aspidistra, startling animals who'd taken refuge in the darkness of their cages. Static from police car speakers cut in and out. The sirens blared.

"It's time to let you go, isn't it?" she asked, knowing the cat would not answer.

She reached for Beth, who tried to sit upright again, this time steadying her against the rock behind them.

She wrapped one arm around Grace, the other around Beth and stared straight ahead, for one last lingering moment with the magnificent feline.

"Go."

A piece of glass fell from the handler's window, and the animal set off. He bounded across the habitat, leaping from one ledge of the back wall to another. A final jump took him over the top.

"What have you done?" Jason said. He was soaked with perspiration, his tranquilizer gun strapped over his shoulder, his phone patch spitting unrecognizable words from his waistband. Three paramedics rushed to her. Jason looked at the foreigner laying face down just a few feet from her, then looked for the cat's cage. He lunged at her, took hold of her shoulders with both of his hands and shook her. "What have you done?"

She pushed him away, stood, and drew in a breath that was unexpectedly rich and sweet as it surged through her like an ocean wave filling every crevice.

"I've made a choice." She picked up a broken branch from the imitation olive tree, drew a fine line in the soft dirt floor and crossed over it.

Chapter Twenty-Eight

The zoo and surrounding Hermann Park area were barricaded for the next three weeks. The National Guard stood watch at the area's perimeter. The HPD Special Shoot Team patrolled the interior grounds for the runaway cat, as did the zoo's veterinary staff that hoped to find Pharaoh's Friend with their tranquilizer guns before one of the sharpshooters did. The entire area was bathed in light from sundown to sunrise from six stationary search beams, police helicopters, security lamp poles and high-powered flashlights. The zoo animals were corralled into their dark interior pens each night to maintain some semblance of routine for them, while Houston residents with new telescopes hosted parties from the high-rise condos that overlooked the unnaturally illuminated tract.

But no one could find the famous cat. Not even Grace's father, who offered a ten-thousand-dollar reward for its safe return. He was interviewed from his hospital room with Grace beside him, both still in recovery from their wounds. He held his daughter's hand, while Mrs. Sutton stood behind them in a cashmere sweater and pulled at the pearls around her neck. He denied involvement with the thieves who'd brought stolen antiquities into the country via Friend's cage. He lauded Grace's heroic effort to save his life by procuring the treasured turquoise necklace for his ransom. "I'm a lucky man to have such a devoted little girl."

Mayor Lafar, Police Chief Gray, the Houston Zoo board, Texas A & M officials, the Museum of Natural Science, the Houston Chamber of Commerce, anyone and everyone even remotely involved felt responsible for the missing cat. Fortunately, there was Jaber al-Sabath, who could be cast as an international villain, and thus blamed for it all.

May lost count of the number of times her husband's picture appeared in the papers. One particular photo became a trademark for the story. It was Jason and Pharaoh's Friend together, taken the day the cat first arrived at the zoo, and probably one of the most flattering portraits she'd ever seen of her husband. The whole ordeal made Jason a reluctant celebrity of sorts. His culpability, much like Grace's father's, was impossible to prove. A local public relations firm took advantage of his notoriety and landed Jason a couple of bit parts in major motion pictures. He was hired for grocery store openings, charity and sports events, and even did an ad for a local furniture store.

May and Beth, on the other hand, did everything possible to dodge the media frenzy. The hospital kept them only two days. Beth had a slight skull fracture, concussion and a huge colorful lump on the side of her head. Though May was unharmed, Dr. Claudia Somners insisted she stay for two days of rest. May refused any credit the reporters tried to give her for saving Beth, Grace and Friend.

When she stopped by Beth's room the day of their release from the hospital, Beth pointed to the newspaper's front-page photo of a powdered-face woman with tightly wound hair standing in front of a chalkboard. "Susan must have told her teacher you have a special way with animals," Beth said.

"I do." She smiled, having also seen the papers. Neighbors and co-workers suddenly eager to tell about the times they'd seen her befriend a runaway dog or walk down the street with a lizard on her head, had called the newspapers and television stations.

"What have you told them?" Beth said.

"As little as possible."

Beth looked back down at the paper she held, her expression now soft and serene.

"You look different," May said. Perhaps it was the lack of makeup.

"I feel different," Beth laughed. "I think I changed my fate without even knowing it."

▲▲▲

A bright yellow taxi waited for May and Beth at a private underground entrance to the hospital. They slipped into the rear seat through the same back door and sat on a bed of weeds. Dandelions sprouted from the ashtrays, mayweed twined around the inside door handles, thistle hung from the overhead light. A garland of clover was draped across the back of the front seat, and a garden of dayflowers blossomed in the back window.

"Where can I take you famous ladies?" A gentle-looking man tossed a bouquet of yarrow over the seat to Beth, who buried her face in its earth-smelling roots.

"May, this is a friend," Beth said. "A 3Q friend."

And May laughed for the first time in a long time.

Chapter Twenty-Nine

Gullcrest, Texas *October 3, 1993*

For an entire year after the night Friend disappeared, May knew if she just looked hard enough on any given day at any given time, she could find mention of the incident in some magazine or newspaper or even on the television. ABC produced a made-for-TV movie about it that was as far from the truth as Gerald Sutton, the co-producer, arranged it to be.

She'd stopped looking for the articles, hoping to rid herself of the memories, but that morning stumbled right into one. It caught her off-guard, like a stubbed toe, abrupt, without warning, she waiting for the pain to set in, but it didn't come.

ANIMALS GO TO COURT
By Philip Sother
of the *Houston Chronicle* Staff

Mr. Buster Walsh had his day in court over a ticket he received from the city while in-line skating to work in downtown Houston.

After having had his car vandalized four times in Primer's Printing's parking lot, where he is employed as head pressman, Walsh began to skate to work from his home four miles away.

Fifty members of the Urban Animals, a group known to skate the downtown area at night for entertainment, came to the proceeding to protest the ordinance against skating on public thoroughfares. When asked about their club T-shirt bearing an illustration of Pharaoh's Friend, the Egyptian cat who disappeared on September 16, 1992, several claimed the famous feline has accompanied them when they skate at night.

Mr. Walsh, representing himself, was ordered to pay the seventy-five-dollar fine.

Now the whole ordeal was as fresh as if it had just happened, but without the hurt. The article's bold print gave the past year of peaceful days numbers and months, a sequence, and an end.

She, Ben, Jerry and the Hit-And-Run Cat had adjusted right away to Gullcrest, at first doing nothing more than napping in the porch shade, the ocean breeze on their faces, watching seagulls. The beach with its sand crabs, ants and lizards eventually stirred the kitties into motion. Employment at the seashell shop across the highway from her home, with the promise of no deadlines, no creative pressures, no co-workers and only an occasional customer, got May off the porch. Stacks of canvases in her spare bedroom grew months later: the rediscovery of uninterrupted painting, time lost in the joy of long strokes with a sable brush.

What had been a long convalescence, with no witness to date or time, had come to rest on a newspaper page with the article. What was once so personal had perspective, a distance, which allowed a broader glimpse of the events that had brought her to the very moment: an ending, or a beginning?

▲▲▲

"Selling seashells by the sea shore?"

She looked up from the newspaper at the customer who'd just walked into the shop.

"Richard!"

He grinned. Standing near him was the same dark-skinned assistant who'd greeted them at the Alexandria airport. He wore a paisley scarf through the belt loops of his Levis and had a large rolled paper tucked under his arm.

"Azzis," he said, and shook her hand.

"You found me," she said.

"It's my profession to find hidden treasure," Richard said. "Well, that, and the letters you sent me had the Gullcrest postmark on them."

She laughed.

"I got tired of waiting for your invitation. I was afraid you might forget to call when your time of recuperation was over."

"As a matter of fact, I think it occurred just a few moments ago." She turned the newspaper on the counter so he could see the article about Friend.

"I read it this morning."

"You believe it?"

"Could be. It's amazing the things people claim for personal possession." He looked at the photo inset of the cat. "I've made an odd friendship with the *omda* of a small village close to where the dig was. He told me he knew of buyers who paid fortunes for stolen antiquities just to keep them in a locked vault. I mean this cat was special, like a treasure. Maybe someone's keeping him."

"You know the whole embarrassing story, don't you?"

Azzis strolled around the room.

"Grace told me," Richard said.

"I can't believe her dad got away with it."

"Hard to charge for a theft when no one knows what's been stolen."

"What about Grace, for taking the necklace?"

"Community service."

"But you know all about my embarrassing story?"

"Grace told me."

She covered her face with her hands. "I don't even understand how it happened. One thing just led to another, and then like a living jigsaw puzzle, it all fit together to make sense."

"I'd like to hear about it all some day."

"That's just it, there's nothing to hear. At the very moment it was supposed to be miraculous, everything fell apart. The legend. The cats. Bast. The transmigration. It all seemed ridiculous. What mattered were Grace and Beth. Not Friend, not the necklace, not even Susan."

"You know, I've been to digs all over the world, and all that's ever found is evidence of man. No gods. No miracles. Only proof of our belief in them, our hope that they exist. What's that saying, 'If triangles had gods, their gods would be three-sided.'"

May laughed.

"From Zeus to Jesus to Pharaoh's Friend, maybe there's something even more powerful," Richard said. "Maybe it's not what or whom we believe in, just our believing that's important. The process."

"I was just thinking about that — where my belief took me."

He pushed a strand of curly hair away from her face; she looked at him.

"Where did it take you?"

"To acceptance. An acceptance nourished by trust and hope. An acceptance that doesn't rely on explanation."

She heard the ocean, and the cars that rushed by on the road outside, movement all around them as they were still, anchored to a quiet moment.

He reached for her hand and held it.

"They've opened the coffin we unearthed. I guess you heard it was empty?"

She nodded.

"Come to Egypt with me and Azzis."

"Egypt?"

"Now that the economy's better, we have funding for another dig." He called to his assistant, who had strolled his way right out of the shop. Azzis ran back in, the screen door banged shut behind him, and he spread the rolled paper onto the top of a glass counter that held hundreds of different-shaped seashells.

It was a copy of the ancient map of the city of Bubastis, an askew triangle drawn around it. Richard touched the southern point of the triangle. "This is where we unearthed the mastaba tomb." Then he tapped his finger on the eastern point. "Our next site."

She stared at the spot, Richard and Azzis on either side of her, positioned around the map so that they formed a triangle of their own. A set of bells near the front door danced and chimed in a sudden gust of wind that may have blown all the way in from Egypt's Delta.

A soft growl surrounded them.

It was Azzis' stomach. They laughed.

"Maybe we should discuss this over lunch," Richard said.

"There's a great Chinese restaurant down the street," she said.

"Good fortune cookies?" Azzis asked.

"Amazingly accurate." She thought of Egypt, the contrast between its arid desert where growth is stunted and alpha grass desiccated, and the intricate irrigated plots where vegetation thrives, and roses, carnations, oleanders and geraniums are cultivated. She thought of the small tour guide with the watch too big for his wrist, the insightful questions he'd asked of her while they played cards on the beach, and the note she'd found later that he'd tucked into her beach bag: *Don't forget me. Bezhad.* She did not tell them that just the week before, the fortune in her cookie had told her to seek out a child she knew in a distant land.

She locked the cash register and pulled the windows shut, but before leaving the store she took a nautilus shell from under the counter and gave it to Richard.

"I want you to have this."

He closed his hands around hers as she placed the shell in his palm.

"I thought you were the one who returned shells to the shore."

She wondered how he could have known this. Jason told Grace? Grace told Richard? But did it really matter? Did any of it, no matter how embarrassing, matter anymore? Richard was there, in front of her. "I've learned it's okay to rearrange things a bit in this world. In fact, I believe it's expected," she said. "Please, take this. It's my pleasure to share it with you."

"Then it's my pleasure also."

Check out these other fine titles by
Durban House at your local book store.

Exceptional Books
by
Exceptional Writers

FICTION

A COMMON GLORY . . . . Robert Middlemiss
A DREAM ACROSS TIME . . . . Annie Rogers
AFTER LIFE LIFE . . . . Don Goldman
an-eye-for-an-eye.com . . . . Dennis Powell
A MEETING OF MINDS . . . . Elizabeth Turner Calloway
BASHA . . . . John Hamilton Lewis
BLUEWATER DOWN . . . . Rick O'Reilly
BY ROYAL DESIGN . . . . Norbert Reich
THE BEIRUT CONSPIRACY . . . . John R. Childress
CRISIS PENDING . . . . Stephen Cornell
CRY HAVOC . . . . John Hamilton Lewis
DEADLY ILLUSIONS . . . . Chester D. Campbell
DANGER WITHIN . . . . Mark Danielson
DEADLY ILLUMINATION . . . . Serena Stier
DEATH OF A HEALER . . . . Paul Henry Young
DESIGNED TO KILL . . . . Chester D. Campbell
EXTREME CUISINE . . . . Kit Sloane
THE GARDEN OF EVIL . . . . Chris Holmes
HANDS OF VENGEANCE . . . . Richard Sand
HORIZON'S END . . . . Andrew Lazarus
HOUR OF THE WOLVES . . . . Stephane Daimlen-Völs
THE INNOCENT NEVER KNEW . . . . Mark W. Danielson
JOHNNIE RAY & MISS KILGALLEN . . . . Bonnie Hearn Hill & Larry Hill
KIRA'S DIARY . . . . Edward T. Gushee
THE LAST COWBOYS . . . . Robert E. Hollmann
THE LATERAL LINE . . . . Robert Middlemiss
LETHAL CURE . . . . Kurt Popke
THE LUKARILLA AFFAIR . . . . Jerry Banks
THE MEDUSA STRAIN . . . . Chris Holmes
MR. IRRELEVANT . . . . Jerry Marshall
MURDER ON THE TRAP . . . . J. Preston Smith
NO ORDINARY TERROR . . . . J. Brooks Van Dyke
OPAL EYE DEVIL . . . . John Hamilton Lewis
PRIVATE JUSTICE . . . . Richard Sand
PHARAOH'S FRIEND . . . . Nancy Yawitz Linkous

ROADHOUSE BLUES . . . . Baron Birtcher
RUBY TUESDAY . . . . Baron Birtcher
SAMSARA . . . . John Hamilton Lewis
SECRET OF THE SCROLL . . . . Chester D. Campbell
SECRETS ARE ANONYMOUS . . . . Fredrick L. Cullen
THE SEESAW SYNDROME . . . . Michael Madden
THE SERIAL KILLER'S DIET BOOK . . . . Kevin Mark Postupack
THE STREET OF FOUR WINDS . . . . Andrew Lazarus
TAINTED ANGELS . . . . Greg Crane
TERMINAL CARE . . . . Arvin Chawla
TUNNEL RUNNER . . . . Richard Sand
WHAT GOES AROUND . . . . Don Goldman

NONFICTION

BEHIND THE MOUNTAIN . . . . Nick Williams
FISH HEADS, RICE, RICE WINE . . . . Lt. Col. Thomas G.
& WAR: A VIETNAM PARADOX . . . . Smith, Ret.
I ACCUSE: JIMMY CARTER AND THE . . . . Philip Pilevsky
RISE OF MILITANT ISLAM
MIDDLE ESSENCE: . . . . Landy Reed
WOMEN OF WONDER YEARS
MOTHERS SPEAK: FOR LOVE OF FAMILY . . . . Rosalie Gaziano
THE PASSION OF AYN RAND'S CRITICS . . . . James S. Valliant
PROTOCOL (25th ANNIVERSARY EDITION) . . . . Richard Sand,
Mary Jane McCaffree,
Pauline Innis
SEX, LIES & PI's . . . . Ali Wirsche & Marnie Milot
SPORES, PLAGUES, AND HISTORY: . . . . Chris Holmes
THE STORY OF ANTHRAX
WHAT MAKES A MARRIAGE WORK . . . . Malcolm D. Mahr
WHITE WITCH DOCTOR . . . . John A. Hunt

SPRING, 2005

FICTION

A COMMON GLORY Robert Middlemiss

What happens when a Southern news reporter falls in love with a WWII jazz loving English pilot and wants to take him home to her segregationist parents? It is in the crucible of war that pilot and reporter draw close across their vulnerabilities and fears. War, segregation, and the fear of death in lonely skies confront them as they clutch at the first exquisite promptings of a passionate love.

BLUEWATER DOWN Rick O'Reilly

Retired L.A. police lieutenant Jack Douglas wanted only one thing after years on the bomb squad—the peace and serenity of sailing his yacht, Tally Ho. But Lisa enters his carefully planned world, and even as he falls in love with her she draws him into a violent matrix of murderers and terrorists bent on their destruction.

BY ROYAL DESIGN Norbert Reich

Hitler's Third Reich was to last a thousand years but it collapsed in twelve. In Berlin, in the belly of the dying Reich, seeds were sown for a new regime, one based on aristocratic ruling classes whose time had come. Berlin's Charitee Hospital brought several children into the world that night in 1944, setting into motion forces that would ultimately bring two venerable Germanic families, the Hohenzollerns and the Habsburgs to power.

THE COROT DECEPTION J. Brooks Van Dyke

London artists are getting murdered. The killer leaves behind an odd signature. And when Richard Watson, an artist, discovers the corpse of his gallery owner, he investigates, pitting himself and his twin sister, Dr. Emma Watson against the ruthless killer. Steeped in the principles of criminal detection they learned from Sherlock Holmes, the twins search for clues in the Edwardian art world and posh estates of 1910 London.

CRY HAVOC John Hamilton Lewis

The worst winter in over a hundred years grips the United States and most of the western world. America's first lady president, Abigail Stewart, must deal with harsh realities as crop failures, power blackouts, shortages of gasoline and heating oil push the nation toward panic. But the extreme weather conditions are only a precursor of problems to come as Prince Nasser, a wealthy Saudi prince, and a cleric plot to destroy western economies.

DEADLY ILLUSIONS Chester D. Campbell

A young woman, Molly Saint, hires Greg and Jill McKenzie to check her husband's background, then disappears. It starts them on a tangled trail of deceit, with Jill soon turning up a close family connection. The deeper the McKenzie's dig, the more deadly illusions they face. Nothing appears to be what it seemed at first as the fear for Molly's life grows.

EXTREME CUISINE Kit Sloane

Film editor Margot O'Banion and director Max Skull find a recipe for disaster behind the kitchen doors of a trendy Hollywood restaurant. Readers of discriminating taste are cordially invited to witness the preparation and presentation of fine fare as deadly drama. As Max points out, dinner at these places "provides an evening of theater and you get to eat it!" Betrayal, revenge, and perhaps something even more unsavory, are on the menu tonight.

THE GARDEN OF EVIL Chris Holmes

A brilliant but bitter sociopath has attacked the city's food supply; five people are dead, twenty-six remain ill from the assault. Family physician, Gil Martin and his wife Tara, the county's Public Health Officer, discover the terrorist has found a way to incorporate the poison directly into the raw vegetables themselves. How is that possible? As the Martins get close to cracking the case, the terrorist focuses all his venom on getting them and their family. It's now a personal conflict—a mano-a-mano—between him and them.

KIRA'S DIARY Edward T. Gushee

Beautiful, talented violinist, seventeen-year-old Kira Klein was destined to be assigned to Barracks 24. From the first day she is imprisoned in the Auschwitz brothel, Kira becomes the unwilling mistress of Raulf Becker, an SS lieutenant whose responsibility is overseeing the annihilation of the Jewish prisoners. Through the stench of death and despair emerges a rich love story, richly told with utter sensitivity, warmth and even humor.

THE LUKARILLA AFFAIR Jerry Banks

Right from the start it was a legal slugfest. Three prominent men, a state senator, a corporate president, and the manager of a Los Angeles professional football team are charged with rape and sodomy by three minimum wage employees of a catering firm, Ginny, Peg and Tina. A courtroom gripper by Jerry Banks who had over forty years in the trade, and who tells it like it happens—fast and quick.

MURDER ON THE TRAP J. Preston Smith

Life has been pretty good to Bon Sandifer. After his tour in Vietnam he marries his childhood sweetheart, is a successful private investigator, and rides his Harley=Davidson motorcycle. Then the murders begin on Curly Trap Road. His wife Shelly dies first. A fellow biker is crushed under a Caddie. And his brother is killed riding a Harley. When Sandifer remarries and finds happiness with his deaf biker bride, the murderous web tightens and he grapples with skeptical detectives and old Vietnam memories.

PHARAOH'S FRIEND Nancy Yawitz Linkous

When Egyptian myth permeates the present, beliefs are tested and lives are changed. My Worth vacations in Egypt to soothe the pain over her daughter's death. She dreams of a cat whose duty is to transport souls to the afterlife. And then a real cat, four hundred and twenty pounds of strength and sinew, appears at an archeological dig. Those that cross its path are drawn into intrigue and murder that is all too real.

SPRING, 2005

NONFICTION

I ACCUSE: JIMMY CARTER AND THE RISE OF MILITANT ISLAM Philip Pilevsky

Philip Pilevsky makes a compelling argument that President Jimmy Carter's failure to support the Shah of Iran led to the 1979 revolution led by Ayatollah Ruhollah Komeini. That revolution legitimized and provided a base of operations for militant Islamists across the Middle East. By allowing the Khomeini revolution to succeed, Carter traded an aging, accommodating shah for a militant theocrat who attacked the American Embassy and held the staff workers hostage. In the twenty-four years since the Khomenini revolution, radical Islamists, indoctrinated in Iran have grown ever bolder in attacking the West and more sophisticated in their tactics of destruction.

MOTHERS SPEAK: FOR LOVE OF FAMILY Rosalie Fuscaldo Gaziano

In a world of turbulent change, the need to connect, to love and be loved is greater and more poignant than ever. Women cry out for simple, direct answers to the question, "How can I make family life work in these challenging times?" This book offers hope to all who are struggling to balance the demands of work and family and to cope with ambiguity, isolation, or abandonment. The author gives strong evidence that the family unit is still the best way to connect and bear enduring fruit.

THE PASSION OF AYN RAND'S CRITICS James S. Valliant

For years, best-selling novelist and controversial philosopher Ayn Rand has been the victim of posthumous portrayals of her life and character taken from the pages of the biographies by Nathaniel Branden and Barbara Branden. Now, for the first time, Rand's own never-before-seen-journal entries on the Brandens, and the first in-depth analysis of the Brandens' works, reveal the profoundly inaccurate and unjust depiction of their former mentor.

SEX, LIES & PI's Ali Wirsche & Marnie Milot

The ultimate guide to find out if your lover, husband, or wife is having an affair. Follow Ali and Marnie, two seasoned private investigators, as they spy on brazen cheaters and find out what sweet revenge awaits. Learn 110 ways to be your own detective. Laced with startling stories, Sex, Lies & PI's is riveting and often hilarious.

WHAT MAKES A MARRIAGE WORK Malcolm D. Mahr

Your hear the phrase "marry and settle down," which implies life becomes more serene and peaceful after marriage. This simply isn't so. Living together is one long series of experiments in accommodation. What Makes A Marriage Work? is a hilarious yet perceptive collection of fifty insights reflecting one couple's searching, experimenting, screaming, pouting, nagging, whining, moping, blaming, and other dysfunctional behaviors that helped them successfully navigate the turbulent sea of matrimony for over fifty years. (Featuring 34 New Yorker cartoons of wit and wisdom.)